ORPHEUS RISING

Also by Lance Lee

POETRY

Elemental Natures – selected poetry, art, and prose

Homecomings

Transformations

Seasons of Defiance

Human/Nature

Becoming Human

Wrestling with the Angel

PLAYS

Time's Up and other Plays

Time's Up

Fox, Hound & Huntress
(in vol. 10, *Playwrights for Tomorrow*)

NOVELS

Second Chances

NON-FICTION

The Death and Life of Drama
reflections on writing and human nature

On the Waterfront – essays: contributor

A Poetics for Screenwriters

The Understructure of Writing for Film and Television
(with Ben Brady)

ORPHEUS RISING

By Sam And His Father, John
With Some Help From A Very Wise Elephant
Who Likes To Dance

by

Lance Lee

illustrated by Ellen Raquel LeBow

Illustrations by Ellen Raquel Lebow
Book, Cover, and Logo Designs by Kate Cooper
Portrait by John Robertson

ISBN 9780578790558 (hc)
ISBN 9780578885599 (p)
ISBN 9780578790565 (e)

Orpheus Rising may be ordered online and through all booksellers.

Reviews and Queries should be directed to poetlee@earthlink.net

Web page: lanceleeauthor.com

 BOOKS

for Jeanne
and
Alyssa & Heather, Hansjorg
and
Milena & Thomas & Sam

The Myth

One day Eurydice dies from a snakebite. Her husband Orpheus in his grief dares to go to hell, to Hades, to regain her. First he charms Charon the Ferryman with his music into taking him across the river Styx, then the terrible, three-headed dog Cerberus, and then the Fates. He even stops the pain of all those in Hades who had faded to gray from their loss of life with his music and longing. Impressed, Hades lets him have Eurydice with one condition: Orpheus can't look back until they both stand in the sunlight of the ordinary world again. Orpheus walks steadily back playing his music for Eurydice to follow until he stands in the sun once more. Then he can't help himself and looks back: Eurydice has followed him, but is not yet in the light, and so he loses her forever.

But, what if…?

CHAPTERS

Prologue

I   A Dream Called Life

II   A Disturbing Book Arrives

III   A Very Wise Elephant Who Likes to Dance

IV   A Dangerous Journey Decided

V   Through the Upside-down Ocean

VI   Wild Dancing in the Sea of Faces

VII   The Breath of Riddles

VIII   A Fearful Place

IX   Biggest, Toughest, Hardest

X   Flesh to Stone

XI   John Finds His Courage—

XII   And Runs from His Dream

XIII   The Voice of Doom

XIV   The Way to Dread City

XV   Dancing from a Dangerous Bench!

XVI   Finding Madelyn in Dread City

XVII   Escape

XVIII   The Battle of Lepanto

XIX   The Long Journey To—

XX   The Heart's Desire

Prologue

The light shatters off the glass facade of the hospital under the noon sun as John stands at a loss, eyes slits against the glare. How did I get here, he wonders?

He can't take it in, the plaza, the people, the buses on three sides, why he stands like an idiot squinting at that blinding facade.

And remembers.

She was gone.

She was so gray....

His eyes water from the light, or is that tears, he wonders? Is this how mourning begins? A confusion of feelings and simultaneously, of feeling nothing at all?

How long have I been standing here in the sun?

A weight on his shoulders bends him down.

He can barely breathe.

How did this happen?

The plaza stretches out around him. The people. The buses....

I need to go far away, he thinks.

To get Sam and go far away.

I

A Dream Called Life

Somewhere an alarm went off; then another followed nearby, and a third more distantly. Soon each room in the house rang. A groan came from a small shape that could just be guessed under the twisted covers in a third story room under a pitched gable from which

a green dragon hung with a too long head, and a two-masted yacht, a schooner, while an unlikely elephant who perilously tap-danced on a flying trapeze hung by them. The elephant was elegantly dressed, and wore spats.

A boy of ten sat up muttering, looked around wildly, and

stumbled to the dresser across the room to turn off the nearest alarm. Somewhere on the second floor a hand silenced another, but these two made little difference to the cacophony of buzzers, beeps and bars of music that filled the house.

Sam—that was the boy's name—disappeared into the bathroom to turn off another alarm, dashed across the hallway into the other third floor bedroom to silence the alarm there, and then hurried down to the second floor to join his father John shutting off the remaining clocks there before they moved to the first to shut off the rest. They ended in the kitchen where an out-of-place grandfather clock stood beside the refrigerator striking deep gongs without relief until John hooked the pendulum to one side.

As he did so a machine took three eggs, a dab of butter and a quart of milk from the refrigerator, cracked the eggs over a bowl on the counter, discarded the shells, added milk, stirred, and then emptied the contents into a frying pan with the butter to make scrambled eggs. When done long arms served two equal portions on plates neatly set out on the small table by the window, and cleaned the bowl and pan— or so it was supposed to—but the machine always stalled early in the process, its motor making a high-pitched, irritating whine. This was, in fact, the last of the alarms which John turned off as Sam rescued the eggs poised over the bowl.

John had never been able to make this machine work, his one great, determined yet failing stab at invention.

At least, having begun to make breakfast, there was no reason now not to continue, which was really the point.

John was a tall man with blue eyes that had lost their light: his blond hair laid limply on his head. His beak of a nose was too small to be called big, but too big to be called small. Sam was tall for his age and looked very like his father. They made breakfast and sat to eat it in silence.

After breakfast John and Sam shrugged on overalls and boots over their pajamas and went out to milk Madrigal, who rolled her eyes at Sam's arrival and moaned in relief as her milk filled his pail. He took that in, then went back for the blue and brown-speckled eggs from the chicken nests in their enclosed henhouse while John spread feed for the chickens and the one rooster who had lost half his comb to a fox a year ago.

In season they visited the garden which always looked thirsty but produced a steady stream of beans and tomatoes, squash and broccoli, carrots, lettuce and chard as the season permitted. They were nearly self-sufficient.

Neither looked up at their Victorian house with its ornate fretwork, gables, and cornices painted a myriad of colors faded to a nearly uniform gray. They called it the "Last House:" it was the only house in a canyon beside an all-year stream that provided their water. Up canyon they could see taller hills, while between the canyon's walls at its foot was a sandy beach and restless ocean.

Fog covered the canyon part of each day for months on end in late winter and spring, sometimes lasting through the summer. Even when it was green and blue, sunny and blowing, the air sharp and tangy, a gray spirit seemed to live in the canyon and look out from behind the sky's blue and the blue of John's eyes.

Sam's, brighter, seemed troubled by some puzzle he couldn't solve or forget. It was impossible to say whether they echoed the land, or the land them.

Their chores done they went back to the kitchen where John lingered over coffee and Sam over a hot chocolate. Finally, still silent, they shrugged off their boots and overalls and went upstairs to dress properly.

There Sam found himself staring dreamily at the elephant on his trapeze. Idly he touched the elephant so he swung back and forth, then set the schooner spinning, as though caught inside a tornado; last he wondered why the dragon's head looked too large for its body.

"Sam! Do you hear me?! Come down for your lessons!"

His father had been calling repeatedly, Sam realized with a start, and slunk downstairs.

John waited at the kitchen table, books piled beside a sheaf of paper. Sam hoped today didn't start with history. He disliked math, but because his father was weak in that they spent little time on it. The lessons in English dragged on, his father's strength, but history was worst. Sam was incapable of remembering anything from the past. He despised Christopher Columbus for starting American History. He hated the Norman Conquest of England for starting English history.

But as he took his seat with a sinking heart he saw today was going to start with spelling.

"Let's begin," John said: "spell ubiquitous."

"Spell what?"

"Ubiquitous. It means something that's everywhere."

"I just want something that's here."

"Like what?" John asked. Sam shrugged helplessly.

"Spell ubiquitous!"

"U-b-i-t-o-u-s."

"Ubitous is not ubiquitous."

"I don't want to spell that word!"

"Tomorrow then," John said with a sigh. There was never more than the beginning of a fight between them.

"T-o-m—"

"No, not tomorrow! Spell—" he looked at his list—"relevant."

"Spell what?"

"Just spell it!"

"R-e-v-e-r-t."

"That spells revert, not relevant."

"What's it mean?"

"Something related to what you are talking about or doing right now is relevant."

"No, revert!"

John sighed.

"I don't want to spell anything today. I don't want any lessons today—"

"It's only Wednesday," John hesitated, not at all sure until he glanced at the calendar.

Sam's face flushed, and he stood up so his chair crashed backwards.

"No," he said, softly, but with an intensity that surprised them both.

"What's gotten into you—" John started.

"Not today," Sam insisted with the same intensity.

John flushed, too, surprised at his own flood of anger, but then nodded his head. What's gotten into us, he wondered? What difference would a day make when they kept to their schedule so routinely?

"Go ahead—go out, play," he said quietly, watching the deepening frown vanish from Sam's face. Sam bounced out of the room. John put his chair upright, then went upstairs to his study. There was a disorderly pile of papers to one side of his laptop he started to thumb through. He went on idly turning pages until he fell into a reverie.... Slowly his head settled on his arms folded in front of his laptop.

Sam drifted downstream towards the beach as the fog deepened and turned the gulls into disembodied cries. Along the shore the surf

was low, the tall, heavy-shouldered winter waves forgotten each spring. Sometimes a storm blew that surf into thirty foot waves crashing onto the beach and, at high tide, drumming at the rocky feet of the bluffs, but now the tide was out, the waves barely more than the ripples you might see on the shore of a protected bay.

If anything, his mind was emptier than usual. At low tide the beach stretched miles north around one arm of the canyon with only occasional breaks in the bluffs: to the south there was a village which had been discovered by tourists that he and his father avoided. The headland ran into the waves, there: to reach the village they had to drive up the canyon to the main road. He turned up the beach and walked along the low tide line, driven by the same unusual restlessness that had made him cut his lessons short, shoulders hunched, head down.

The wind blew softly, gulls cried, surf lapped the shore.

He had no sense of time, simply turning on his heel and walking back abruptly, surprised at how far the tide had let him walk. By the time he reached their canyon the water was up to his knees as he came around the bluff into their valley. He was hungry, and hurried home. There he found his father setting out their usual turkey sandwiches. Four empty hours had passed.

More passed before with unspoken, precise timing the two walked up the long drive to the main road. They soon heard a badly mufflered roar, then Mr. Nicholas drove up in his newspaper delivery truck, faded, dented, and without bumpers. Even though he saw them waiting he beeped his horn, a sly smile on his face. Then he leaned out the window.

"Good afternoon, John. Got yer paper." When he handed it to John Sam saw yet again that one of his arms was longer than the other.

"Oh."

"Maybe there'll be udder news t'morra," Mr. Nicholas said, relishing the doubt in his voice. "How's the novel goin'?" He knew John was a writer. He seemed to know a great deal about everyone without asking.

"Oh, great! Just great," John lied.

"Ya been workin' on thet a long time, must be the biggest novel eva'," Mr. Nicholas rasped. Mr. Nicholas had a purple nose too big for his beet-colored face, his wild red mane of hair a clashing shade. He smelled of whiskey, salt, and wet wool. Just now he screwed his eyebrows together: he didn't believe John was writing anything.

"Each word has to be right," John said to that stare. "Takes a long time to do it right. Like anything."

"Oh, yeh." Mr. Nicholas' eyebrows were still screwed together. Sam wondered how often they had said just these words to each other. He shuffled his feet.

"Y'know, thet boy oughta be goin' t'school in ter village."

"I don't want to," Sam said, horrified at the thought, then angry at himself: how often had Mr. Nicholas taunted him this way, too?

"Do'im sum good," added Mr. Nicholas, "looks gray around the gills, if ya get me meanin'. Needs ter be with others his age." Sam shuffled his feet and choked off his reply. Mr. Nicholas' eyebrows screwed together tighter.

"Darned shame about his muther: lad needs mutherin'."

John stepped back as if slapped. Angrily he said good day to Mr. Nicholas and headed back down the canyon. Sam looked at Mr. Nicholas, half wanting to stay and ask, "Where is my mother?" But he didn't dare. She was a closed book. One look at his father's face whenever the subject of his mother came up made sure that book stayed closed. Yet each time Mr. Nicholas offended his father this way Sam ached with curiosity and sadness.

"See yas t'morra!" Mr. Nicholas ground out, and gunned away with an unpleasant laugh. "Same time, same news!"

"Mean man," John muttered as Sam caught up with him. "He's the kind of person you have to take with a grain of salt, Sam," John added; "what else does he have to do out here but deliver papers and make meaningless small talk?"

"At least he does something. We never do anything."

"What do you want to do?" Sam shrugged, the moment of rebellion gone with his words.

Afternoon dragged into evening and the slow process of preparing dinner: vegetables washed and sorted, fat sliced from the meat, potatoes in the oven. Each step was a ritual, each knew his place, each knew without thinking how this too made time pass. A silent eating followed, and the reverse rituals of cleaning, putting away, and resetting the machine for the morning as the last of the light faded.

They moved into a small room with a fireplace where they laboriously built a fire: then John as laboriously filled and lit his pipe.

"You shouldn't smoke, Dad," Sam said, almost by rote, sighed, and read a little of this or that or drew. There was no television or radio. The phone was turned so low it had to be checked for messages, and never had any. On a Tuesday or Friday night Sam took a bath, but not tonight. His father made no effort to shoo him off to bed, but a hazy, gray sleepiness soon sent him upstairs, automatically turning the alarms back on as he went.

With a start he found himself standing in the middle of the room in his pajamas, hair combed, teeth brushed. Idly he touched the dragon with the too long head hanging above him, spun the yacht, and set the elephant swinging back and forth as he danced on his flying trapeze, watching their shadows mingle and separate on the walls. Then he turned off the light, asleep as his head hit his pillow....

Sam was in a dense forest, its leaves earthy reds and shades of orange: the sky was red. He took a step, amazed, bounced, and fell. Carefully he got up and tested the ground: it looked like a yellow rug piled with dark leaves and was so resilient he had to learn to walk by bouncing, and soon found himself bouncing ever higher through the trees. This would have been exhilarating except that he didn't really like heights, but couldn't stop himself.

Then he bounced by a platform high in a tree and saw three misshapen men, one with a mane of red hair, one with a beet-colored face with a purple nose that was too big, and the third with arms of different lengths smoking a fat cigar.

"Bid," said one.

"Three more, and two bits," said another, but instead of tossing chips into the pot, they tossed what looked like disembodied, rolling eyes.

"Two pair, aces high!" said one eye, looking up at the cards held by the man with the purple nose. Sam had no idea how it spoke, but the sound of the words was startling in its sharpness.

"Three kings!" said another about the cards held by the man with red hair.

That set off a terrible row. Again and again Sam bounced high enough to witness their play, and saw the men throw in their hands, disgusted. They could never finish a game with eyes used for chips giving away their cards.

Then the one with red hair saw Sam.

"Not you," he said.

"Not here," said the second with uneven arms who blew a cloud of smoke into Sam's face.

"Soon!" shouted the third with the huge purple nose. Sam tried to wave away the smoke as he choked. When he could see again he was on the bare expanse on a plain baked by a violet sun so hot he gasped for air. He didn't dare move—the ground was covered with sharp pieces of glass and piles of springs, gears, hands and shattered near-human clock faces almost as big as himself.

Not far off was a little out-of-place Victorian house. Sam heard shouting, a crash, and silence. The violet sun deepened to purple and the house flaked away. He reached out for the last flake as it blew towards him, although it seemed to take years reaching his outstretched hand. When it did he held what at first he took to be a card, the Queen of Hearts, except he found himself staring at a living woman's face he could not take his eyes from, her eyes searching his even as she turned to dust.

"No!" he shouted—and sat up, drenched with sweat. His room turned around him before it stilled, full of dark shapes. As it stilled he got up, unnerved, touched the elephant dancing on his flying trapeze

as if it was a talisman, and changed into fresh pajamas. He was afraid to fall asleep and sat in a chair until the first gray light touched the windows and he dragged himself to bed with only a few minutes to go before the alarms began to go off.

Downstairs the fire waxed and waned as John read. His head sank slowly, the book slipped from his hands onto the floor, and he slept, until a crackle from the fire made him start. He stared blindly for a moment, picked up the book and marked his place and went to his room.

That could have been a monk's in its bareness. Bed, night table, lamp, clock on a dresser, an uncarpeted wood floor needing refinishing, a wooden chair, and a single picture of himself and Sam at an amusement park from some years ago. With a start he found himself standing in the middle of his room in his pajamas, touched the picture lightly, turned off the light, and was asleep as his head hit the pillow....

John found himself beside Mr. Nicholas in his truck, but his seat was a bathtub, and Mr. Nicholas scrubbed him with one hand as he steered around corners with others.

"Gotta work the gray in," he snarled illogically, and with every pass of his brush John turned grayer. They careened off the road. Calmly they stepped out of the truck onto the floor of a small, one room house. Out the window John saw they were flying. Mr. Nicholas laughed and stepped off onto a platform where three men played cards with eyes for chips.

John was alone. The air around him filled with houses like his, barely missing one another. Closing his eyes, he stepped out. When he opened them he found himself in the middle of a rain of clocks as large as himself, colliding as they fell ringing, as if to say:

"Time to go!"

. "Time to be up and away."

"Time's up!" before they crashed into a pile of springs, gears, hands and shattered faces. John couldn't avoid the springs: he found himself bouncing on one in a forest whose leaves were ochres and siennas. He bounced right past where Sam was having an argument with the three men. They reached for John.

"That's the one!" shouted one.

"Mine!" shouted the second.

"I'll take him!" shouted the third.

"No!" John shouted—and sat up, drenched with sweat. His room turned around him before it stilled, full of dark shapes. As it stilled he got up, unnerved, and changed into fresh pajamas. He was afraid to fall asleep and sat in a chair until the first gray light touched the windows when he dragged himself to bed with only a few minutes to go before the alarms began to go off.

Every night John and Sam dreamt the same dreams. Sometimes they switched dreams. They never spoke of this but went on one day after another each in exactly the same way as the alarms broke into their exhausted sleep and started a new round of repetition.

They would have been surprised to be told they were unhappy—sadness would have been exciting. They simply thought of this gray existence as life.

II

A Disturbing Book Arrives

S am and John waited by their mailbox on a day of unusually heavy fog. They couldn't see Mr. Nicholas approach, only heard the muted roar of his muffler before he materialized from the gray.

He leaned out the window when he stopped, his eyes already screwed together.

"Same news fer ya today," he grinned, handing John the paper.

"I suppose," muttered John. The only news that mattered to him were his occasional royalty checks that kept them going. But Mr. Nicholas didn't drive away and just kept looking at John with an odd smile twisting his lips before going on.

"How's the novel comin'?"

"Oh, great! Really getting into it now," replied John automatically.

"Ya been workin' on thet novel fer years. Must be the biggest book eva'." Mr. Nicholas smiled so maliciously that John choked off the words on the tip of his tongue.

"Y'know, thet boy oughta be goin' ter school in the village."

"Too far to go," John said automatically.

But Sam choked off his usual reply, sensing Mr. Nicholas was up to something unusual.

"Darned shame about his muther: needs sum mutherin'."

John spun on his heel, dragging Sam with him.

"Don't be in such a rush!" Mr. Nicholas laughed, his purple nose flushing. With that he tossed a book into John's arms. "See ya t'morra. Sure you'll have written somethin' by then!" He laughed so hard they

could hear it over the muffler.

He thought the book was a grand joke on John and Sam, and only wished he'd thought of it himself. But he had just found it sitting on the seat beside him with a note,

"Give this to the father and son gray around the gills. You know who." He'd known instantly that meant John and Sam.

John opened the Book to see what it was all about.

"Mr. Nicholas is the kind of person you have to take with a grain of salt, Sam—" John said, then: "the nerve." He muttered something else under his breath, and gave the Book to Sam as they walked back.

The Book was heavy, its covers sheathed in red leather with a gold-embossed pattern of intertwined leaves and branches, with a space on the front where there should have been a title, and another, also blank, for an author. Curious, Sam looked inside. The pages were blank, each blank page facing one ruled. He shut it, disappointed and puzzled too.

At home he decided to stay in and sat down before the fire they had lit earlier, let the Book slide to the floor, and nodded off.

When he woke up to begin dinner, he found it beside him, and doodled half-heartedly on the first unlined page. He couldn't make sense of his picture, until it dawned on him the stick figure in it was himself going to bed. Impulsively he wrote, "No dreams." He looked a moment at his handiwork, shrugged, and went to help his father in the kitchen and after before he finally climbed into bed, idly spinning the dragon and swinging the dancing elephant on his trapeze. He was asleep as his head hit the pillow.

He groaned from under his covers the next morning as the symphony of alarms broke into his sleep. He groaned again, stretched luxuriously, his head appearing from under the covers, then abruptly sat up, and stared around the room. Something was wrong. Something was different. It wasn't the alarms.

"I didn't dream," he muttered.

He hurried to tell his father as they traced the alarms down to the kitchen, stopped the grandfather clock, and rescued the eggs poised over the bowl.

"Might as well make breakfast," said John.

Suddenly not dreaming didn't seem so important to Sam.

"Last night..." Sam trailed off.

"What about last night?"

"I didn't dream."

"There's nothing surprising about that." He had, but hadn't noticed anything.

"But I always dream: didn't you miss me, Dad?" John stared. "You always bounce by when I'm arguing with the three strange, misshapen men playing cards in the tree. Was I there?"

John was dumbfounded. If their dreams weren't so familiar he might have claimed he forgot them, but that wasn't the case. He could have denied they shared dreams, because that was just too strange, but didn't say anything because he suddenly remembered very clearly Sam had not been in his dream last night for the first time in—he couldn't say how long, because—because—he had not dreamed either. Sam saw the bewildered look on his face, but all John said, closing off discussion with a swift frown, was: "We better milk Madrigal."

Sam followed his father out to the barn to milk the cow, fetch the eggs, scatter the feed, and pick the vegetables. The Book was forgotten as their daily rituals set in.

But one evening soon after as John smoked after Sam protested again by rote, Sam found the Book beside him and picked it up again. Idly he flipped the empty pages, then turned to the beginning. He saw the page with "No dreams" was different. His stick figure drawing had been replaced by a fine pen and ink sketch of himself sleeping peacefully in his room.

Facing his image was a printed narration about how their dreams had stopped from that moment, which they had accepted without question, not even altering the way the alarms woke them, or changing any other part of their routine.

Sam looked at his father. He must have done this, he thought, to tease me. He decided to say nothing and wait for John to say something, who glanced up from his book to see Sam holding the Book Mr. Nicholas had brought sometime last week.

He said nothing as he turned away.

Outside the wind blew like a beggar trying to warm his fingers on a cold night yet only succeeding in making them feel colder. Sam let the sound of its rush fill him, and the fire's crackling flames, and the occasional puffs from his father's pipe.

Then he picked up a crayon.

On the next blank page he drew a yellow door in the middle of the air floating over a pool in their canyon stream. He drew some green grass under the door, both floating over the water, as if the door gave entrance to another world, one where, as he drew, a violet sun hung in a red sky. Above the door he drew a big yellow banner that whipped in an invisible wind, and wrote the word "Fog" in red, blue, and green. He drew fog streaming from its tip like smoke.

Then he thought this was silly and shut the Book and stared into the fire until his head nodded and the Book slid to his feet. With an effort he shook himself awake and went upstairs for another dreamless night.

He had to shrug on a jacket against the cold the next day after his lessons when he went out into a heavy fog. At a loss for a moment, he followed the stream towards the ocean, searching for the quick, silver minnows who skirted the edges of small pools. Slowly he worked nearer the beach, absorbed yet with an excess energy he had no idea what to do with thanks to their peaceful nights.

He moved from the stream towards the canyon's wall looking for wildlife in the low growth. Sometimes he surprised a ground squirrel into a noisy flight up the cliff's side, or a sparrow into the air from a bush he jostled. Sometimes he found the tracks of larger animals that hunted in the night. Slowly he circled back towards the stream, wondering about the night and animals' secrets.

The stream had reached a level stretch before the final descent to the ocean, and the water seemed thick and gooey. He looked back, and couldn't see the Last House, then heard something flap behind him. He squinted into the fog but saw nothing so edged towards the sound, closer to the ocean.

"Oh," he breathed after a few steps, and stopped.

Hovering over the stream was a banner whipping in a strong wind. "Fog" was written on it in red, blue and green. Fog streamed in smoky swirls from its flapping tip. He looked away, then back. The banner remained. He picked up a rock and threw it, missing. His next hit the banner solidly, falling back with a dull splash into the water.

The hairs on his neck rose, and he turned, certain someone was there.

Nothing but the stream, bushes, and barely guessed canyon walls in the fog met his gaze. He turned back.

"Oh," he breathed again.

A yellow door was firmly anchored to a patch of green grass that floated above the water. It was ajar, and he could just glimpse a red sky with a violet sun beyond. He stood still for a long time. Then he splashed into the water, gingerly touched the firm ground hovering there in the air, and clambered up. He pushed the yellow door wider. A dull meadow stretched out as far as he could see, with dull shadows cast by brown clouds. He walked through the door.

The violet sun gleamed in the sky. The hills, mountains and canyon were all different shades of red that half faded, half darkened to varied browns, hard to tell apart from the sky and merging with the dull meadow. In the distance he glimpsed an unexpected, emerald sea.

When he looked back through the door his canyon was gray with fog.

He walked into the meadow.

ꙮ

John was impatiently tapping his foot at the dinner table when Sam arrived home many hours later.

"Where have you been?" He was annoyed their routine was disturbed.

Sam opened his mouth to tell him, then thought better of it, and shut it wordlessly. John's eyebrows arched.

"Well? Explain yourself." Sam took a breath.

"You know the Book Mr. Nicholas brought the other day?" he began hesitantly.

"What's that got to do with anything?" John asked impatiently.

"Nothing," Sam said.

"Start eating. Don't be late again. You have your share of chores to do, too."

"When I drew 'No Dreams' we stopped dreaming," he blurted suddenly. "You know, you wrote in it."

"Wrote in what"

"The Book!" Sam hurried on before John could say anything. "Last night I drew a yellow door in the Book, and a banner with the word 'Fog' in red, green, and blue, with a red sky and a violet sun. Beyond the door."

"Eat your salad."

"They were on grass floating over the stream."

"A yellow door and a red sun," John repeated, humoring him.

"Violet!"

"Well, that would make a banner day," John laughed.

"No, 'Fog' was on the banner, and came out from its tip."

"Ah."

"Well, when I was outside…" He trailed off, pushing lettuce side to side on his plate. "I heard this flapping sound, and—." He broke off, and pushed the lettuce around on his plate again.

"Well?"

"I heard this flapping sound and there really was a big banner flapping in the wind with the word 'Fog' on it in red green and blue."

"Was it attached to anything?" John asked, not sure what to say.

"No."

"Why didn't it blow away?"

"That's just it, Dad! It was all there like I drew it! Including the yellow door! I climbed up on the grass and went through it! Everything was red, or brown, or both, except the sun, and the clouds were brown. That's why I was late. I kept looking around. When I came back through everything was like—"

"Like it really is," John said flatly. "You fell asleep and had a dream."

"The Book makes things happen!" Sam insisted.

"Books don't make things happen, Sam. Books don't do much of anything."

"You write books."

"I know."

"Or you did before you started using the computer for a pillow." John stared into his salad. "It really happened," Sam said. "Look, I've even got a sunburn." John stared at Sam's red face, which gave off waves of heat.

"That's ridiculous, Sam," he said. "You've been out in a cold wind and gotten wind-burned. You're being very silly!"

Sam seethed with hurt and rebellion as he ate, angry because everything his father said made sense, except for one thing: he did go through the door into—oh, that was impossible. He dropped a glass. Silently John swept it up. Later as he remembered how that violet sun had burned him he dropped the dried plates. That was too much.

"Go to bed Sam, now! Maybe tomorrow you can draw us a cabinet full of new china!" He instantly regretted his words as Sam dashed out, and shrugged, surprised at himself. But a red day: really! And the dreams stopping: that gave him pause, but he didn't know how to think about that.

Sam dashed upstairs and flung himself on his bed fighting off tears at his father's mockery. Then he couldn't help himself: hot tears scalded his cheeks, and he felt very alone and small. What was going on, anyway? The red day had happened! He had run in that meadow! The dreams had stopped! But how could drawing things in a book make them happen? They couldn't. But they had.

And why was his father so angry just because he dropped some plates? Why did he sleep on his laptop? Everything seemed wrong to Sam. At that moment he longed for an embrace and a sweet voice to murmur, "There, there."

"Moth—mother," he wept, crying that word for the first time in many gray years.

John admitted to himself that Sam taunting him over sleeping at his desk had stung. Then he wondered how often Sam had seen him like that, and the scene filled his mind. There he was at his desk. He saw his head fall into his arms, his breathing turn soft and steady, and then after a moment, Sam appear at his doorway on some errand, stop abruptly, "Dad" dying on his lips as he saw him asleep. After a moment he turned and tip-toed away.

John shook his head. What difference does it make anyway, he thought, we're still living off my past successes. Past, he mocked himself, past. He threw the last cutlery down instead of putting it away and stormed out of the kitchen. A knife fell to the floor and bounced end to end before it settled.

He stopped in the hallway. There wasn't anywhere in particular to storm off to, and it was too cold to go outside. He paused a moment at the stairs, thinking he should go comfort Sam, but then walked into the small living room and sat in his chair by the fireplace.

What had gotten into that boy, anyway? Confusing reality and fantasy? He took a breath to calm himself: patience he thought, patience. Unbidden words slipped into his mind: "Thet boy needs a muther," with Mr. Nicholas' laughter somewhere behind them.

"Madelyn," John breathed involuntarily, and saw a soft face with warm brown eyes framed by brown hair with natural, coppery highlights. Hers was a pretty face, if not beautiful, the face, once, of love. His fists clenched: he shut his eyes and banished both thought and memory.

Deliberately he made the fire and resumed their evening routine, except alone tonight. He unrolled his tobacco bag, filled and tamped his pipe, and lit up. Somewhere in the back of his mind he heard Sam say, "You shouldn't smoke, Dad."

"Ah," he breathed, defiantly. His mind settled as he watched the flames gather strength. He looked around the familiar room, the fire crackling, comforted—and noticed the Book propped by the window. He got up and settled down with it on his lap. He lifted the heavy cover.

There on the first page was the neat narration of Sam's "No dreams" with a fine illustration. He didn't know Sam could draw that well, but how else could that be there? He turned the page, baffled. A neat narration finely illustrated met his eyes, this time of the events following Sam's drawing his door and banner, "No fog." The last illustration showed Sam crying in his bed tonight. John stared, then slammed the Book shut, shaken.

He turned the Book over in his hands, looking for something to give away its secret, some part of his mind all the while saying "No." Sam must have let someone do this, he thought, then looked at the last picture of him crying. No one could have.

"Books don't write themselves," he said angrily, certain of that at least, and threw the Book on the floor.

John stared into the fire. His eyes grew into still mirrors reflecting the flames. Hardly realizing what he was doing he reached for the Book again, turned to a blank page, took the pen from his pocket, and drew a large two-masted schooner-rigged yacht tossing in a storm.

Then he caught himself, slammed the Book shut again and again tossed it on the floor. He drew deeply on his pipe and exhaled with a deep sigh, sat back, and stared into the fire, watching a line of sparks dance down the length of one of the logs. His head sank slowly.

He woke with a start being rolled on a hard surface. Stunned, he saw he was on a large schooner-rigged yacht wallowing in a strong sea, the booms of its two masts swinging back and forth, the sails slapping thunderously in the wind. He could barely stand on the lurching deck, too astonished for words, and ducked just in time as the aft boom swung by wildly. A green wave broadsided the yacht and took his feet out from under him, the water almost sluicing him past the port railing he clung to desperately. The water was cold as a slap to his face and brought him fully awake.

There was no time to think: he would drown if he didn't do something as another wave tried to roll the yacht over and catch the booms and sails in the sea. I have to get it into the wind, he thought, lurched to his feet and swaying side to side like a drunkard staggered towards the great tiller that guided the schooner.

Another wave knocked him down, and his fingernails clawed against the deck to stop his slide. Then the water was gone, and he flung himself at the tiller. It was alive, filled with malice, and nearly jerked him off his feet, but he forced it to port and held on for all he was worth.

Slowly the bow swung into the wind, half pushed by the waves, and with a thunderous clap of the sails the booms' wild swings stopped. He knew he had only moments and lashed the tiller in place and hurried forward to the jib.

He had the presence of mind to seize two lengths of coiled rope from just inside the cabin before he did so, and these he now secured to the bow and tossed overboard. As they uncoiled with the yacht's drift their drag kept the bow to the wind.

Thankfully the jib was on a roller, and its sheet released cleanly from its cleat and he was able to roll it until only a small triangle remained to help steady the yacht. Wind-driven rain lashed his face, green water sucked at his feet as the waves broke over the bow and drenched him as he worked. If the first crisis was past as the lines held the yacht into the wind and waves, it was a nightmare, nonetheless, the yacht heaving as the waves passed under it while the larger broke down its length.

"Time, time," he muttered, full well knowing the next gust or wave could set the yacht into wild motion again and sweep him off with the sails still up. In desperation he struggled to lower and reef each great sail as the salt from wave and wind began to blind him.

The knots holding the sails' halyards in place at their cleats were so water-tightened he cursed and more then once thought he ripped off his fingernails as he worked to loosen them. At last he worked first one free and lowered the sail until, reefed to a storm sail, he began the same struggle with the next until that too was reefed. He lashed both booms in place.

Even as the yacht steadied the waves increased and threatened to wrench the booms free, as though determined to catch one in a swell and capsize the yacht. The wind too increased until it wailed through the stays and shrouds in a fine, high-pitched voice he had never heard before as the water continued to wash down the length of the deck.

"I could drown," he groaned in fear, and clambered into the cabin to find some extra lines to reinforce the lashings on the booms. Just then a rush of water washed him down the cabin's length until he came up hard against the wall to the head. He staggered to his feet, clutched fresh lines he found in the chaos, and hurried back on deck, sealing the cabin behind him just in time to keep out the next wash of water.

He was in a turmoil of waves, wind, rain, booms, lashings, knots and whipping lines on a tossing deck. Now, with a nightmare's logic, first one lashing slithered loose, then another, and a particularly forceful wave washed him off his feet as he struggled to redo his handiwork. Now a boom gave a sudden sharp jolt to port or starboard despite his handiwork, once nearly knocking him across the deck and over the railing into the waves.

Slowly he succeeded in lashing one again, and then the next boom firmly into place. He was nearly blind now from the waves' wind-driven spray. He heard someone laughing hysterically then caught himself laughing, and fought to control his fear.

"Why don't you help?" he shouted at the boat, and almost gave way to crazy laughter again as a wave washed down the length of the deck and tore at the lines holding the tiller in place.

"Help yourself," laughed someone, as if standing beside him. He stared wildly to see who it was. Was it a shroud keening? He saw no one, yet the thin, cruel, metallic voice laughed at him again, "Help yourself!"

He clung grimly to the tiller. Then to his horror the lines holding the bow to the wind untied themselves and snaked overboard, then his boom lashings followed suit as though with a life of their own as the next wave swung the bow around and the booms swung out madly. Nothing made sense, unless a nightmare's.

Then he saw the largest wave yet bear down on him broadside as the booms caught in the water, tipping the yacht over: no time, no time to do anything he thought. A great wall of green water arched over him as the deck tilted vertically. He was falling, falling into that sea's embrace.

"Help!" he shouted in despair. "Help!" he shouted again.

He was in his chair before the fireplace.

The logs were embers, the room stifling.

"Are you alright, Dad?" Sam asked behind him. His father's shouts had drawn him downstairs. "You shouted for help."

"Just a bad dream," John got up, too stunned by this turn of events to take in where he was, still seeing that great wave arch over him. Sam stared at him.

"A dream?"

John nodded, beginning to realize where he was, taking in the concern on his son's face.

"Why are you all wet?"

John looked down at himself. His pants were in tatters. His shirt was torn. Cold water dripped from him and puddled on the chair and floor. He shuddered at its coldness, unable to feel the numbing warmth of the room. He brushed wet hair from his eyes, winced, and held up his hands. His palms were covered with rope burns, his skin raw and cracked and oozing blood.

III

A Very Wise Elephant Who Likes to Dance

"I told you it does things," Sam said. John looked at his hands, then at the Book. He picked it up and threw it into the fire. "No!" shouted Sam, but John held him as he lunged after the Book.

"I don't know what's been going on—I mean this can't go on!"

"No, no!" shouted Sam, still trying to rescue the Book.

"You leave it alone, do you hear?!"

Sam saw John's angry face, heard his angry tone, and stopped struggling. He hung his head. John let him go, and with another disbelieving look at his wet clothes and painful hands, and a quick glance at the Book in the fire where the flames began to lick around it, hurried out of the room.

The moment he was gone Sam pulled the Book from the fire with the pair of tongs that leaned against the fireplace. The leather was barely scorched on the back, despite the flames licking its edges. Sam hesitated, then lifted the cover at the foot of his father's chair and slipped the Book underneath. He threw a magazine into the fireplace in its place, poking its pages and puffing on the fire until they curled into flame. He took the poker and kept stirring the pages to be sure they all burned until he heard his father coming down the stairs, and hurried back to his room.

The last flames flickered over what had been the magazine when John returned in dry clothes, his hands bandaged. He stirred it with the poker, and sat down as it crumbled in curled, black ashes. He could make no sense of his adventure. He tried to tell himself it was all psycho-somatic, but that seemed far-fetched even to himself.

His head ached.

His body was all sprains and sore muscles.

His hands burned.

He gave the dying embers a last poke, laboriously went up the stairs and threw himself unchanged onto his bed.

He dreamed for the first time in many days, except he dreamed Sam's dream. When the Queen of Hearts dissolved into flakes that stung his hands, raw and unbandaged in the dream, he woke with a groan in the dark, stood up, and paced back and forth in his room until dawn when the alarms began to go off.

Sam hardly slept, his mind racing from his father's hurt hands and soaked clothes to the "No Dreams" and "Fog" in the Book, and back. He felt exhausted when the alarms started. He staggered downstairs shutting off one alarm after another, saying nothing to his father in the kitchen after one look at his face and bandaged hands.

He soon discovered his father's remedy for the strange goings on. Sam had to do all the chores, milking, feeding, gathering the eggs, tending the vegetables, cooking, washing up, carrying, lifting, and stacking, for days.

Few words passed between father and son during that time. Sam cast only a surreptitious glance or two at where the Book was hidden as the evenings passed before the fire in dead silence.

Lessons too became rigorous, although after a few days of relentless chores he could hardly pay attention. John avoided his study and laptop, hanging around to see that if Sam wasn't doing a lesson he was doing some other long neglected chore around the house.

John did have the excuse there wasn't much he could do with his bandaged hands, but Sam soon seethed with unspoken resentment as he milked Madrigal, fed the chickens and hoed the vegetable patch with only the barest exchange of words with his father.

One thing was subtly altered, however: Sam no longer looked gray around the gills. He looked, if not bright and eager, like a coal the slightest breeze could fan into flame.

Mr. Nicholas noticed the change too one day not long after these events as he handed the paper to Sam.

"What's new, m'boy?"

"Nothing, Mr. Nicholas."

"Why hasn't your Dad cum up fer the paper as usual? Thought he looked fer'ard ter the help wanted ads!" His eyes screwed together as he laughed meanly.

"He hurt his hands."

"Must've been typin' up a storm!" Sam didn't smile.

"He went sailing in a storm and they got raw."

"Didna know you folks had a boat. No storms aroun' here recently, neither."

Sam shifted from one foot to the other. Mr. Nicholas' eyes had a coal-like intensity. Sam almost blurted out the explanation just to see Mr. Nicholas' befuddled expression when a voice said softly but quite clearly in his head, "Don't." After a moment it added, "Go home."

Sam shut his mouth and turned back down the canyon.

"Hey! Wait a minute!" Mr. Nicholas called after him, but Sam picked up his pace. He was about to shout, "Thanks for the Book!" when again he heard, "Don't." He ran down the path and into the house, slamming the door behind him. Mr. Nicholas stared after him with an ugly frown before he ground the truck into gear without using the clutch and roared off.

Even as John's hands got better and their bandages lessened he was still forbidding, driving Sam through his lessons. He didn't know how else to deal with his near-death adventure except by making their routine as formidable and unchallengeable as possible.

"Spell matrilinear," he ordered. "Ma-tri-lin-e-ar," he sounded off, seeing the look on Sam's face.

"What does it mean?"

"It means descended from the female side."

"Like from your mother?"

"Yes." Something stuck in Sam's throat at that, and his seething resentment abruptly spilled out.

"M-o-t-h-e-r. Mother! Where's mine?" he gasped, then shouted: "Where's mine!" Surprise filled John's face. "Mr. Nicholas always talks about mothering, mutherin', when we get the paper," Sam added: "why don't we ever talk about her?" There were tears at the edge of his father's eyes. John closed the spelling book.

"You go out and play now. No more chores. I'm going to

work today."

"I want to know!"

"Get out! I mean go out! Now!" John shouted back.

The pause filled with a shared anger and pain and confusion. How gray he looks, Sam thought while John thought, looking at his son's defiant face, how vivid, how young, how full of life he looked.

"I'm sorry," John murmured. "Not now. Another time." He walked out of the kitchen. Sam stood there, clenching and unclenching his fists, his breathing calming. He heard John hesitate, then go slowly upstairs. After a moment the door to the study closed.

Sam didn't know what to do or where to go, released from days of drudgery. All the strange events in their lives since the Book's arrival raced through his mind. An image grew in his mind of a woman's face with brown hair with natural coppery highlights that blew across her face as that faded, her eyes lingering on his. He was rooted to the spot by their sadness.

He tried to shake her impact on him. First he focused on the kitchen: its pale blue walls, the table with two chairs, the old refrigerator whose paint had begun to bubble, the machine that wound around the walls which never made breakfast, and the old stove that once burned wood and looked like it had been rescued from the witch's house in the fairy tale of Hansel and Gretel.

He looked at the grandfather clock with its sunburst face and deep gongs they stopped every morning. He walked circles around each second, got bored, took a rest, and finally moved around the next.

Nothing added up. He had no idea what to do.

Then he hurried into the living room and pulled the Book out from under John's chair, turning it over in his hands, examining the superficial fire damage. The front cover was unharmed, still with spaces for a title and author's name. He turned the pages, wondering at the drawings and neat writing. Now opposite a yacht tossing in a storm was a neat narration of John's experience that ran several pages, each page of text faced by an illustration showing one of his predicaments: the last showed the great wave about to break over the yacht.

"Who sent it," he murmured, "and why?" And because he was a bright boy and agreed with his father that drawing in books didn't make things happen, he almost closed it for good.

But he didn't.

Instead he turned to a blank page and reached for his crayons. This is silly, he thought, but began to draw, his disbelief making him exaggerate the absurdity of the picture that emerged. First he drew the bluffs along the shore and their canyon's walls, but far taller than they were and leaning forward dizzily. Under the worst overhang he drew a tent like something out of the Arabian Nights, tall and with a pinnacle rising from its bulbous top from which rose a finger of smoke that twisted into fantastic shapes.

He left a big flap open so he could see inside the tent. There he drew a large Elephant wearing spats and an elegant Edwardian suit with an embroidered, green vest. Great tusks curled outward from his mouth. The Elephant was the source of the smoke as he sat on a tiny circus stool and with a pipe that looked like a tea kettle with a hose coming out of it in place of a stem in his mouth. Smoke streamed upward from his mouth, his upraised trunk, and his ears.

Sam gave him a caption: "Very Wise and Likes to Dance."

He laughed as he looked at his drawing, shook his head—and sighed. He stopped mid-motion from sliding it back under the chair, straightened up, then put it squarely where his father couldn't help but see it on the cushion before he sat down. Then he grabbed a jacket and went out.

John as defiantly deliberately tried to sleep on his laptop without making any pretense to work, but he couldn't find a comfortable place for his hands. He didn't want to think about anything but couldn't stop from wondering why Sam asked about his mother after years of silence.

He was puzzled at his son's new vividness, too, although he thought that was a good thing. But his irritation deepened; his hands were an all too visible reminder that something he couldn't explain was going on. It was a long time since he had been a child and could cross the boundary between imagination and reality effortlessly. Long ago like everyone else he had learned to make that boundary an iron wall. Suddenly it seemed transparent and full of holes.

He was glad he'd burned that Book, anyway! Who had sent it? Mr. Nicholas? He didn't think so: he was too mean spirited and cheap to give anyone anything. Who else would want to hurt either of them? Haven't we been hurt enough?! he thought abruptly: didn't I do enough hurt? slipped into his mind next. His head jerked erect.

"No," he muttered aloud. There were some things he just would not think about. He stared blankly out the window.

There he saw Sam wander down the oak-bordered stream towards the beach. I've really been much too hard on him, he thought. He's just a child! After a moment he headed downstairs and grabbed his jacket from the coat-stand by the front door; as he turned to go out the Book sitting on the cushion of his chair in the living room caught his eye.

He went in and, after a moment of hesitation, picked it up. He turned it over, seeing the scorch marks, and realized with growing anger Sam had defied him and rescued it from the flames. Then he opened it.

He thumbed past the neat narration of the earlier adventures to his own on the yacht with new illustrations. The last showed him cowering by the tiller, helpless as a great wave arched over the yacht.

He was too dazed to think. He turned the page—and saw Sam's new drawing of the canyon and the Arabian Nights style tent with an Edwardian, great-tusked elephant smoking in its middle on a tiny stool. The Book dropped from his hands.

"What next," he muttered to himself, his anger building, and raced out after Sam in fury.

"Sam! Sam!" The fog which had inched its way up the canyon chose that moment to gather itself and pounce on house and canyon. It muffled John's words in its thick swirls. Angrily he walked towards the beach, sure of his direction in the thick fog only by his steady descent.

"I'll teach you to deceive me," he muttered, making the mistake of flexing his hands. "Just let me get my hands on you!"

Sam was well ahead of him, nearly to the beach. He didn't really expect to find an elephant in a tent, but pushed on. After all he still wasn't dreaming, not his old dreams anyway, and it had taken days for his sunburn to stop bothering him. But near the bluffs' end he stopped, and half turned to go home. Suppose nothing was there? Worse, suppose something was!

He felt a moment's weakness: wasn't it better not to put his imagination to the test? After all, an elephant in a tent on his beach! Better to turn back, better to be able to think, well, maybe I'd have seen it if I went on! Better to have hope.

Besides, it was so cold as the sharp wind blew off the always cold ocean that he clenched his teeth to stop their chattering. It was almost impossible to see anything in the thick fog, anyway. Then he glimpsed a figure slip behind one of the wind-bent cypresses to one side of the stream where that emerged from the bluffs onto the beach.

"Dad?" There was no answer. He stared forward.

There! The figure slipped from one tree to another. It wasn't a man at all, but an old lady bent half over.

"Who's there?" Two more old ladies dashed after the first. He didn't remember ever seeing anyone like them in the village. He edged cautiously after them through the lupine and wildflowers edging the creek, pushed past a wind-bent cypress, and saw no one. He hopped from stone-to-stone to cross the creek.

"Who's there?" he called again. His voice was flat and heavy in the fog. The ocean thumped on the shore like an old woman beating a rug with a pole. Lower down the stream he saw the three old women slip around a large boulder that blocked his view of the beach.

"Wait a minute! Who are you?" he called.

"Come and see," replied a barely audible voice, but at its sound Sam leaped uncontrollably through the underbrush towards the boulder. His heart pounded. His hands were clammy.

"Coming, coming!" he heard himself shout. He wanted to stop at the boulder in sudden fear, but his legs carried him breathlessly around it as if they had a life of their own.

The kindly old women had vanished. Instead, the beach was an expanse of eyes like those used by the three misshapen men in their card game in his dream, but of every imaginable size. Some hovered above small pyramids whose tips floated above them: some were encased in the floating tips. Some rested on posts, some lay in the sand, all of every conceivable size....

They made no sound but he could sense their thought, "Come and see..." Far worse than these was what Sam saw galloping towards him.

"That's the one!" shouted one figure.

"Mine!" shouted another.

"I'll take him!" shouted the third. Sam couldn't move as they raced towards him. He couldn't make sense of their appearance, half horse, half men, with no heads where there should have been heads,

and heads where there could not have been. A scream rose in his throat.

"What have we here?" someone said behind him, and like a bubble bursting the frightening creatures disappeared. He stared, breathing hard: only a fog-shrouded, empty beach with the surf barely visible through the gray remained.

"What have we here?" repeated the voice behind him. He turned around slowly in dread.

"Ohh!"

ᏯᎧ

"Sam!" John shouted into the wind, hurrying down canyon towards the ocean. Soon he realized he had gone far enough to reach the beach, yet was still in the lupine and oaks along the stream, not even as far as the bent cypresses nearer the shore. How could he get lost in a downward sloping canyon?

He saw a gray, fleeting shape across the stream: a will-o-wisp bit of fog, he thought, but the hair on his neck rose, and he whirled, certain Sam was behind him, playing tricks. He saw no one. He walked on and the hair on his neck rose again, but again no one was behind him when he turned. He turned back but tripped on a stone and fell into the stream, hurting his hands as they slid on rocks to break his fall.

"Ow," he muttered, then worse, the water soaking him in an instant. He pulled himself up dripping, seething. When his hair stood on end on his neck again he ignored it, still edging towards the beach. He thought he heard voices ahead arguing and, alarmed, he picked up his pace, careful where he put his feet. For all that he stumbled constantly, automatically reaching out with his hands to a branch or rock to steady himself until his bandages were in tatters and his hands' sensitive skin turned raw and bled in places.

That made him even angrier and more determined. He gritted his teeth and drove himself on in pursuit of the voices that always seemed only a few steps away. With a final lurch he fell into the midst of three misshapen men playing cards. Their skin was wind-burned from constant exposure. One had a face like a beet with a too large purple nose, another a mane of flaming red hair that clashed with his skin, and a third possessed arms of different lengths.

"Not yet," said the one smoking a cigar, and blew a puff of smoke into his eyes. John staggered up only to fall backwards into the stream again. He groaned with pain, and wearily got up. The men laughed.

"You're a sight," someone said behind him. The three men disappeared. John turned slowly in dread.

"Ohh!"

෧෨

Sam sat on a pile of rugs and took in the great tent whose ceiling was woven with bright, abstract designs that went up to the distant, bulbous peak. A twisted band of red, blue and green circled the tent ten feet off the ground. The lower walls were plain. Several Persian carpets spread across the floor, one with a brilliant red Tree of Life design, one green with gold flowers, one blue with filigrees of foliage.

Smaller piles of rugs were near the tent's walls for seats, as well as an odd assortment of ottomans and heaped cushions amid a few large, well-worn chests. A central pole went upwards, bright brass rings showing where its segments had been fitted together. Finally he forced himself to look at the tent's occupant.

Gimme that old soft shoe I said
the old soft shoe a razza-ma-tazz
a raaaaaza-ma-tazz! Ah-one, ah-two,
a doodle dee doo! that old soft shoe
nothing else will do oh raazza-ma-tazz!
That's the dance my darling used to do!
Razza-ma-tazz oh ma-taaazzz!

this individual sang freely, dancing as though this was the most normal thing in the world.

'He' was an Elephant dressed in an elegant Edwardian suit with a fine green richly embroidered velvet vest whose pockets bulged with objects Sam could only guess. The Elephant happily worked his way through the dance routine Sam had drawn earlier. He kicked a cane with one spat-shod foot and let it spin in his hand, his body heaving in merriment. His trunk waved gaily side to side as his ears fanned back and forth and he bobbed to his own beat, light-footed despite his great size. His eyes were tiny in such a large head, though they

had a lively brown and amber-flecked gleam. He never blinked. His tusks gleamed.

"Who are you?" Sam finally asked, suspended between denial and delighted belief.

The Elephant danced towards him.

"You had a narrow escape, young man. Your adventure almost ended there and then." He was serious, but his dance was so comic Sam laughed. "I'm glad you're happy!" said the Elephant. "As for who I am..." He uttered a rhythmic chant without words to which he shook and jolted in the middle of the tent. "Wonderful," he sighed, and stopped.

"I wouldn't say anything for awhile," he said, looking closely at Sam: "wait until your mind's not in such a daze. Words can be useless. Ubiquitous things, though. U-b-i-q-u-i-t-o-u-s. Relevant only sometimes. R-e-l-e-v-a-n-t. Like that word matrilinear. Only special to people with matrilineal problems." He laughed at Sam's expression, trumpeting as his belly shook and he stamped on the ground.

Then he looked so hard at Sam he felt as though the Elephant was inside his head fingering his thoughts, saying "this one's good" or "here, this is rubbish."

"Stop that," demanded Sam.

The Elephant nodded, and stopped. They regarded each other. Finally the Elephant settled down on a circus stool that seemed far too small to hold him, and began to smoke from a hose leading from a large tea kettle with a lid and safety valve held over a small fire on a plinth placed between two of the Persian rugs.

Little fingers of steam pried at the lid. Smoke poured from the Elephant's ears, mouth, and trunk, forming arabesques as it rose. At Sam's expression he murmured,

"Caravan tea. I'm very fond of it." Sam nodded, fascinated.

Some time went by with only the sound of the kettle hissing and the Elephant's puffs as Sam watched the smoke take on one strange shape after another as it rose and floated out the hole at the tent's top.

He wondered why the tent was so bright, for there were no candles or lamps or torches. Then he realized everything had its own glow, creating a diffused lighting.

Suddenly the Elephant stood, putting the hose to one side. Wrinkles piled up on his forehead as he stared out the tent's entrance. Without a word he went out. Sam stayed motionless, though he wondered what had drawn the Elephant's attention. He had no desire to be on that beach again. The little fingers of steam redoubled their efforts to pry open the kettle's lid.

"Stop that!" ordered Sam. The fingers hesitated and then withdrew into the kettle. As he got up to inspect this contraption more closely the Elephant threw open the tent flap and his father walked in, drenched, ragged, dazed, holding his hands out awkwardly from his sides.

"Sam!"

"Dad!"

The Elephant stepped in behind him.

"A very interesting day," he murmured. John stared at him.

"Sit down by the kettle, my boy, it will warm you." He gestured towards a pile of smaller rugs by the fire under the kettle: John obeyed with a dazed expression. The Elephant did an intricate dance step over to one of his trunks and rummaged through its contents.

"Are you okay?" Sam whispered to his father. John was silent. "I drew him in the Book," he added. Their eyes met, one glance bright and eager, one confused.

"I can't sort all this out," sighed John.

"It's real," said Sam, "he's real!"

"I know, but I don't believe it."

The Elephant turned with a smile, then went back to rummaging in the trunk. "Must fix you up," he murmured, "must do some maaaajor repairs, a raaaaza-ma-tazz!"

IV

A Dangerous Journey Decided

The Elephant found what he was looking for and turned to John.

"Hold out your hands," he ordered. John obeyed, continuing to stare at him.

The Elephant took them in his own, dwarfing John's, and carefully applied a foul-smelling yellow paste first to one, then to the other.

"Phew," sniffed Sam.

"Help your father pull these on," he ordered next, holding out a pair of embroidered gloves. Sam carefully edged the gloves over his father's fingers and palms. Then the Elephant handed John a pack of cards. "Shuffle them."

"How can I do that?" exclaimed John, holding up his hands.

"Shuffle them."

Awkwardly John took hold of the cards. He cut the deck.

"Ouch!" someone said. John almost dropped the cards. Then to his surprise he shuffled them easily as someone else said, "Whee!"

"You can do more than you think," the Elephant murmured. John knew he meant more than just his hands could do. "There are some clothes in the trunk that should do. Those are useless."

John looked at his torn pants and jacket. His shoes squelched with water. Hesitantly he pulled at their laces and took them off, handing the cards to Sam so he could rummage in the trunk for a new pair.

"I'm the Two of Diamonds," announced that card when Sam turned the pack over and looked at the last card. "Who are you?" it asked.

"Sam," he laughed, amazed.

"No! What's your suit!"

"I don't have one."

"Everyone is a heart, spade, club or diamond!"

"Hearts," he said on impulse, with a grin.

"Which one?"

"The Sam of Hearts," wisecracked the Elephant. Sam laughed.

"No such thing!" shouted the Two of Diamonds.

"There is now. He said so," replied Sam. John froze by the trunk at this exchange, one leg into a new pair of trousers.

"Here," said the Elephant reaching for the cards, "we'll play a game of poker." He dealt five cards quickly so that their cries were buried under each other. He inspected his hand. Sam copied him, not sure what to do. He had the Two of Diamonds, the Six of Clubs, a Three of Hearts, a Nine of Hearts, and the King of Spades.

"Throw the two and three away," whispered the Nine of Hearts.

"You bet," added the Six of Clubs.

"You big guys are always ganging up," said the irrepressible Two of Diamonds.

"Get lost, peanuts!" replied the Six. The King was silent.

The Elephant replaced two unhappy cards with two happy new ones. A sigh of relief breathed from his hand.

"Come on, Sam," the Elephant said.

"He went out of turn!" cried the three.

"Quiet!" the King of Spades spoke finally. He looked at the bemused face of Sam. "Throw them all away." He ignored their protests. "Now." Sam tossed four cards away and picked up four new

ones. By now his father had returned in dry clothes, although he looked vaguely like an Argentinean cowboy, a gaucho, with a satchel filled with ropes and a bola—a rope with heavy balls at each end to throw and tangle someone and bring him down. If possible he looked even more incredulous as he watched the game.

"Take a hand," said the Elephant. "Go ahead, turns don't matter here." He handed John five cards. No sound came from his hand.

"Call," said the Elephant.

"You haven't bet anything," said Sam, knowing that much had to be done in poker. The Elephant shrugged. He laid down two Twos and two Nines, with one Jack left over.

"Better one Jack than no John," it cracked. "Let's see your hand," it added, to Sam. He laid down a Five of Hearts, and the Kings of Spades, Diamonds, Clubs, and Hearts.

"Oh no," groaned the Elephant's hand. They turned to John, but he only sat there looking at his cards. He felt their eyes on him, looked up, and after a moment laid down one blank card after another until only one was left. Then he laid that down.

"Ohh," breathed the other cards. It was the Queen of Hearts. She took off her crown and shook loose her long brown hair with its natural coppery highlights. For a moment a smile almost touched her face, then she faded to gray and vanished.

"Come and get me," she whispered just before disappearing.

"Make her come back!" Sam shouted, standing abruptly.

The Elephant put the cards away thoughtfully. John covered his face with his gloved hands. Sam could still hear her words. Very faintly they were drowned by a babble of soft voices crying "Sam, Sam." Then her face appeared in his mind again, except now she looked at something beyond him. Sam strained to see what it was, blind to all else, and walked towards the tent's flap. The Elephant watched Sam closely. Now Sam saw what she was looking at: a young child in bed.

"Sam," she whispered.

"Mommy!" cried Sam, and lunged forward towards the vision.

"Stop!" trumpeted the Elephant. Sam did, blinded by tears. The babble of soft voices faded. Now they had a cruel edge: they were just beyond the tent flap.

"Don't go out there," the Elephant breathed. "You have a ways to go before you can tell the difference between the true and false." He looked larger and a great deal sterner than Sam's first impression. His father on the other hand looked sadder and smaller. The tent's stillness was broken by a violent flap as a strong gust struck. Drafts raced about, touching them in unguarded places, making them shiver. Dark shadows loomed from the tent's edges.

"It's too dark for my taste," murmured the Elephant. He took a colorless globe the size of a softball from one of his vest pockets and gave it to John. He held the globe gingerly, a puzzled look on his face.

"Just look in it," ordered the Elephant. John did, but he saw only the distorted curvature of his gloved hands cradling it. Then he saw a small flicker of light to one side, and twisted the globe to get a better look. The flicker grew into a disembodied twist of flame, but the globe stayed cool and heavy, and the flame's glow didn't deepen further.

"Give it to Sam." A greater gust struck the tent; shadows stepped towards them from the walls.

Sam took the ball curiously. He could see the little flicker of flame, and squinted trying to see it better. When it rushed towards him he dropped the globe with a startled cry.

The Elephant picked it up. Red and gold twisted brightly in the globe. "That's good for a first time," he smiled. Then he looked at it briefly and tossed it up towards the tent's pointed peak. There it floated, its warm yellow light erasing the shadows before they had time to retreat and hide. The next gust was much weaker.

"This has been a pleasant meeting," the Elephant said, hesitating over his choice of words, "but some decisions are in order. To go back to the Last House would be hard. You would have to cross the beach." They remembered what they had seen there. "And there is no telling who, or what, will be waiting in the canyon now." They exchanged looks. "Even if you could get home I don't think it would be safe."

"What are those—creatures—?" Sam asked.

"They are—they want to enforce how you have been, or been getting. Gray around the gills. Grayer."

"Like the Queen of Hearts!" Sam said.

"Yes. They are here now because you have started to change," he said to Sam, "while you" he looked at John, "are almost in their grasp."

"You mean," Sam asked, "we were fading out like—like—her?"

"Yes, you were, until you began to desire again, young man. You cannot desire without hoping to get what you want so badly. Life is desire," he breathed, "and desire creates the future." Sam understood instinctively, but John just shook his head.

"I don't think either of you will find peace or safety until memory is laid to rest and hope realized."

"What does that mean?" John asked, noticing with surprise it was to Sam whom the Elephant spoke.

"It means I have to find what I need," said Sam, understanding at once.

"And what is that?" his father asked. Sam took a deep breath. Oh yes, he understood very well!

"I want my mother."

"I've had enough of this nonsense!" John said, stung, standing. "We're going home."

"But he said we can't."

"He's not there!" shouted John. "Neither is that globe up there, or this tent, or those cards—"

"Or the clothes you're wearing," continued the Elephant—"or those men who scared you on your way here, or those gloves on your hands, or the rope burns under them, or that sailboat you couldn't handle."

"That's right," insisted John: "They're all delusions!"

"You're not crazy, Dad!"

"Little by little you've got me seeing what you want to be real because I'd prefer that rather than decide you're—that you need help," John said angrily in response: "it was wrong to isolate you like I've done. You need to be in a regular school with regular children and to be—"

"Mothered!"

John ignored that.

"I need to do the right thing and get some reality back into our lives!" He grabbed Sam and headed out of the tent. The Elephant sat in silence.

Sam cried out and struggled to twist loose. But John held him firmly and dragged him across the tent, ignoring his painful hands, and flung open the flap. There he stopped. The beach of eyes had

returned, each again floating over its own post, some over pyramids of different sizes, some encased in their floating tips.

Their collective thought beat on John and Sam: "Come out, come out, come out to us!" They stood turned to stone. Careening through these was a herd of stony figures driven by the weird centaur-like creatures Sam had seen earlier with their misplaced heads. There was something else too that John saw that made him step back into the tent. He let the flap shut the vision from his eyes.

"Everything you say makes a great deal of sense," the Elephant sighed behind them. He rose and came to them. "It's just not true." He flung the flap open over John and Sam's protests. There was nothing except fog and a sandy shore, and the gray surf pounding towards the bluffs as the tide rolled in. Then he let the flap drop again. "You see," he said, returning to the kettle and beginning to smoke again, "they are afraid of me, for now. But they want you. Does your hand hurt?"

John's hand throbbed from holding onto Sam against his will. He let him go.

"It's time for simple truths," the Elephant challenged him.

"Yes, it hurts," John conceded.

"I want my mother!" Sam said, undaunted by John's anger.

"Indeed you do!" cried the Elephant. He jumped up and cut some steps, delighted now that things had taken a turn for the better.

"CHA cha Cha

CHA cha Cha

CHA cha Cha" he sang, dancing to his new rhythm.

"Cha CHA cha

CHA cha cha

cha cha CHA!"

The fingers of steam beat the changing rhythms on the kettle's lid. John and Sam stared.

"And now," panted the Elephant as he came to a delighted halt, "you tell your son why he can't have his mother!" He tried to snap his fingers, always difficult for an Elephant. Sam did it for him. "You really should have years ago," he added, mopping his brow with a fine silken handkerchief. "How in the world have you avoided talking about it so long?"

"I wanted to shelter him from the hurt," John said.

"How could you do that except by lying and dying?"

"What do you mean?"

"We live in the truth! But to live getting gray around the gills—is—wrong!" The whole weight of the Elephant's personality was in "wrong" as it gusted out. "Tell him the truth now."

"I want my mother. Why are you keeping her from me? Everyone has one. Are you divorced or something?"

"No."

"Did she run away? Did she do something wrong?"

"No."

"What, then!?"

This was the book John had promised himself never to re-open. Now here he was—wherever that was, he thought in a daze—feeling the weight of that book oppress him as he opened it.

"Simplest is best," sighed the Elephant, and John had the same feeling Sam had earlier, that he was in his mind and could read his thoughts. He shook his head, and took a breath.

"Your mother is dead, Sam," he blurted out. "She got very sick when you were a little boy in a way that no one understood. She almost faded from sight."

"Just like the Queen of Hearts? That is her, isn't it!" he said accusingly.

John nodded. He had loved her desperately, yet she was also someone he had taken for granted, like the ground, or the air in his lungs. He had written his way to fame living in her yet not realizing her importance.

When she got sick he had been confused, and helpless when he should have been the opposite. He remembered the grief in her eyes, and how she turned ever grayer. Perhaps that had started sooner and he just paid no attention until it was critical. Maybe—…. He forced his memories down and met Sam's glance. How could he explain any of this to his son? He could hardly explain it to himself.

"She's dead," he repeated finally.

"But I saw her just a little while ago!" Sam insisted. "She's the Queen of Hearts, isn't she? That's her face, isn't it?" he said desperately.

John nodded. "And she said 'Come and get me'!"

"Oh, Sam."

"And that was real—real—as your hands!"

"Mmm," murmured the Elephant.

"How can that be, I ask you?!" John demanded, turning on the Elephant.

"People," the Elephant replied tartly, "ask questions they've already decided can't be answered reasonably, to prove their point of view. Like you. So you ask, 'How can that be?'—when the answer is right in front of you. And when someone else nods and says, 'Of course it can't be', you nod your head as if you're hearing something else besides your own prejudice being confirmed. It's just like asking," the Elephant added hotly, "'how can there be a talking deck of cards?,' although you've just played with one! Do you think if I say, 'You're right. There can't be!' this deck will go silent?" He held the cards up and shuffled them.

"Whee!" they said.

"Worse," snapped the Elephant, "you pretend things that happen all the time don't happen at all. Here. Choose a card," he said to John, holding out the deck. "I can tell you right now what the card will be, and so can Sam. Here, take the whole deck and shuffle it." John did.

"Whee!" the cards cried again.

"Now choose." John picked a card.

"It's the Queen of Hearts," Sam said. John turned the card over. She fell to dust in his hands.

"Now explain it," demanded the Elephant. John shook his head. "But there she is! The queen of your dreams!"

John stood helpless, understanding nothing.

"A wise Elephant knows when to stop asking and accept, while the foolish pretends he's got the question and answer for everything."

John's head ached. What had happened to their careful routine? He realized in the same moment it had been breaking down since Sam first refused to do that spelling lesson, and then…the Book arrived. That stood everything on its head! Perhaps, just perhaps, the thought slipped into John's mind, perhaps more is possible than he dreamed?

The next moment the absurdity of such hope made him dismiss that thought. He again took in the tent, remembered the creatures on the beach, and eyed the Elephant: and fell into hopeless confusion.

"Madelyn," Sam whispered into the silence, "that was her name." He sighed, and looked towards the tent's flap. "Is the Queen of Hearts really my mother? Can I—I want her!"

"Ahh," sighed the Elephant. "Really?"

"Yes."

John dropped his eyes when the Elephant's gaze shifted to him. "And do you still want her?" sounded clearly in his mind.

John realized with a shock the Elephant knew how he failed her when she was ill. For the first time he didn't wonder if the Elephant was real, but who he really was. He couldn't meet his gaze but, slowly, found himself nodding yes even through his confusion.

"Sure," he said bitterly, "who wouldn't want a second chance?" The Elephant leaned back.

"Very well. Those—eyes on the beach?" They looked at him. "I know those Watchers," he sighed. "I can't tell you about them, except they are much worse than you think." His shudder made them shudder.

"As for the three misshapen men, I suspect we have not seen the last of them. Nor of those strange women you chased, Sam. Nor those centaur things, with their odd heads. I can't say who they really are, whatever I may guess." Sam looked disappointed. The Elephant weighed them. "What's hanging from the ceiling in your room, Sam?"

"What?" Sam was startled by the sudden change of subject. He shut his eyes and summoned a picture of his room, everything there taken for granted for so long he could barely remember anything in particular. "From the ceiling," he breathed. He saw them now. "A green dragon with a big head, and—a sailboat—"

"A schooner rigged yacht—" John said, startled in turn, "like the one I was on…"

"And a dancing Elephant on a flying trapeze," finished the Elephant.

He and John looked at Sam.

"We are living in Sam's imagination," said the Elephant.

"You mean Dad's right? This isn't really happening at all?"

"Oh no," smiled the Elephant, blowing a long string of arabesques as he resumed smoking, "just the opposite. We always live within our imagination. Nothing in the world has any meaning at all aside from our imagination, from what we make of whatever it is," he added, "and it is your imagination that has caught us." He laughed. "Oh yes, I'm very real, though I hardly recognize myself!" He blew another string of arabesques. Sam laughed. John stared at the smoke and kettle.

"Caravan tea," sighed the Elephant with a touch of impatience at his look.

"He's very fond of it," said Sam. The Elephant smiled.

"Such rich steam," he explained.

"What about the Queen of Hearts?" demanded Sam.

"She is your mother, and not: your mother is in—in Dread City. That can only be reached through a Far Land of Fear which none can bear to cross."

A silence drew out. Finally the Elephant added, "All these who have frightened you are the servants of Dread City, seen in your own way. They are coming for you now because you've almost faded into their land and they don't want to let you go. You spend the nights trapped in the same dreams, and you sleep most of the day," he added to John. "Both of you do nothing new or go anywhere. You talk about nothing. You imagine nothing. Or not until very recently. You hid from pain, from disturbance, from hope. Until the Book came."

"The Book!" exclaimed John.

"Who sent it?" demanded Sam.

"I have no idea." The Elephant smiled a vast, inscrutable smile.

"It writes out all our adventures!" Sam exclaimed, "and draws pictures."

"And is it full?"

"It's almost empty."

"Hmm," the Elephant nodded, and sat back.

The truth of how he had described their lives struck both John and Sam powerfully now, too. John thought there was a poetic justice in his turning ever grayer, like Madelyn.

At that moment a powerful gust of wind nearly tore the tent from the ground. The globe dimmed perceptibly.

"We haven't much time," said the Elephant, uneasy for the first time. Another gust tore at the tent. A rope snapped outside and slapped against the tent's side. The globe dimmed farther. They could sense the elements gather their forces for another blow.

"What can we do?" asked John. "You said it would be hard to go home up the canyon." The Elephant nodded. "Is there anywhere we can go to avoid them?"

"I don't know, not for long, anyway."

"We can't go home, at least not safely, and we can't avoid them, at least not for long," said John.

"We have quite a problem," the Elephant observed unhelpfully.

"And I want my mother," added Sam. But now a thought crept into his mind, triggered by mention of the Book.

"This all started when I began drawing in the Book," he said. First one, then the other turned to Sam.

"Mm hm."

"And each thing I drew happened, and ended up being drawn and written even better in the Book."

"Mm hm."

"And it's all led to my coming closer to my mother."

"In a way of speaking," the Elephant nodded.

"In a way of speaking," Sam echoed, angry at words, a desperate resolve swelling. He didn't know how, but he knew what he wanted more than anything else and that here, now, the impossible was possible. He took a deep breath. "Then let's go to Dread City."

The gust just about to break against the tent stopped at that.

"Go to Dread City," repeated the Elephant, the wrinkles piling up on his vast forehead in astonishment.

"Yes! But not just that. Let's go get her, my mother," he said to the Elephant, "Madelyn," he said to John, "and bring her home!"

The globe went dark. Only the tent's original dim glow remained.

"So many have tried," murmured the Elephant in the silence, "names like stars, Gilgamesh, Orpheus, Aeneas, Dante…" John just stared in disbelief. "You have the worst case of doubts," the Elephant trumpeted at him. "Everything will happen that must happen whatever you want or believe."

"Dad, let's go," Sam pleaded: "let's go!"

"I don't know how such a thing is possible! Even if you believe the stories," John added for the Elephant's benefit, "those who get there can't stay, not living—…"

"Noooo," agreed the Elephant.

"And when they've tried to bring someone away they've always failed."

"Yessss."

"Well?" John demanded, as if he had proved his point.

"Because they lacked belief. Like you."

"It's all just myth!" John exploded. He struggled for a damning word, but all he could add was, "It's all nonsense! Nonsense!"

"Myth is the story we tell to make sense out of what happens to us," smiled the Elephant. "Nonsense is the word we use to deny anything we don't understand." It was more than John could bear.

"Maybe Madelyn's going was because I failed her in some crucial way. Okay, I admit it!" he said, amazing himself. "I failed her! Or maybe things were so good and that made her a target and she would be taken away from me again even if we found her! I couldn't bear that." The Elephant looked at John and nodded. That at least was a fear which deserved respect.

"But we don't have to fail," Sam broke in. "There's something new this time." They looked at him. He'd sat silent through his father's words, hardly understanding them except for their despair.

"You said it," he said to the Elephant, "and don't know it. You're not as smart as you think!"

"Well now!"

"I'm new. Me," he said. "We're living in my imagination you said. I'm shaping events. And I say we go." He turned to his father. "We go, and we get her, and we make things different. Better."

"And—if we went—and even got there—" John said, fighting his incredulity, "just how do we come back?"

Sam laughed with sudden inspiration. "We can leave that to the last page in the Book!"

The Elephant laughed. Even John smiled, shaking his head, touched by Sam's enthusiasm. That stirred a muted hope in him in response. The hardest thing for anyone to believe is that their life is a story, he thought, and that we make up our stories. Sam's eyes were fixed on him.

"I'll help, however I can," he said at last, "although I'm not sure what I can do." Sam impulsively threw his arms around him.

"Then it's decided," said the Elephant. They looked at each other, and nodded, sobered by Sam's choice.

"How do we go?" Sam asked, stepping back.

The Elephant frowned. "I don't know, I've never been."

Outside the tent there were countless small, cruel laughs.

"I doubt if we have much choice, though," added the Elephant. The laughs grew louder. A sudden urgency struck them. They felt the next gust long delayed like a withheld breath was about to strike the tent.

"We have to get out of here," said Sam: "if only we could fly!"

The laughter grew in intensity. But the Elephant perked up.

"Ahh! An excellent idea!" His eyes caught Sam's, who laughed in turn.

"Find a flying trapeze! An Elephant dancing on a flying trapeze! That's what hangs in my room!" he shouted gleefully.

The Elephant began to rummage through his vest pockets and produced an inexhaustible variety of items, though none of any use now. Sam hadn't realized just how many pockets he had, or how bottomless each appeared to be. But when none proved to be what he was seeking, the Elephant dashed to a trunk, and threw up its lid.

It was crammed with books, a trumpet, packets of seeds, two small rugs, a shovel with a folding handle, a horsehair crested helmet, a spare tea kettle pipe he looked at briefly before tossing it aside, a set of vests, and at last brandished with a cry of triumph a flying trapeze whose ropes shot into the air as he held it out. When he let it go it hovered in the air. The Elephant looked pleased, and laughed

at their expressions.

It was an unusually broad trapeze, but still not wide enough to fit them and an Elephant. Any elephant! Yet first the Elephant stood on it, then Sam and John sat together, the trapeze extending just enough for them to fit.

"Now, if I only knew the right words to make it fly," the Elephant said as the long-delayed gust hit the tent. Its walls strained inward, then they heard ropes snap and saw the tent begin to cave in on them, the central pole slowly twisting and falling to one side. Strange shapes pushed against its canvas.

"Hurry!" said Sam. The Elephant sat there mumbling one word after another in his trunk. "Fly!" Sam finally shouted in frustration.

"Fly you blasted contraption, fly!" shouted John as the tents' walls fell towards them.

"Too late!" a thousand voices roared outside.

"Please, fly!" yelled Sam, and as the tent collapsed they twisted up and out of its central hole.

Up and up rose father and son and Elephant as the voices below cried out in thwarted anger. They rose through the gray fog until at last the sun shone and they looked down on the fog's brilliant white surface.

"Wow," said Sam, his fear of heights forgotten.

"Well done," the Elephant said to Sam. "That's always the magic word."

Sam laughed.

John's hands hurt from clutching one of the ropes.

Through the Upside-down Ocean

How amazing to be on a flying trapeze with a dancing Elephant thought Sam, then John. At this height the day was clear, its light a white glitter on the waves. What a transformation from the gray beach and canyon.

They could barely see the Last House through the fog. No one thought of going there. They guessed as soon as they arrived there the fog would thicken and be full of more than mere menace. Still, John looked down wistfully, wondering what he had gotten himself into. Sam looked ahead full of hope. Then they noticed they were slowly sinking.

"You're heavy," a voice squeaked.

"Who said that?" asked Sam.

"You're sitting on me!" said the Flying Trapeze.

"Ohh..."

"I've never carried any kind of Elephant before, certainly not a dancing Elephant. What a monster!"

"Monster!" repeated the Elephant, indignantly. But he felt so good he stepped out a rumba beat as John and Sam held on tightly.

"Stop that!" they shouted.

"Oof!" said the Flying Trapeze, and sank lower. That sobered the Elephant, and he stopped.

"Let's get going," said Sam. The others nodded assent. But they hung motionless. Which way was Dread City? And the Far Land of Fear?

"I'll tell you," said the Flying Trapeze, as if able to read their minds. "To go either place you have to leave this world for the next."

Wrinkles piled up on the Elephant's brow. John couldn't look more astonished.

"And to do that," continued the Flying Trapeze, whose voice made everything sound ordinary, "you need to sail through the Upside-down Ocean."

"What's that?" asked John.

"How do we do that?" Sam asked.

"Simple," said the Flying Trapeze, answering Sam: "just before I dropped because Mr. Bigness can't keep still—"

"Oh, really!" exclaimed the Elephant.

"I saw a very pretty schooner tossing about with no one aboard."

"Dad's boat!"

"I doubt it," said John.

"Then it must be so," replied the Elephant, giving John a look.

"How do you know all these things," asked Sam, "while he doesn't?" indicating the Elephant.

"You learn many things when you live life at a great height."

"Ohh," groaned the Elephant. Sam laughed in delight.

"Let's go then!" Sam turned to the Elephant:

"But no more dancing!" The Elephant nodded.

Slowly the Flying Trapeze arched back.

"No, go forward!" ordered Sam.

The Flying Trapeze ignored him, pulling back in a slowly rising arc until he quivered, unable to go back farther, then released himself forward so suddenly they cried out in surprise. They swung forward a great distance, but finally their forward motion slowed, then stopped. The Flying Trapeze again arched backwards until he quivered—and again released himself forward. Their stomachs heaved.

"Oof," gasped the Elephant. John's jaw clenched.

"Can't you go straight?" asked Sam.

"I'm a Flying Trapeze, not an airplane," was all the answer he got. John groaned. After a few more swings even the Elephant began to seem less brown than green, while Sam was green: but he could see they were drawing closer to the yacht his father had drawn in the Book.

"Can't you at least go a little faster?" Sam demanded.

"I'm doing my best," replied the Flying Trapeze peevishly. "Carrying the three of you is a lot!" With each swing the Flying Trapeze sank a little lower until they felt they were skimming the waves. The large schooner-rigged yacht was close now, and John did recognize it from his dream with an odd blend of incredulity and familiarity, the booms swinging side to side, although gently here.

"Just a little more," Sam groaned in encouragement to the weakening Flying Trapeze. Then, inspired, "What good's a Flying Trapeze that can't make the connection?" he cried. At that the Flying Trapeze shouted,

"Failure just isn't in my ropes!" and pulled himself back and regained altitude until, shuddering, he let go forward, whizzing through the air but also sinking so their feet just cleared the water. He slowed just before they crashed into the side of the yacht, again pulled himself back, and with a last effort swung forward. The yacht raced towards them.

"On no!" shouted Sam.

"Hold on!" trumpeted the Elephant.

The Flying Trapeze slowed itself with a groan and dumped them exhausted amidships.

"Oof!"

"Ow!"

"Ouch!"

John winced, lifting his hands from the deck where they'd broken his fall. Sam rolled forward, and lay still for a moment before sitting up, dazed.

The Elephant landed on his back, and wheezed a breathy "Thank you" as he picked himself up, then found a pocket the Flying Trapeze slid mysteriously into. John and Sam couldn't tell how he made the long trapeze fit, but after the day's events that was too small a mystery to worry over.

The schooner was big, a good thing with the Elephant on board. The sails hung lifelessly, a far cry from the storm that had tormented John in his dream. Quickly he checked out the rigging, cleated the sheets properly, and stationed Sam and the Elephant, explaining their tasks.

"At least I know how to sail," he said, "all we need is a breeze." As he looked astern he saw the coastline was obscured by a low, gray cloud full of odd twists and eddies. A brilliant ocean stretched forward. They were very much in the world John had always known, and all his doubt returned. Sail through the Upside-down Ocean? Wherever was that to be found? To a Far Land of Fear? Then the mirror surface of the sea rippled.

"Pay attention, now," he said, "a breeze is coming." The sails flapped, flapped again, and filled. Slowly they gathered way. Sam stood near the bow, the Elephant amidships keeping a careful eye on everything. "Which way shall I steer?" asked John.

"The straightest way," said the Elephant with a shrug, and gestured ahead out to sea. That meant a dead downwind course away from the land, and as John heaved on the rudder to set them on course he told Sam and the Elephant which sheets to release, which to haul in, and how to set the mainsails wing and wing, one on each side of the schooner.

Soon they were surging ahead. He watched the sails' tell-tales until he was sure of his course and a thrill ran down his back. He grinned broadly despite himself at the brilliance of the day, the breeze, their fine wake, the sea's glitter. Sam and the Elephant wore the same grins as the schooner steadily breasted the low waves and the water creamed at the bow.

"This is the thing!" trumpeted the Elephant, and had to restrain himself from dancing. Sam looked back with the wind tousling his hair, eyes gleaming.

"This is great, Dad!" he shouted.

The water gurgled and sloshed as it rushed by, almost echoing Sam's delighted laughter. Seagulls shrilled overhead, and then a pair of dolphins leaped beside them before they flashed ahead, their bright forms arching through the waves.

"Look!" Sam shouted, and pointed as dolphins crested the wave raised by their bow. John smiled at his son's happiness. Their white, straight wake stretched astern as the land steadily shrank into a blur on the horizon, hung there for a time, and then was gone. Fleets of white clouds filled the sky so one moment they were in shadow, the next in the bright light. A weight lifted from John's heart. This is now, he thought, this is happening, let come what may we'll at least have a fine sail!

Sam and the Elephant felt his exhilaration: they were truly off! The menacing figures they had fled seemed insubstantial as these cloud shadows, the yacht showing a fine turn of speed despite the weight of the Elephant as the breeze strengthened.

Hour succeeded hour in this way, the schooner slicing through the water, a straight wake gurgling aft, and now and then dolphins racing beside them or cresting their bow waves.

After a time Sam began to feel his aches and bruises, and shifted uncomfortably. Relief from strain combined with the steady motion of the yacht to make his head heavy. The Elephant was already asleep amidships, trumpeting an occasional shuddering snore, while his father had lashed the tiller in place and half-dozed off beside it, his head dropping then snapping up, only to drop again.

Sam sank down in the shelter behind the bows. John fought his sleep despite his exhaustion and aches, enjoying himself. Either Sam and I are two crazy people sharing an imaginary journey, he thought, and together hallucinating a talking dancing Elephant, or…it's our wonderful adventure.

He nodded off again, then snapped to and saw the satchel he had carried with him from the tent. Idly he pulled out its contents: several ropes, a bola, a knife, a compass, a bottle of wine, a loaf of bread, a lump of cheese, and at the bottom, the Book.

He shivered.

He flipped its pages. There were Sam's "No dreams" and "Fog" written out and illustrated. There was John's struggle to survive the storm. He read each story with interest: every detail was there, with a good deal more as he turned the pages. Next was the story of their meeting the Elephant: one illustration showed the Queen of Hearts, with the caption, "Come and get me."

He remembered how she had faded in his hands and flaked away. No worse than memory, he thought. There followed their council, clearly narrated in the same neat handwriting, their escape, and now himself steering the yacht in brilliant weather, holding the Book by the tiller.

The following pages were blank. He slipped the Book back into his satchel, as mystified as ever. His mind drifted into vague reveries and fantasies, then his head sagged down again. As they slept the wind weakened, then died. The yacht coasted slowly to a stop and began to wallow in the swell.

A crash followed by a blast from the Elephant woke Sam. The sea had steepened, and the booms swept side to side as the yacht wallowed. One such swing gave the Elephant's shoulders a good whack: anyone smaller would have been injured and swept overboard. The commotion woke John too. He was bleary-eyed at first, but his mind cleared fast as he saw the Elephant's danger.

"Watch out!" Sam shouted at the Elephant.

"We must rig preventers!" John added.

The Elephant looked dazed at Sam standing in the bow as a gust of wind made his hair stream out, then turned to look where John had shaken himself awake.

"Watch out!" Sam shouted again, but too late as a boom again smacked the Elephant's massive shoulders.

"Ow!" he trumpeted. But John now shouted out instructions to attach lines to the booms to control their swings as he threw off the tiller's lashings and set them back on course in the new breeze. The yacht gathered momentum in the steadily freshening wind and began sending arcs of spray over the bow, swiftly soaking them.

"Ooo, that's better," a strange voice said. John looked around.

"Who said that?"

"Me," said the main sheet. John simply stared in astonishment. "What's wrong," it added, "you've heard of talking a line," the main sheet said.

"Well, not of a talking line," he managed to get out.

"Same difference."

"Never mind!" snapped the Elephant. "Do whatever it says." John was miffed: he knew how to sail. But he couldn't handle everything in the freshening weather.

"You'd better—no, send Sam back here," he said. To the Elephant's look he added, "You know. Balance. Stay in the middle. If we heel one way or the other, move to the opposite side." The Elephant nodded.

First Sam had to loosen the jib and genoa sheets to spill wind.

"I'm the genoa, loosen me first," said one.

"We shouldn't have you up," said the jib sheet, "loosen me now!"

Sam did as he was told. But it wasn't enough for long: the wind kept strengthening. Once in the cockpit he held the tiller as his father instructed, while John loosened the main sheets farther. Each sheet happily identified itself, now.

"We'll have to bring her into the wind and shorten sail," John shouted over the wind and waves.

The Elephant waved his trunk in agreement, and John again took the tiller and sent Sam forward, then carefully brought them into the wind. In a confusion of talking lines, halyards and sheets they struck the genoa and bundled it below, where John tossed the satchel and Book. Then he told Sam to reef the jib into a storm jib while he reefed the two great mainsails.

The Elephant's efforts to help made things worse, as each shift of weight to port or starboard heeled them over. John finally shouted at him to stay still. He did as he was told a bit sulkily, not used to taking orders, but being on a yacht, even one this size, was no place for an Elephant.

John paid off and under shortened sail they began driving forward again. If anything the wind's force had reached gale strength: the seas steadily mounted.

"If it gets too rough we'll have to turn into the wind again and throw out a sea anchor and ride this out," he shouted.

Sam and the Elephant said nothing, staring at the sea ahead.

John followed their gaze. Where the air started and the sea stopped was hard to say. When did it get this bad, John wondered, bemused? The tiller struggled to swing free under his arm: he had to grasp it with both hands no matter how they ached.

The sails gave a sharp slap as the wind veered unexpectedly, and the boom swung across the deck in an unplanned gibe. Only the preventer saved the Elephant from another blow as he hung on grimly.

The next moment the wind veered again, and the other boom tried to snap back across the deck in another jarring gibe. Then first one, then the other preventer, broke with painful cries.

"This won't do," muttered John.

"What did you say?" shouted Sam. John shook his head, for even if he wanted to turn into the wind he no longer knew which way to turn, now: it seemed to come from every direction, while a wave now broadsided them from starboard, another rolled under the rudder, and the next came at an angle to the bow from port. One blast of wind almost capsized them to port, and only the Elephant frantically flinging his weight to starboard kept the yacht from going over.

"We must get the sails in!" he trumpeted.

John nodded. What followed was a nightmare of effort. He lashed the tiller amidships, since no course made sense, then had Sam make his way to him, and lashed him to the aft mast so he wasn't washed over. Then he and the Elephant struggled against wind and wave to loosen the aft sail's halyard as the yacht pitched sickeningly.

Once the half lowered sail blew over them, blinding them: then it ballooned to port as a sharp gust lifted and filled it, then snapped back towards them as the wind veered entirely around. It caught them a stinging slap with the next gust, then sagged on them. Stunned, they fought to free themselves from the canvas. A moment of stillness let them clear it away and lower the sail altogether and fold and tie it to the boom. Then they struggled to the foremast.

"Hurry, hurry," whined a stay supporting the foremast. "I can't hold on much longer!"

"Hang on!" grunted the Elephant. John said nothing, tearing at the sail's halyard despite his hands' pain.

"Hurry, hurry!"

But the halyard was sea-watered slippery, and its hitch as tightened as it was in his dream: it was like trying to untie a knot made of steel. Finally the Elephant crooked an arm around the mast and searched his pockets with his free arm, at last pulling out a long knife.

"Hurry!" shouted John.

"No!" screamed the halyard. But the Elephant sliced through the line and the sail crumpled towards the deck as a tall wave lifted the bow, ran under the yacht so it lifted and shuddered on its crest, then slipped past the rudder so they shot down a wall of water as another rose over them.

"No!" they and all the lines screamed as that wall broke over them. The yacht shuddered under the endless pour of green water.

That stilled their voices, clogged their ears, blinded their eyes, and would have choked them if they'd opened their mouths to shout, even to shout a warning to Sam. Then the water was gone and the yacht broke into the clear—and John and the Elephant were empty handed, for that surge of water had taken the sail with it.

"Watch out!" yelled Sam, pointing up. In horror they saw a wave falling from the sky. John dashed aft, threw off the tiller's lashings and flung himself against it: as the boat slid to port down a hill of water the falling wave crashed in a long line to starboard.

Now waves rolled and smashed into them and one another from every direction, while blasts of air blew tunnels through the waters now in this direction, now that. They had found the Upside-down Ocean, and there was nothing funny about it except its name. Only luck could save them now. Luck, and...John shook his head to deny the thought, but desperation won out.

"Sam!" he shouted. "The Book is in my bag! Go below and draw us a safe course!"

Their eyes met across the deck even as a wave jarred the bow so sharply the yacht almost spun on its axis. They grabbed at anything near to keep themselves on their feet, and held on grimly as the yacht lurched, shuddered, and straightened. But now there was nothing underneath them, and the yacht dropped so that they grew light and their stomachs heaved: then it splashed into the water again. There was a moment of shocked stillness, then Sam hurried below once John set him free.

There he saw a spacious main cabin and galley with sleeping quarters fore and aft—or it would have been spacious if the storm had not tossed everything into such a jumble on the floor that he could barely move. But he found his father's satchel, pulled out the Book, and clambered onto the table to find a blank page to draw a safe course on. He had no intention of lingering over their earlier adventures now, but to his horror he saw nothing with which to draw.

He let the Book slide, searching through the bag for a pencil or pen. Nothing. He stared around the cabin, then lunged over the clutter towards the shelves lining the galley. The boat lurched, dipped, and rose dizzyingly, each motion flinging him off his feet. There was nothing in the shelves or drawers he searched through next.

Despairingly he dove into the clutter on the floor, fishing through sail bags, mattresses, pots and pans, cans of food and bottles of water, and a chest he emptied of once immaculately pressed suits for the Elephant that scattered with each lurch of the yacht.

A wave lifted the bow steeply and flung him backwards. As he lay on his back a long, thin drawer holding charts broke free and sailed over him, crashing against the wall. As it tumbled down he saw a felt-tipped pen drop into the confusion. He crawled where it had disappeared and reached down blindly, his fingers at last tightening around the pen.

Then he crawled to where he could see a corner of the Book sticking out from the jumble where it had slid, pulled it out, and on the first blank page drew a tunnel through a tall wave as they slid down another's crest.

"Tunnel!" he wrote jerkily, and "Past the—" before the boat's motion pitched him forward. He had to retrieve the Book: he never lost his grip on the pen. "Storm!" he wrote. Past the storm. He leaned back. A wicked thought carried him away. "More sail!" he drew, and laughed.

He struggled back to the deck.

"Well?" shouted John, struggling to avoid a wave coming at them down a slant of air.

"More sail!" Sam shouted. "There's a tunnel!"

John stared at him.

"More sail!" he shouted at the Elephant.

That set off a reverse nightmare as they raised the genoa and jib, a new halyard and a new mainsail fished out of the chaos below, re-rigged in a daring ascent of the foremast by Sam, and last the aft mast's great sail.

"Madness!" trumpeted the Elephant.

"Madmen!" screamed the lines, halyards, stays, and sheets: even the shrouds keened.

Luck preserved them from the wandering waves as they worked: one by the sails filled and emptied as the boat rocked crazily, one moment dead in the water, another almost driven into the face of an approaching wave by a mad gust filling the sails to near bursting. Then the wind steadied from astern and they surged forward.

"Ahh!" they cried with the lines and sheets and halyards that were taut with strain. They feared the sails would shred from the strain—or the yacht would be driven straight under. But even as a wave bore down on them from aft, with a larger one visible behind it, and an even larger ahead, nothing gave way. They saw a circle of darkness in the face of the wave rising over them—.

"Steer for that! It's the tunnel" Sam screamed.

John threw himself on the tiller, then Sam added his weight against its stiffness. Grudgingly the tiller moved. They surfed down the wave reaching them aft, straight towards that rising dark spot. There was no time to adjust the sails. They gathered such speed they were blinded with spume and spray; then every sail shredded into a thousand tatters.

"Ohh!" the three shouted, terrified. But they shot into that dark spot, a tunnel of green water whose walls collapsed behind them as they shot forward.

"Ohh!" they shouted in fear and from the wild thrill of the ride as they just stayed ahead of the tunnel's collapsing walls. A small circle of light appeared ahead.

"Look!" trumpeted the Elephant.

"Whee!" shouted the lines.

"Dad!" shouted Sam.

John and Sam hung grimly onto the tiller, sick from the strain. Then with a final roar of crashing water the circle of light grew large enough for them to shoot through as though spat out by the tunnel. They drifted clear with frightened shouts. Groaning, they looked about for the next menacing wave, their heads twisting in every direction. But the sky cleared quickly, while the sea, with a last parting broadside from a rogue wave, remained choppy.

But that was almost as bad as what they had escaped, for with torn sails and a dying wind they wallowed uncontrollably. They turned green and at last hung over the sides, desperately ill. Each second felt like hours. One by one they thought they would rather just roll off and drown than go on being sick this way.

"I'll never finish this adventure," Sam groaned. He looked longingly at the waves. All he had to do was let go and slide down: cool waters would close over him, and he would sink into blessed stillness. His hands relaxed: then a little warning went off in his head, and his grip tightened.

"No," he ground out, took a great gulp of air, and set his jaw. "You can't stop me!" he shouted at the sea, at the air, at the sky. "I'm going to Dread City and you can blow all you want or not and make us sick but you can't stop me!" He shook a fist defiantly.

"Stout fellow," trumpeted the Elephant, but not very strongly. John simply hung on.

But it seemed Sam was understood. As abruptly as the storm

had begun the wind died, the sea calmed and the wallowing stopped. Soon a wide blue sea stretched in every direction, light glittering on its barely rippled surface. Soft clouds raced across the sky. The wind breathed pleasantly.

"Well," Sam breathed, and sat back, his queasiness dropping away. As he took it all in he realized something was strange. They all had the same feeling, but no one could put his finger on what it was. After a time the Elephant breathed,

"This just isn't the same sea we were in when the storm hit."

"Skippingly, skippingly, skippingly," breathed the breeze as the three looked around bewildered. Then it hit them: it was still morning here, although it had been afternoon when the storm struck. They had seen no night.

"The sun is different," said Sam. It was violet and had a red tinge on its edge, as if older, and fading. The shadows the clouds threw were a dull, unlikely red. And the ocean turned an emerald shade never seen in any known sea. John, however, recognized it. That emerald had been in his first adventure with the schooner. Sam too remembered his glimpse of it after he went through the yellow door.

"Skippingly, skippingly, skippingly," said the breeze again.

They wondered what was going to happen next, and waited—and waited—and waited. They began to relax, then to set things in order, found they had replacement sails, and set those in place of the old torn ones some instinct made them stuff into a bag instead of throwing over the side. The torn sails sighed audibly as they were stowed away.

They set another course that kept the wind astern, going where the wind willed, and only then realized how hungry they were. But they lingered, not quite believing in their good fortune, until finally John went below and lit the galley stove, and made them all a full meal.

Afterwards they stood on deck, and as the same breeze blew and blew, began to feel there were no strange dangers lurking near them. One by one each yawned in turn, the Elephant's going on forever. Evening fell with a tropical rush. Wordlessly Sam and John staggered below and fell into their now neat berths. The Elephant sagged amidships. Their dreamless snores mingled in the breeze.

"Skippingly, skippingly, skippingly," the breeze hummed soothingly all night long.

Though each woke with a start, looking around wildly in certainty some disaster must be near, nothing happened to disturb the night or the soft, steady breeze. In fact, now one day followed another monotonously. They ate, slept, spliced damaged lines so that they hummed with the breeze, explored the boat, counted the birds in the air, and gazed dreamily at the stars at night, though unable to recognize any familiar constellations.

Nothing changed.

"Skippingly, skippingly, skippingly," the breeze hummed.

At times they wondered if they were moving at all, one day was so like another. But the breeze held, and after each repeatedly stared astern to reassure themselves there was indeed a wake, their mood changed, and they began to take their good fortune at face value. They began to feel secure, and set the great spinnaker, exhilarated at their increased speed.

Day after day after day they sailed in brilliant light and weather although the colors were strange, until: they got bored.

A Far Land of Fear seemed very far: Dread City seemed even more nebulous. Thought of either did not raise even a casual shiver. After a few more perfect days either of those places seemed preferable to this pleasant monotony. John even caught himself in a reverie where he once again, now happily, wrestled with the Upside-down Ocean.

He looked down shame-faced at a glance from the Elephant, certain he had read his mind. Sam began to wonder if he would be an old man before they crossed this pleasant sea.

No one, not even the Flying Trapeze, knew how far they had to go.

Finally John decided to resume Sam's lessons.

"Not here," he protested, incredulous.

"You've got a lot to learn," the Elephant said.

"None of you would be here without me." Sam said flatly. This was true.

"So?" asked John.

"No one does homework on an adventure," Sam said.

"He does have a point," the Elephant muttered. Sam looked at him gratefully.

"We don't have any books here, anyway," Sam added. "Not those kind, anyway."

"There's a first time for everything," said John. "For starters, spell Elephant."

"Aww, I don't want to," Sam said, sulking. Imagine ruining an adventure this way!

"Spell Elephant!" John insisted. Sam gave the Elephant a mute glance, but that individual now pretended to be distracted with a search through his pockets. Sam took a reluctant breath and opened his mouth—and heard a strange voice spell,

"E-L-E-P-H-A-N-T!"

Sam grinned. The Elephant and John stared about. There was no one.

"You spell Elephant," said John insistently to Sam.

"E-L-E-P-H-A-N-T!" someone spelled again.

They thought it might be a line, a sheet, or a halyard, even a shroud, but those were all happily humming.

"It wasn't me," said the Flying Trapeze whom the Elephant had pulled out for a breath of air.

"Who then?" asked Sam, grinning even more widely. "This is great!"

"ME!" they heard distinctly from the ocean beyond the yacht to starboard. They peered over the side just in time to see what looked like a man's pleasant face floating on the surface drift by.

"GOODBYE!" it shouted.

"Hmm," murmured the Elephant.

"Gee," breathed Sam. John stared.

VI

Wild Dancing in the Sea of Faces

Each described the face differently, and each wanted the other to accept their description. Soon the Elephant trumpeted and John and Sam shouted.

"What are we arguing over?" said the Elephant suddenly. They stopped, sheepishly. "Perhaps there are others," he suggested.

They looked over the railing again, but there was only the emerald sea in every direction.

Then they saw their own faces looking up at them from the waters, but blurred almost beyond recognition.

"Time to start your lesson again," John said.

"Since you've already had a little help, spelling Elephant should be easy."

"Aww..." And he spelled Elephant, but only in his mind.

"That's cheating," murmured the Elephant. Sam's face had a set, stubborn look.

"Alright," sighed John, "spell his name—" he began, gesturing at the Elephant, and paused. They didn't know his name. They were dumbfounded: how had they gone through so much together and not yet been properly introduced?

"What's your name?" they asked together.

"Hmm, yes, it's—" and a puzzled frown settled on the Elephant's vast forehead. "I don't know the name that goes with—" and gestured helplessly at himself.

"I didn't give you a name when I drew you."

"Let's not start that again," said John.

"You wanted me to draw a course to safety and here we are!" Sam said to his father. He turned to the Elephant. "I know what to name you," he grinned, "something like what you sound like when you dance. Lepanto!"

"Lepanto?"

"Lepanto?" repeated John. He was surprised, and a little worried: that was the name of a famous battle. But he kept that to himself.

"Le-Pant-o," Sam breathed, emphasizing the pant.

"I've been called worse." Then the Elephant—Lepanto, now—had the same thought as John, but said nothing, too.

"Le-pant-o! Le-PANT-o! LE-pant-o! Le-pant-O!" Lepanto chanted. Soon he jiggled in time to his name. "Oh! It's really very good! I like it!" He drummed his feet in time with his chant. "Le-PANT-o! Le-PANT-o! Le-pant-O!" The yacht bounced up and down: Sam had drawn Lepanto large.

"Spell his name now," demanded John.

"L-E—" he began.

"L-E-P-A-N-T-O!" spelled a voice.

"Who said that!" they cried.

"ME!" replied a voice to the port side.

They rushed over to the port side railing ignoring how Lepanto's weight made the yacht tilt. There was another face in the water, round and a little green, but with piercing gray eyes and a shock of flaxen hair. He smiled up at them.

"L-e-p-a-n-t-o!" he spelled, laughing. "That's too easy!"

"Who are you?" the three asked.

"Myself," exclaimed the face, surprised at the question.

"Wait!" they cried as he fell astern.

"You're the ones moving." That left them stumped for a reply.

"Freshly, freshly, freshly," said the breeze. The yacht picked up speed.

"GOODBYE!"

"Are there more?" shouted Sam after him.

"Of course," said someone from the starboard side. They hurried over there now, the yacht righting itself, then tilting to starboard. A pretty face with long black hair floating around it quickly fell astern.

"OW!" they heard next from the bow, and watched as an angry face was caught up in the bow spray before falling back into the water.

"WATCH WHERE YOU'RE GOING!" it shouted.

They debated whether they should stop to avoid hitting more faces, but couldn't see the point of just wallowing in place: they had somewhere to go. So John tried to steer around them with Sam in the bow calling out directions while Lepanto stayed safely amidship, but John soon realized there were too many to avoid.

They apologized profusely to each in turn, until they saw the hopelessness of that too and sailed on silently however a face complained as they swept by.

Soon Lepanto, Sam, and John saw faces of every imaginable variety dotting the ocean, round, flat, wet, floating faces that kept up a continuous chatter unless disturbed by the yacht.

"Fine day," one said.

"I've seen worse," another replied.

"Beautiful."

"Ohh... How I like to crest!"

"I like the troughs, myself."

"Never down but up."

"Never up but down."

"Fine weather."

"You're looking well."

"Same to you."

"Only a few clouds."

"I get the chills when one goes over."

"Just shut your eyes and pretend it's not."

"I still feel it!"

"Up, down, up, down, up, down…"

"Down, up."

"Up, down."

"Up!"

"Down!"

And so it went until one would shout, "IT'S ALL THE SAME!" Then there would be a pause—and the chatter resumed.

"I like violet days better than purple."

"Green are my cup of tea."

"It's been so long since any of us had a cup of tea…" Their voices fell silent. A great ripple of silence and sadness spread. Then someone said,

"Where are you off to?"

"I'm staying right here!"

"Never down but up!"

"Never up but down!"

Sam, John and Lepanto's fascination wore off as this repetitiveness went on and on. It crossed Sam's mind that if this was the beginning of the Far Land of Fear, there didn't seem much to worry about.

"If you've seen one, you've seen them all," Sam said at last with a shrug as he watched the bow slice through a stream of protesting faces.

"No!" said a face.

"No!" said another. That "No!" spread out and grew in volume as uncounted numbers of faces took it up. John and Sam and Lepanto put their hands over their ears to block the sound. The "No!" grew so loud they fell to their knees, clutching their heads, Lepanto especially squirming from pain with his great ears.

"Stop!" he trumpeted, "STOP!"

"Sssh…" whispered a face nearby.

"SSSH!" trumpeted Lepanto.

Now one, and then another face went "Sssh" until that sound too spread outward growing steadily in volume. Again they squirmed in pain from the deafening hiss all around them.

"Do something," Sam shouted at Lepanto. He stared at Sam at a loss, then smiled with sudden inspiration.

"FINE WEATHER!" Lepanto trumpeted.

"Who said that?" asked a face.

"It's been worse," said another. Soon that conversation spread like the "No!" and the "Sssh" until once more the faces calmly repeated their mindless exchanges.

Sam and John and the Elephant exchanged looks: the faces no longer appeared so harmless.

"Strongly, strongly, strongly," said a deep voice with a quiet but unrelenting strength behind them.

The schooner shuddered as the wind strengthened, the sheets groaned from the increased pull of the sails, and the sails grew taut as drums. A purple haze spread over the sky. Anxiously they loosened the sheets, and checked the rigging. All was still well. But they brought in the spinnaker.

"We may be in for another storm," said Lepanto thoughtlessly.

"Storm?" cried a face,

"Storm?" cried another, terrified.

"STORM!" shouted another, and another, until they shrieked together, "STORM! STORM! STORM!"

The sound knocked Lepanto, John, and Sam flat. The yacht

vibrated under them. Lepanto stared at the deck as he saw its members begin to tremble and separate from the vibration. He took a deep breath, then trumpeted,

"BEEAUUUUUUUTTIIIIIIIIFULLLLLLLL DAAAAAY!"

"Beautiful day," someone said.

"Fine weather," said another. And then another and another and…. The three travelers relaxed. The deck stilled. They had escaped another danger.

The sea was no longer visible through the dense number of faces. Great patterns began to be evident among these: here they saw a band of red-haired faces, there, brown. There were brown faces, and red, and black, and yellow. There was a swath of blonde faces, followed by a stretch where all were mixed together and jostling noisily. These areas they called quilts.

Then there were cliques of faces where all you could see were sad faces, or happy faces, or angry faces, or even, though rarely, silent faces. Multiple conversations went on, one band caught up in one strand of chatter, another band in a different. The edges between were uncertain, the faces there jumbling different conversations.

Sam, John and Lepanto exchanged a meaningful glance: what a terrible place, they thought, not daring to speak. Nothing ever happened here except the same meaningless cycles of chatter. Under the surface they heard other faces rumbling in discontent, trying to force their way to the surface past the others. Their efforts to rise made the sea choppy, and sparked waves of anxiety in the faces on the surface that periodically over-rode their chatter so there would be an outburst of confused cries that, thankfully, would settle before they became contagious.

Then off to port they saw a gust of wind blow a violent hubbub into the air that turned in on itself, then careened as a tornado of faces over the ocean towards them. After a stunned moment, John dashed for the tiller.

"Hurry!" shouted Lepanto.

"Tacking!" cried John.

"Hurry!" shouted Sam.

But the tiller wouldn't budge for John; a glance over the stern revealed it was jammed with weeping, cursing faces. The tornado of faces bore down on them.

"Gale! Gale! Gale!" ground the wind, as if chewing stones. The schooner lurched forward. Still the faces bore down on them.

"Oh no," breathed Sam.

"OWWW! ARRGH! NOOO! OOOO! OOFFFF!" the faces screamed as they slapped against the masts, slid down the sails, bent in half on the stays and shrouds and slapped into Sam, Lepanto, and John who frantically brushed them from their heads, arms, chests, and legs, and kicked them clear of the deck as they held on for dear life to whatever was near.

"FULL GALE!" moaned the wind. John took one look at the straining sails and knew they would shred in turn if not swiftly reefed.

"Lower the sails!" John shouted. "Help me bring her into the wind!" he added, and flung himself against the tiller. Sam flung himself against it too and now the Elephant edged aft, discovering they were so thickly embedded in faces the schooner didn't sag to rear as he threw his weight against the tiller, too. That did it.

The schooner slowly turned into the wind. John held it there as now Sam and Lepanto scrambled forward and between them lowered and reefed the great sails until only enough remained to give them steerage as they fell off the wind and resumed their forward motion with the wind dead downwind again. Wherever it willed.

The genoa they stored away, and left only a corner of the jib showing, for added balance. Then Lepanto took up his position amidships again and Sam lurched back to help John hold the tiller as even the greatly reduced sails filled with gale wind. All the while faces screamed behind and ahead of them as the bows again drove through the heavy, face-filled swells.

The wind caught faces up off their crests and flung them against the travelers. Peeling one off was like trying to grasp a large flat jelly fish, one that spoke angrily at you during the process as it tried to slip through your fingers. But they felt no pity, given their own danger, and had no intention of stopping and throwing out a sea-anchor to ride out this storm.

Even with so little sail set, and such resistance from the densely packed faces, they went at a surprising clip that provoked a steady wail from the bow and stern. They thought their ears must burst from that wail, but now Lepanto searched his pockets until he found wax to plug their ears. That kept the racket just bearable.

"STOP!" shouted the faces.

"No!" trumpeted Lepanto.

"Stop hurting us!" they demanded.

"We can't stop," Sam answered grimly, "or we'll never finish our trip!"

"STOP!"

"We won't stop!" shouted all the lines of the boat, and the shrouds, and the stays, even the anchor chain in a grating voice. "We can hear below what those dark faces are saying, and we'll never stop!" The three stared at the yacht, then at the Sea of Faces.

"What are they saying?" asked Sam.

"Swamp them, sink them, crush them."

"STORM STORM STORM," roared the wind.

At first the sea was full of cries and groans, screams and moans.

But they let the wind drive them as they were, for it was strong enough the schooner clove through the Sea of Faces who in turn dampened the height of the waves. But that fearful groaning infected them: even Lepanto quivered with fear, while Sam, after standing it as long as he could, broke down and sobbed. John ground his teeth together to control the waves of renewed disbelief that were close to paralyzing him.

Lepanto fought fear off longest, but finally a tear formed, almost immediately whipped away by the wind, then another. Soon he was wracked by great sobs. Night fell, and if anything the storm was worse and the terror deeper in themselves and the faces they could barely make out that now filled the air, slid down the stays, or slapped into them.

Sam sobbed and felt hot tears run down his cheeks.

"I should never have listened to them and none of this would be happening," John groaned.

"Oh for my pipe and tent and a warm rug over my knees," Lepanto sobbed to himself, peeling several flying faces off his own.

Despair filled Sam's heart at how unlikely his hope was to find his mother, let alone bring her home. He sobbed even harder. All around him now he heard the faces crying and shrieking:

"Let her go! Let her go! Turn Back! Go home!"

Let her go? Didn't she say come and find her, flashed across his mind? The dark, the storm, his Dad sobbing at the tiller, Lepanto sobbing amidships, the faces sobbing their despair all weighed on Sam. For a moment he almost gave up. He only needed to say, "I want to go home," and he knew the storm would soften, the faces grow friendly, Lepanto and John no longer be filled with grief. All I have to do, he thought with great clarity, is give up what I want most.

The words formed on his tongue almost too thick with grief to

shape them. He thought he felt a hush in the storm, a pause in the faces' wailing, in Lepanto and John's sobbing. He swallowed as he heard that momentary hush and knew what that hush wanted to hear him say.

He had never felt so alone, or been so aware of how, after all, he was just a boy, not some great adventurer, not a magical creature like Lepanto, not a man, like his father; who was he to dare the impossible? A little boy who wanted his mother?

"I am going to rescue Madelyn!" he muttered, using her name. He drew a deep breath, and let go of the stay he was clinging to and stood on the edge of the pitching deck and shook his fist over the railing at the Sea of Faces.

"I'm going to rescue my mother no matter what you do!" His voice strengthened into a shout that filled the eerie silence his words had caused.

"You can't stop me! Nobody can! You can moan and blow and complain all you like but I am going to the Far Land of Fear, wherever it is, and to Dread City, wherever that is, and find her! And then I'm going to bring her home!"

The wind stopped. There was a dead, stunned silence that spread ever outward from the yacht. Lepanto stood, regaining his self-control, as did John.

"This is no ordinary storm," he said.

"This is no ordinary storm," the nearest faces now laughed maliciously. That laughter spread out in turn from the yacht until a storm of laughter echoed back from the dark horizon. The wind slapped the yacht, then returned again in full force, driving them through helplessly laughing faces.

Sam, John, and Lepanto fought that laughter off, but soon one, then the other, chuckled, and in a moment they began to laugh helplessly until their sides ached. Laughing faces sprayed into the rigging, laughing faces slid across the deck, laughing faces were stuck in the yacht's nooks and crannies.

"No," Sam gasped, "No more." And stopped. Then Lepanto took a deep breath, and stopped, and finally John. They looked at each other—and burst out laughing again. But Sam stopped again. Suddenly it just wasn't funny any longer. Then Lepanto stopped. But John laughed with a growing hysteria until finally Lepanto edged towards the stern and gave him a stinging slap. That stopped him. Anger flared in his eyes.

"I'll get you for that!"

"I'LL GET YOU FOR THAT!" roared the faces. For a moment it was touch and go whether they would fight each other, but Sam grabbed his father's hands.

"No Dad! No, we won't fight each other!" he shouted repeatedly until John relaxed. There was a lull in the storm.

"This storm is being directed against us," Lepanto breathed. They nodded, mutely. "But even the worst storms end!" he trumpeted defiantly at the Sea of Faces.

"Le-PANT-o!" the Sea of Faces whispered in response. "Le PANT-o!" the sea muttered loudly.

"Le-PANT-o! Le-PANT-o! Le-pant-O!" shouted the Sea of Faces.

Something odd happened then: Lepanto shook a leg. His body gave a little twist. His other leg tapped in time to the rhythm.

"Le-PANT-o!"

"Mmmmm," Lepanto breathed. He stamped his feet, waved his arms, and jiggled his hulk. His ears waved back and forth.

"Le-PANT-o! Le-PANT-o!" he echoed. The chant rolled over them.

"Le-PANT-o! Le-PANT-o!"

The yacht shook to his movements, the deck timbers groaned beneath his stamping feet.

"Le-PANT-o! Le-PANT-o!"

In another moment he was in an ecstasy of motion, oblivious as the deck boards started to splinter and John and Sam shouted and waved at him in alarm. Faster he danced, harder he stamped, trumpeting, "Le-PANT-o! Le-PANT-o!"

"LE-PANT-O! LE-PANT-O!" the faces and he chanted, his trunk waving madly. His belly heaved up and down and he flung his arms wide, stamping in an ecstasy of movement. The deck groaned, its planks cracked, and then splintered.

"Watch out!" shouted the lines and the sheets and the halyards and the keening stays and shrouds in their knife-edged metallic voices.

"Watch out!" shouted John.

"WATCH OUT WATCH OUT WATCH OUT!" echoed the faces.

Lepanto crashed from sight into the cabin below. A wave of faces broke over the bow and rolled down the deck, pouring into the cabin in their hundreds. A few such waves John realized and the schooner would founder and they would find themselves joining the Sea of Faces.

"Oh, no!" groaned Sam. Lepanto trumpeted with rage from below. Painfully he climbed up. Another swell rolled over the ship, and more chanting faces sloshed below. The chanting stopped.

"Help yourselves," the voices whispered maliciously: "help yourselves" a male chorus chanted, "help yourselves," a female chorus jeered.

An angry glow burned John's cheeks. "We'll see about that!" He started the pumps: they stuttered, then ran steadily, spewing out jeering streams of faces.

"Find the genoa!" he ordered next. He and Sam dashed around Lepanto, who tossed items out of their way, and found the genoa safely in its bag. They pulled it out, found the toolkit, and came back on deck. John found some spare planks and they nailed those in place, then nailed the genoa over those, covering the hole.

It was makeshift, at best, but all the faces from the next wave that rolled over them sluiced over the sides and out of the cockpit into their wake. John and Sam happily slung the few remaining into the air over their fellows' faces. All the while jeering faces sluiced from the pumps to join the others now taunting them from all sides.

Sam stood with a flush of triumph on his face and shook his hammer in the wind.

"You can't stop me!" Sam shouted. "I won't give up!"

The faces still jeered, but they had tried their worst, and failed. What heart they had wasn't in it anymore. Their volume dropped, turned into a whisper, and that into a silence that spread towards the horizon.

Far to the east a pink tint deepened, and then, the wind entirely gone, the faces still, the yacht wallowing in their midst, a rim of light appeared under the pink. The sky went from twilight in reverse to a pale, pearly white, and the few remaining clouds lost their angry edge. The day strengthened as the violet-red sun shone as brightly as it could, the pink clouds not whitening but turning shades of pale brown.

"Skippingly, skippingly, skippingly," breathed the breeze.

The sea settled with an unlikely swiftness as John set course as they took the storm reefs out of their sails with their course still dead downwind. The tiller was ever easier to control. They said nothing more, just stared at each other, then out at the Sea of Faces. That thinned quickly now; none of them could sense any anger left beneath the keel. John lashed the tiller in place, then went into the cabin and tossed faces up to Sam to toss overboard. He brought the last up himself and threw it in their wake.

"Good riddance!" he said.

"Pity us and stay," a face wept, then another, as they swept by.

"Never," Sam said firmly. The lines laughed in the breeze, a little maliciously.

"Tough luck," they said.

"Tough luck," the faces echoed, and then one breathed: "Beautiful day."

"I've seen worse," answered another. Soon the senseless chatter they had first heard swept across the thinning bands of faces. The sea resumed its emerald glow.

The three of them sank down, too tired for words, let alone for repairs: John had just strength to lash the tiller into place before their heads nodded, and one by one they fell asleep. When they woke it was past noon. The wide emerald sea stretched all around them, with hardly a face in sight. Soon what proved to be the last drifted astern.

"Hi," it said. They didn't reply. "It's me!" it said. They ignored it. "Goodbye," it said sadly.

"Good riddance," said Sam.

VII

The Breath of Riddles

The hours, then the days, passed without event though at first they scanned the sea and sky nervously for some new threat. But it seemed now all they had to contend with was peacefulness.

"Merrily, merrily, merrily," hummed the wind tirelessly.

They couldn't have said why, yet they remained sure this was the right way to go. They carefully replanked the deck Lepanto had broken with his wild dance with spare planks from the hold, checked the rigging for storm damage, pumped the last face out of the bilge, swabbed down the decks, and set the cabin to rights, and with all shipshape at last pulled out the torn sails from the Upside-down Ocean and painstakingly sewed smaller versions together from their remnants for spares. All the needles and threads they needed came miraculously from Lepanto's pockets, including, against all hope, battens to stiffen the sails' edges.

That chore done, they stowed the new sails away and looked for something more to do, but now all that was left was to listen to the wind hum "Merrily merrily merrily" under a sun that went on smiling.

The wind continued to blow from dead astern without variation, and they set the great mainsails wing and wing to maximize their pull, then the great spinnaker that billowed out from the bowsprit and foremast, noticeably increasing their speed. They lashed the tiller into place and relaxed if with a sense of growing monotony. John's hands healed entirely. But he gave up resuming Sam's lessons after

careful thought, remembering all too well how the last attempt ended in disaster.

So Sam larked around the boat, studied the stars at night with Lepanto, and began to trace out and name the unfamiliar constellations.

"There," he pointed one night, "see? We'll call that The Umbrella." Carefully he pointed out the arches and the long curved handle. Lepanto chuckled. "And that one…" Sam traced out the hefty form, the long curving line for the trunk. "That's you. The Elephant."

"I see," said Lepanto after a pause. "My turn." Idly his trunk waved about, and then he carefully pointed out a round circle of stars with a little cluster at their top, and a long curling line coming to one side. "That will be The Kettle."

With that he fished out his kettle and pipe line, set it on a little burner, sprinkled some of the intense caravan tea leaves he so liked into its water, and soon was smoking with delight. John shook his head.

A week passed.

A second week passed….

At the start of the third peaceful week Sam came back up from the storage area under the cockpit and told them there was only one keg of pickles, ten pounds of salami, three boxes of crackers, one tinned ham, and thirty-four hamburgers left. Given the way they ate, especially Lepanto, they would soon starve. Worse, since the day of the storm there had been only a few swiftly passing showers, and their water was low.

"We were so worried about one danger or another we never thought about food and water," John said, "at least not for a long voyage. How much farther is it to land?" Lepanto was silent. "For someone who knows so much, it is amazing how little you know!" he snapped.

"Great knowledge goes with great ignorance," Lepanto replied with dignity. "The more of one, the greater the other."

"Oh, great," muttered John.

Sam laughed.

But John wasn't ready to give up: he had a great deal more color than when this journey began, and was not as silent and morose or sleepy as before. He stared at the Elephant. "Have you looked in your pockets?"

"My pockets?"

"Everything else seems to be there," he said, irritated: "maybe you've a spare gallon or two of water!"

"No need to be testy," replied Lepanto. He had been reclining against the aft mast, but now sat up and rummaged in his vest pockets. "Ah," he said suddenly, and pulled out several large bags of peanuts. John examined one carefully.

"Salted," he muttered.

"My favorites," smiled the Elephant. He resumed his search, moving from one pocket to the next. "Oh," he said, "what can this be?" He pulled out a long, round package. It turned out to be a hard but tasty salami.

"It's salty too," Sam laughed.

"Of course," said Lepanto. "Spice of life!" He rummaged in another pocket. There he found six cans of baked beans, a can of peach halves, and a tin of sardines. "Mmm," he sighed, "we'll save the peaches for a special occasion. They are not in character, but they are my favorite. Especially the sweet juice."

"Is that it?" asked John.

"Heaven's no!" Lepanto replied, and in another pocket found two ripe melons, while yet another yielded a ten pound sack of sugar.

"Let me guess," said John: "you have a sweet tooth."

"Tusks," grinned Lepanto. He waved his two gleaming tusks in the light. John and Sam looked at them, suddenly not taking them for granted as usual: they were formidable! Then they met the Elephant's bright, amber-brown glance. Despite this being another clear, perfect day the hairs prickled on Sam and John's necks.

"Who are you, really?" breathed Sam.

Lepanto looked at him. "I am what you wished for—" he began.

"No! Really!"

"But I am really that. Ohh!" he cried, having moved to his pants' pockets, and drew out not two but four two-gallon containers of water. "I am afraid that's all," he sighed, leaning back, clearly not intending to answer Sam's question further.

"We'll have to start rationing supplies."

"It's a good thing I eat on the fly," quipped the Flying Trapeze, sunning on top of the repaired deck. They looked at it with frowns, then at the stores Lepanto had found. They would help, but for how long?

"I'll find the Book," said Sam inspired, "and draw us a full supply!" He could already picture the result of writing "Food!" and drawing an abundance of everything they needed. "Where is it?"

But no one had seen it when they straightened out the cabin after their deck repairs. Thunderstruck, Sam rushed below and ransacked every cabinet, shelf, cubby, and storage bin on the yacht. After a while John joined him, occasionally shaking his head as if in some private argument, but persevering.

They came back on deck. To Lepanto's look Sam said, "It's lost."

John thought if there was one thing of theirs any enemy would want to destroy, it would be the Book. He remembered how their chant had set Lepanto dancing. "You crashed through the deck," he said.

"Then the waves started washing over us," added Sam.

"They wanted the Book," John said, "not us."

"And got it! Now what will we do!" said Sam. Lepanto shook his head.

"I doubt very much if anything can happen to that Book it doesn't want to happen," Lepanto said: "I doubt very much if it's lost," he added. "I suspect it has its reasons."

"What reasons?" John's incredulity had surged up again. Lepanto shrugged. "We could starve!" father and son said.

"Perhaps. But what I think is…" He pondered a moment, looking around. "We have a fine little ship," he murmured, "a tested crew, a delightful companion," he smiled, clearly meaning himself, "fine weather, a steady breeze, and a set course going where the wind wills. Mm hm," he nodded with satisfaction.

"We are through the Upside-down Ocean," muttered John.

"And past the Sea of Faces," added Sam.

"And we are 'in' wherever 'in' is," said Lepanto, "on our way to you know where." John and Sam were silent. "So what I think is…" He let the pause draw out, then reached his conclusion. "Yes, I believe the Book helped us come this far, but that what follows we must do on our own."

"Whatever that is," sighed Sam.

"You don't want to think everything works out just because you draw it that way, with the result you wonder if it's all real, like your father still does, do you?" Lepanto asked Sam. Sam shook his head.

"But I don't know what I can do."

"All anyone can do is try his best when he must, and usually we don't know what that is—"

"Until put to the test," Sam finished.

"That's not very hopeful," John said. "I mean helpful."

"Oh, but I think it is," smiled the Elephant. He very much

approved of how much both had changed since the beginning of their journey. "And besides, if it is gone, then we must simply use our heads and—and ration the food," he conceded, looking at John, coming back to where this conversation had started. "I leave that to you." John nodded. Sam turned away and stared out to sea.

"I know," he laughed suddenly, "I'll go fishing! Here's an ocean, and it has to have more than faces swimming in it!" Nonetheless he gave an anxious look over the surface to make sure no faces unexpectedly reappeared. None did.

"Now why didn't I think of that!" Lepanto exclaimed, striking his endless forehead with the back of a hand.

"Because your brain is so large it can't think of anything obvious quickly!" quipped the Flying Trapeze.

"That will do for today," Lepanto said, and stuffed the Flying Trapeze into one of his pockets over its protests.

Sam soon had a fishing rod set. For lack of anything better he took a piece of salami, set it to the biggest hook he found, and cast aft, letting out all the line as the yacht moved steadily on. He waited eagerly for a strike, but as time passed and nothing happened his shoulders sagged, and finally he passed the rod to John who, after a patient wait, sighed and carried the rod amidships to Lepanto until he tired of it and it was Sam's turn again.

The hours dragged by as again they passed the rod from one to another.

"Maybe we should try hamburger," John muttered after they had reeled it in, seen that the salami was still untouched, and let the line out again.

"Salami really is too salty." But so much time had passed Sam felt rooted to the deck, unable to hand the rod to John and go below to find hamburger meat.

"We should just tie the rod to something and leave it until something happens," he suggested. He was about to tie it to the aft railing when the rod gave a little jerk.

"Something took a nibble," he breathed.

The others looked. He felt another nibble.

"Yes!" John cried out. Carefully Sam walked forward followed by John until they stood by Lepanto. There was another jerk of the line, but before he could say anything something in the depths nearly tore the rod from his hands. Quick-thinking Lepanto saved the day by grabbing Sam with his trunk, and taking the rod himself. But even he was hard put to hold on.

"Hmph" was all he said. They could see his muscles flex and stiffen under his suit.

"What can it be?" Sam wondered.

The rod was bent double. Lepanto huffed and puffed, pulling back with all his strength, letting the rod go forward suddenly and reeling in the slack, then repeated the process as the minutes stretched out and became hours. For all the strain Lepanto didn't weaken. A frown marched across his vast forehead, the lines deepening with his struggle, then set into fixed determination.

John and Sam got anxious as they saw the yacht tip to Lepanto's side each time he pulled the line taut, the railing almost dipping into the sea, then rising abruptly as Lepanto released the tension and hurriedly reeled in some slack.

"Do you think this is safe," John asked after awhile, his feet now in the water with Lepanto's before the Elephant let the yacht right itself again as he reeled in more slack. The Elephant grunted.

"Maybe it's only a gigantic boot," Sam added. Lepanto paused, stared at him, then resumed his efforts.

"I'll get it, whatever it is," he grunted.

Father and son exchanged looks. Once Lepanto decided on something, now pulling, but a few weeks ago, dancing, there was no stopping him. Whatever he had, and John was starting to get very worried about what it might be, Lepanto was going to bring it to light, or else.

The struggle wore on. Back Lepanto pulled the rod, bending it double, then swiftly reeled in a length of line as he let the rod sink down, then heaved back, the rod bending as he pulled: pull, release, reel, pull, release, reel, pull, the yacht tilting and righting itself with each release.

"Water," he breathed at last.

Sam got him a large bottle. Lepanto took it with his trunk and poured some over his head, and drank the rest. Pull, release, reel, pull.... The sun slid down the sky: Lepanto's suit darkened with sweat. Pull, release, reel, pull.... After a time Lepanto could not remember a time when he had not been reeling in this monstrous weight. The day felt like it had extra hours to John and Sam, while to Lepanto it felt like the sunset somehow was deferred....

At last the sun fell towards the horizon and, as Sam, blinded and half-hypnotized by Lepanto's rhythm, glanced to starboard, he thought something had changed. He snapped alert, staring. Something had darkened the water. The darkness expanded and the tension on the rod gave way so suddenly Lepanto fell backwards.

"Uh oh," said Sam. John stared. The shrouds and stays keened, high-pitched, and the lines squealed, as if let loose too suddenly. The yacht was a cacophony of warnings, including what sounded like dark muttering from the keel below. Then everything went quiet.

"Calm, calm, calm," sighed the breeze and died. They coasted to a stop, the sails flapping helplessly, and began to wallow in the swell.

A shape greener than the water broke the ocean's surface to

starboard, its eyes green too, but flashing. The scales on its long, serpentine neck glittered in the late light below a head that looked too large despite the great size of the rest of the beast's body. The only sound as it rose beside them was of water pouring from its body until it towered over them.

They heard water falling to port, too, and when they looked they saw another coil of the beast's body had broken the surface there after running underneath their boat. If it chose it could wrap its body around the schooner and crush them.

"Oh no," said Sam. He stared at the fishing line glittering in the air: they had hooked one of the triangular, spiny ridge scales running down the beast's neck.

"This is the end," murmured John.

"Oh my," said Lepanto as he too stared. They did not think of escaping on the Flying Trapeze in the middle of this watery desert, and the monster did not seem to be in a rush. His look was neither friendly nor hungry as he stared down at them, done rising, and they stared up. Sam's memory flashed back to the green sea dragon hanging from the ceiling in his room so far away: it seemed a riddle with no solution—Lepanto, the schooner, and now this beast.

"I like riddles." The words didn't come from the monster's mouth but sounded in their minds at the same time, they realized, as they glanced at each other.

"Really," muttered Lepanto, "a riddling sea monster!" How fortunate he's not hungry, he thought. Something like a smile touched the monster's lips. At least not yet, his thought ran on. The monster's smile grew.

"Careful," Lepanto breathed, "he can read our minds!"

Sam looked back and forth between Lepanto and the beast. Before he could stop himself, he blurted out, "We like riddles, too. My

father is very smart and Lepanto is the smartest Elephant anywhere!" They felt rather than heard the serpent's amusement.

"A plump fellow, that one," sounded in their minds, the monster clearly looking at Lepanto as a farmer might at a prize pig.

"I'm quite tough," Lepanto said, "and my hide is very thick!" The sea serpent smiled, baring long rows of razor sharp teeth.

"Who is most handsome of all?" echoed in their heads. They looked at each other: what kind of riddle was that? "Me!" The beast gnashed its teeth, offended they hadn't said so right away.

"That's not fair!" Sam said boldly.

"What's fair?" Sam stared, at a loss for words.

"That's not right!" answered John.

"What's right?"

"This will get us nowhere," said Lepanto.

"What's nowhere? Answer my riddles!"

"Those aren't riddles!" Sam said.

"Me! Me! ME!" came the angry reply.

"Me me me," Sam mocked, then greatly daring: "you're just a big stuffed shirt!"

"Am I?" The thought echoed in their heads, but with an amused edge to it. "You're very small to say so."

"Rightness has nothing to do with size," answered Sam.

"Hahahaha, hahahaha, oh hahahaha!" the serpent convulsed, his coils setting off choppy waves that made the schooner rock and wallow in a way that soon made them queasy despite their sea legs.

"What can be embraced, but not held; held, but not kept; kept, but must be surrendered?" They looked at each other: the beast had turned serious without warning, and they had no doubt about the warning in its thought if they failed to answer his riddle. Sam and John were stumped.

"Easy," muttered Lepanto without looking at them. "Life."

The serpent clashed his jaws, his laughter again in their heads, and rose up higher, beginning to coil around the boat.

"Wait!" shouted John. "That's a trick riddle. It has two answers!" The beast paused.

"Yesssss." But a coil slid over the stern even as his mouth widened.

"Love is the other," said John. Lepanto gave him a level look.

"Yes," thought the sea-monster. The coil over the stern loosened. The beast did nothing fast: it had all the time in the world for them to admire the sharpness of his teeth and the size of his maw.

"Okay!" Sam cried. "You said answer your riddles first. Now answer mine!"

"Must I?" But he knew he did. Riddling games had their rules, thought Sam.

"Hahahahaha... Rules... Hahahahaha..."

"And there's a prize for whoever wins!"

"A prize? I like prizes! If I win, I eat you. If I lose, I eat you. Hahahahahahahahaha!"

"No. If we win you have to—"

"Have to—what?"

Sam glanced at his companions.

"To let us go to the Far Land of Fear and Dread City."

"Hahahaha! Hahaha! HAH!" roared the sea serpent in their minds, convulsing again, the yacht lurching on his waves. They clung to the railing grimly. "Hahahaha! Oh, that's a good one! That's the best I've heard in hahahaha! a very long time." The great serpent, sea dragon, beast, finally stilled. It lowered its great head so it seemed to float on the water, level with Sam.

"And if I win?" rolled through their minds.

"You already know. You get us."

"That's nothing I don't have now!"

"You dared us to riddle."

"Did I? Did I? DID I—"

"Besides," and Sam laughed, "we're not much to eat. Even him," he added, with a gesture to Lepanto. "We're tidbits. He's no more than a bite or two. Wouldn't it be better for you to lose?" John smiled: Lepanto's look of indignation gave way to a laugh.

"Oh, very good! Very good! Hahahahaha! Well," sighed the beast at last, "he is only one or two decent mouthfuls." He looked at Lepanto again: his eyes took in Lepanto's great tusks, which seemed larger than usual in the late light. "It won't do you any good," the beast added mockingly, but his head lifted. "I never lose."

"You've never played me!" Sam said bravely.

"Stout lad!" exclaimed Lepanto, trying to look small.

"Oh very well," sighed in their minds. For the beast was intrigued despite himself. No one as small as Sam had ever dared challenge him. He nearly felt an unusual emotion for the boy, one of liking for his bravery. But the folly of bravery sent him into fresh convulsions which this time sent water lapping over their feet. When he settled down, he searched Sam silently, and found only a wall of determination in the boy's mind.

"Oh very well," he repeated, "if you lose, I eat you, and that boat, and whatever is in it. But if you win—! Hahahaha!" He found even the thought funny.

"If we win you let us go where we want to. In fact, you help us."

Yes, the beast thought, yes, I rather like this boy. Nonetheless, I'll eat him in the end.

"Oh very well," he hissed aloud. "What is your riddle?" sounded in Sam's mind.

Sam opened his mouth, but nothing came out. He'd talked them from one menace to another, but now he needed a winning riddle he couldn't think of a thing.

"Yes, what's your riddle, Sam?"

"Indeed," murmured the Elephant.

"Well?" demanded the beast.

"Well?" asked Lepanto.

"Think, Sam!" his father said.

"No riddle?" thought the beast, its smile deepening, a coil again lashing around their stern.

"I want my mother," Sam blurted, unable to think of anything else.

"Hahahaha! Hahahaha! Oh hahaHaHA!" roared in their heads so loudly they clutched them in desperation. "He wants his mother! HahahahaHaHA!" The yacht heaved again from the waves set off by the sea monster's convulsions.

"Here now," Lepanto said sternly: "we're depending on you." The wisest of Elephants and his own father were looking at him grimly. Sam took a breath. The beast's jaws began to descend, opening as they came, and Sam stilled. Then he knew. The beast stopped, sensing the sudden, utter certainty in the boy's mind. Before he could bend down and snatch the boy from the deck Sam blurted his riddle.

"Where does everyone go but no one comes back from, but where we are going when we can't, to rescue someone who we shouldn't be able to, But Will?" All his defiance was in those last two words.

The beast froze. Its jaws snapped shut with a sound of teeth clashing that was frightening.

"Whom," murmured John.

"NONONONONO," the beast shouted in their minds, so they again clutched their heads. "That is impossible!" rang in their heads. Wholly impossible, thought the beast. He had been charmed when

119

the boy said where he wanted to go, but this was quite something else. He felt, for the second time, a novel feeling: surprise. His head lifted. Liking…. Surprise…. He startled himself by a third feeling now, one even rarer: curiosity. He suddenly very much wanted to see if the child could do what he said.

"Wrong!" shouted Sam to the beast's 'nos'.

"Dread City across the Far Land of Fear," the beast replied, "where all go when life is done, never to return," he added, temporizing, weighing his admiration for Sam's bravery, weighing his surprise, and curiosity.

"But we are not dead, and we are going there!" They could feel the beast's confusion, for Sam had spoken the truth which until now the beast had not fully taken in.

"You can't succeed," it hissed aloud, stunned by this fourth novel feeling: confusion.

"You have to wait for us to succeed or fail before you can be sure. We've already come here through the Upside-down Ocean and the Sea of Faces!" added Sam. Then, bursting with triumph, "You lose!"

And that too was something new for the beast to contemplate. Five things, in one hour, he thought. He was dazed. The boy's logic was ironclad. And not just that: the beast's curiosity swiftly became all-consuming. Oh yes, he would see, yes, and the boy would not find it so easy. He made no effort to hide that threatening thought from their minds. If John and Lepanto were sobered, Sam was unaffected.

"You have to help us!" he insisted.

"Yes," sighed the beast aloud, releasing the schooner from his coils. "Yes," he breathed again as he moved his head behind the boat. He took a long, deep breath so that his body filled with air and almost surfaced in its entire enormity, bearing the yacht on its back. "Yes," he breathed: then let his breath out in a steady stream that filled their sails and drove them forward.

They had to grab the stays for support with the sudden motion, then hurriedly adjust the rigging to take full advantage of the monster's breath as they slipped off its back and flew ahead. That being steadily receded, but his breath continued and, if anything, grew stronger.

"Yes," lingered in their minds, in the air, in the steady forward thrust of the yacht into the night, "yes, go and see." A last "Hahahaha" faded from their minds.

VIII

A Fearful Place

They surged over the waves with that breath in their sails, the spinnaker set, the great mainsails ballooned wing to wing, taut but safe.

So great was their surge they surfed down each wave's crest, which would have been exhilarating except for its strangeness, for outside the beast's breath the sea was windless, its surface mirror clear. Two suns danced in their eyes, the one above, the other mirrored, and both so intense they nearly lost their red edges. They kept to their stations uneasily, not sure they could trust the beast's breath, ready for any sudden change. But that breath held all day and through the night although they kept four hour watches in their wariness.

That breath held true the next day, filling any other sail they could rig as well. As the days wore on with that relentless breath carrying them forward a smudge on the horizon one morning raised fresh anxiety: were they being blown helplessly into another storm? They had barely survived the storm in the Sea of Faces! But the smudge rose steadily as the hours passed and began to resolve into recognizable features.

"Land," whispered Sam from the bow with a dry mouth. He made himself swallow. "Land!" he said clearly, pointing. The others nodded, for the smudge that filled the horizon resolved slowly into a wall of ever taller cliffs. All that day the cliffs rose forbiddingly. Only directly ahead did a break open and two headlands separate and grow in definition. Those dull headlands and cliffs were shades of red and brown, tumbled stones, precipitous heights, and lifeless as far as they could tell. Only as they drew abreast of these did the monster's breath weaken.

"Skippingly, skippingly, skippingly," spoke the breeze, and they maintained momentum into the channel between the headlands. At the foot of forbidding cliffs on either side they saw some distant objects that after a time they realized were signs. Lepanto took a pair of binoculars from a pocket and stared, then passed them to John, who stared in turn before he gave them to Sam without comment. He read, "Dread City: 920 miles," "Dread City: 5,000 light-years," "Dread City: 40 meters," "Dread City: 200 years" and so on.

"Someone put them there," he muttered: "why couldn't they make up their minds how far it is?" No sign said so, but they knew they had reached the Far Land of Fear.

The forbidding cliffs on either side of the channel gave way to a wide body of darker, cliff-fringed water opening before them that steadily lost its emerald hue. They were somber, for there was no current, no change in the breeze, just dark water, somber cliffs, and the violet sun. Silence was a wet blanket on a drooping line.

As they took in the size of the great bay these cliffs enfolded they were soon reduced to binoculars to search for a beach or rocky cove to pull into. No paths were visible along the cliffs by which they could reach the land above. Sometimes they did glimpse narrow beaches, but they offered no temptation to land and explore: they could see their steep, enclosing walls.

They sailed straight into the widening bay as long as the breeze held, and the breeze blew only down the center of the channel. Still, shining dark water stretched away to the shores on either side of the rippled path the breeze created down that bay's center. There was no sign of life, neither of fish in the water nor of vegetation or wildlife on

the narrow shores or on the cliffs, nor any sign of the bay's end ahead.

At length the wind sighed, and died. They glided slowly to a stop. Astern they could see a faint ripple on the water where there was still some breeze, but they had coasted beyond its reach. The sails shuddered, and hung slack.

They waited for a breeze to start up again as the violet hue faded from the sun that grew large and darkly red as it sank below the horizon. The sky, empty of stars, deepened to purple, and then to night. Quietly they furled and lowered and stowed the sails, ate, then bunked down, the schooner motionless in the profound silence.

Morning found them still motionless in dark waters. They looked at each other without speaking and understood they had come as far as they were going to by sail. But on which side should they disembark? They scanned the distant shores with the binoculars, but all looked harsh. All they had to go on was the faintest sense of trembling reaching them from starboard.

"I'm portside, myself," said John.

"I think we should go right," said Sam.

"Right would be left in this case," his father asserted firmly.

"It gives me the creeps," Sam said. "I don't believe it's as calm as it looks. I don't think the right could be as bad as we're afraid. Who knows what that shaking is from?"

"The fact is," offered Lepanto before father and son got into an argument, "I don't like the looks of either. I would like to go ahead, except we can't."

"Left," said John.

"Right!"

Lepanto looked from one to the other.

"Get your satchel," he ordered John, as if in agreement. John did as he was told, stuffing what was left of the salami into it as well.

The Elephant pulled out the Flying Trapeze. Its ropes shot up in anticipation. "Everyone on!" Lepanto cried merrily.

"Which way?" asked the Flying Trapeze.

"Starboard!" Lepanto ordered, smiling at John's look.

They shot up in the swiftly heating air as the sun rose higher. Soon they were high enough they could see wide plains stretch beyond the cliffs on either side, but speculation was cut short as the Flying Trapeze arched back and up and then abruptly surged forward to a collective, "Whee!"

The shore was farther than they thought, the Flying Trapeze soon huffing and puffing in the warm, still air. Slowly it lost altitude until it just skimmed over the water from which waves of heat reflected. It strained up just enough for the last swing to drop them with a thud just past the high tide line on a pebbly beach. They found themselves at the foot of a canyon that rose steeply towards the plains above.

"Let's go!" Sam shouted, excited to be on land again. They had come so far Dread City had to be near! Despite the glimpse of wide plains above he half expected once up the canyon to be able to see the city in the distance. He raced forward.

"Wait!" warned Lepanto, but Sam ran with a sense of glad release from their schooner's confinement. The canyon was rocky and barren: piles of red rocks lay everywhere, washed into great fans by sudden floods from above. He raced by these up a dry stream bed, sluggish rivulets appearing as he climbed higher.

Then he saw little clumps of cacti almost the same color as the rock, covered with sharp spines, some larger in squat, barrel-like shapes with brown flowers between their needles. On he raced, the others' shouts growing faint as he left them behind. He took care to avoid the cacti, but now and then stumbled and scraped himself on the stones. Each time he picked himself up he ran faster, like one possessed.

Ahead the canyon's steep slope leveled briefly, and turned to the left. He hurried to the bend.

"Ohh," he breathed as a low grove of palm trees with red-veined fronds hanging over clusters of coconuts came into view. Small pools of water flowed into each other and out into the stream working its way down the canyon. Then he saw something moving down the steep canyon wall towards the water and flung himself behind a boulder.

The figure had a horse's body, with a braided tail swinging from his rump where a very human head looked backwards. A man's torso was where a horse's neck should have been, with arms where a man had arms and two more where there should have been a head. Under each normal arm was another head. The creature looked like it was carrying those, although it wasn't.

Now and then it paused to scan the grove, then moved forward, again. Finally it knelt down by one of the pools. The three heads started a noisy argument.

"Me first!" said one.

"No, me!" said the other.

"Turn around for me!" shouted the third.

"Shut up!" said the other two, and took noisily disputed turns. The beast stood alertly when it heard a rumble above, all three heads staring anxiously at the cliffs where the plains ended. Clouds of dust appeared over the canyon rim, then Sam heard countless cursing, shouting voices. As his eyes widened a few bodies appeared on the ridge, but apparently made of stone: heads, torsos, limbs of like but different sized stones, and as he took them in he thought of some of the figures he had seen on the beach outside Lepanto's tent.

These wavered on the edge bellowing in anger and fear as more pushed into view behind them—then they began to fall, smashing themselves to pieces with anguished cries against the canyon's walls and the cliff's base. At length a line of the three-headed centaurs appeared on the cliff's edge, screaming with laughter. Not one of the stony mob survived.

"What a mean thing to do," he said, angry.

"Who's there?" shouted one of the centaur's heads by the pool of water: there was nothing wrong with their hearing! The herders on the ridge fell silent as their comrade trotted towards Sam's hiding place.

"Who's there?" shouted another of the centaur's heads.

"Turn around!" demanded the third, straining to see ahead. "I can't see anything!"

"Thrash him whatever he is! Thrash him hard!" all three cried.

Sam looked around for a weapon but could see nothing but smashed rocks. He trembled with fear: if he moved he'd be seen in a flash.

"He must be behind that boulder," said the first head.

"I'm not dumb!" said the second. "Beat him up!" bellowed the third, still twisting to look forward. "Oh, why do I miss all the fun!"

But just as the figure came near Sam's hiding place, he heard his father and Lepanto calling as they neared the small oasis he had found. The three-headed centaur stopped: the others on the ridge crowded together and stared down.

John and Lepanto called more loudly, then came in sight. The strange centaur-like figures let out a collective gasp. But there was not time for more because as soon as Sam saw Lepanto and his father he picked up two smashed fragments and jumped onto the boulder.

"Take that!" he cried, and hit one of the heads between the eyes. "Ow!"

"And here's one for you!" he cried as he threw the other rock: at this distance he couldn't miss.

"OUCH!"

"What's happening?" the third head cried. Sam jumped down and grabbed two more rocks.

"Watch out!" cried a head, but now a rock hit the one in the rear.

"Smash him! Smash him hard!" it screamed.

The centaur readied to charge, but it was Lepanto who trumpeted angrily, lowered his tusks, and charged. The three-headed centaur took one look at the sight of a great elephant in his elegant suit in full charge and fled up canyon with frightened shouts.

The others on the ridge above milled about, half-enraged, half-stunned by this turn of events while Lepanto stopped, satisfied with his impact, cut a few quick dance steps, and trumpeted at the milling figures. After a moment filled with a confused babble of voices they too turned, and fled.

"Well," said Lepanto, turning to Sam, "it was a fool thing to run away from us like that in a strange place. What got into you?" Sam hung his head. He had just had to run. But Lepanto was right.

"I'll be more careful," he said.

"Good lad," nodded the Elephant. Before John could say anything the cries of the centaurs drew their attention. They reappeared on the ridge in greater numbers egging one another down the steep path towards the travelers with clubs in their hands.

"Quick," said Lepanto. "Onto the Flying Trapeze." He pulled it out from his pocket, watched the ropes shoot straight up, and got on, John and Sam to either side. "Up!" shouted Lepanto: "swing by those coconuts as you go! We need supplies!"

The Flying Trapeze did as he was told without a word, first allowing Lepanto to stuff coconuts into his pockets, then arching back before sweeping forward over the canyon's rim, above the astonished centaurs, soaring over the plains. They set off inland with long swoops after steep recoils, the undulating plains passing beneath until they could see nothing but plains everywhere.

"Couldn't we go the other way?" asked John. "This is a mistake."

"What if it is worse the other way?" Sam asked.

"Too far now," the Flying Trapeze said, speaking finally. "This is hard work. This air… There's nothing refreshing about it at any height."

All three nodded. The air felt, well, thick—and the heat was stifling.

"These dangers we begin to know," breathed Lepanto, "which is something. I very much doubt going back would be a good idea."

"But where will this lead?" asked John.

"Here all leads to one place."

They looked at Lepanto, then at the dusty plains below. On they swept towards a distant range of mountains, while mesas began to rise below them and dot the plains like empty tables set in a desert. Worse, steadily lowering their spirits even more, were the groups of centaur-like creatures herding stone people, always in the same direction towards the cliffs they'd left behind.

None noticed them flying above: none looked up. Between that and the thick, hot air, a silence deepened in them as the miles sped by. The flying Trapeze too remained silent, going on without complaint until they felt his recoils lessen and swoops grow weaker.

"I'm very tired," the Flying Trapeze huffed at last. He had flown farther than expected, and that on top of the morning's flight to the bay's shore.

"Very well," replied Lepanto, "find a good place, and land. On one of those mesas, where those centaurs don't seem to come."

The Flying Trapeze swung towards a small red mesa to their left that rose from the plains with reassuringly sheer walls. A few moments later they dropped down, landing roughly, thirsty and tired.

"Oof!" said Lepanto, while the Flying Trapeze gave a happy sigh as Lepanto stuffed him into one of his pockets. John and Sam dusted themselves off, then looked around.

The mountain range they had seen in the distance was closer now, and not a range but one great, solitary mountain whose haunches spread over the plain. Red mesas dotted the plains at its feet, just like the one they had landed on. Here and there they saw swirls of dust on the plains: just below their cliff they made out figures through the dust, with more of the centaur-like herders driving their stony charges towards their end. They turned away from the grim spectacle.

Lepanto drew some coconuts from his vest, cracked them open and handed them to Sam and John, slurping the juice from his own with a sigh before immediately cracking another open, and then another. Sam and John stared at his endless supply as they drank down the sweet juice from their own and pried the sweet flesh loose from the shell.

No one spoke for some time: then Sam leaned back with a sigh, followed by John, while Lepanto methodically split and drank, smashed and ate, split and drank. The pile of shells grew before him.

"How come your pockets hold so much?" asked Sam.

Lepanto paused, surveying the wreckage at his feet, and smiled. "Because that's how you imagined me," he replied to Sam; "it is most convenient." This answered and didn't answer, except Sam's eyes widened, and he suddenly wondered how else Lepanto or his pockets could have been imagined.

But, "You hung from the ceiling," was all he said.

Lepanto shook with laughter even as something like the same thoughts as Sam's raced through John's mind, and he wondered again not whether Lepanto was, but who he was, really. Before he said anything, he felt the Elephant's gaze on him, and met Lepanto's brown, amber-studded glance with a deepened sense of mystery, for as he looked around he realized mystery was a fact, and everywhere, here and not any less in their home they had left behind, which now seemed like an oasis filled with the magic of peace compared to this.

"Very good," was all Lepanto said, as if he had read his mind: "I am what I am partly because of you, too," he said, surprising John as he swept his trunk about, "if mostly because of him," he added, nodding towards Sam. "I hardly know what I am outside his imagination and your doubts." He said no more, shrugging off their questions in silence.

John sat back thinking how expectations could determine a man's action—thoughts of failure could lead to failure, thoughts of depression to depression, and of action to action. He knew he had lost his way before this adventure began, had sunk deep into lethargy, and acted lethargy, as it were, dragging Sam down with him. Thoughts of fear, of loss, of impotence had come within a hair of breaking his spirit. He looked around again full of wonder, and realized whatever his rational doubt might be about what was in fact happening that he didn't want to fail Sam again.

Finally the sun ceased to set, its rim hovering in what they thought, somehow, was the northeast, while now in the far west the sky was dark enough for ruby stars to be visible in constellations no one recognized, not even those they had named on their voyage. Everything felt upside down. Everything was red, too, the mesas and plains, the deep, somberly red mountain before them, and the reddened clouds. They looked red to each other in this light.

"This is like the red day I drew in the Book," Sam sighed.

"Yes," nodded the Elephant. John sighed and shook his head. One by one they yawned.

IX

Biggest, Toughest, Hardest

They decided keeping a sentinel would be a good idea. Lepanto drew the first watch; John and Sam slowly drifted off after squirming on the hard ground trying to get comfortable until, exhausted, a darkness free of any reddish tint swept over their minds.

Lepanto settled down, only his ears betraying life as they fanned slowly back and forth. Faint cries rose from the plains below: otherwise time flowed by thick as honey. What passed for midnight arrived and started to fade, but Lepanto made no effort to waken John for his watch.

Suddenly he straightened.

"What is it?" Sam whispered. He had slept profoundly at first, but then vague, unsettled dreams made him restless, and Lepanto's movement brought him to.

"I'm awake too," muttered John, twisting uncomfortably.

"There are voices over there," Lepanto whispered, pointing towards the center of the mesa. "Nice sounding voices," he added in response to the alarm in their faces.

"Let's go see," whispered Sam, "no one's sleeping anyway."

"Alright," whispered Lepanto, "but softly, and do as I say."

The mesa sloped gently downwards towards its center, and they began to pass small, bowl-like depressions in the ground. As they carefully edged forward John and Sam could hear a murmur in the distance that slowly resolved into gentle voices. They didn't think the three-headed centaurs could speak that gently even if they tried. At last they saw a small pool of water bordered by an unexpected edge of brown grass and pink, almost coral wildflowers.

The still water reflected the ruby stars, and, bringing them up short, they saw a ring of heads circled the pool, all perfectly normal, the rest of their bodies, if they had bodies, encased in stone. All had kindly, serious faces and were in earnest conversation with one another. As Sam and the others listened they saw no one ever lifted his eyes from the pool.

"Whether there can be a mind without a body," murmured one.

"Whether there can be a mind without a head," corrected another.

"Mm...mm...mm..." the others hummed.

"Whether there can be a head without a mind?" another asked.

"I've never seen one," said a kindly old head.

"Mm...mm...mm..."

"I have!" exclaimed Sam.

"Who's that?" the heads asked in unison.

"Me!" said Sam.

"Keep still," John warned.

"Mmm," murmured the Elephant.

"Who's that? What's that!" the heads asked.

Sam stepped forward. "Us!"

"Who is 'us'?" they cried.

"Look!" Sam said impatiently.

"We are!" But they kept their eyes fixed on the pool where the red stars shone.

"Look up!" Sam demanded, frustrated.

"Up?"

"Whether there is an 'up'?"

"Whether there can be anything that isn't visible in the pool?" said another. They stared into the water.

"Mm…mm…mm…"

Sam and the others were stunned by these wise old heads' behavior. Finally Lepanto leaned over the pool, followed by Sam and John. The heads exclaimed in surprise.

"How strange!"

"Monstrous!"

"Full-bodied!" said a third, revolted.

"And moving!" added another head with an expression of fear and astonishment.

"Mm! mm! mm!" Then they fell silent and stared at the reflections. Sam stood back.

"Ah! One has gone!"

"I'm still here!" Sam shouted.

"Whether something can be here that is no longer visible," queried one head.

"Whether something that is no longer here can still be heard," added a second.

"Whether being so extraordinary while here, and so insistent when not, can it be anything but a delusion?" added a third.

"Mm...mm...mm..."

"Whether a delusion is anything?"

"Whether a delusion is anywhere?"

"Whether—."

"You're all crazy," Sam said: "you only see what you want, and call that real!" The heads were unfazed, and came to the conclusion no one had been here at all. John and Lepanto stepped back. Sam wasn't done.

"You'll never know anything this way."

"Whether there is anything to know beyond what we can see—" started one.

"We're going to Dread City across a Far Land of Fear," Sam shouted angrily.

"Whether there is anywhere but here?" one started

"Whether there can be any here that is not here?" added another.

"There is my mother," Sam said with a sudden, cold passion. "Who we lost and are going to find."

"Whether what can be lost can be found?" one began.

"Whether if lost it was ever here to lose?"

"Whether a delusion can have further delusions!" interjected a third, impatiently.

"Mm! mm! mm!"

Lepanto tapped Sam on the shoulder, and with a nod indicated they should go. Sam was furious at the heads dismissing his existence, let alone failing to react to the nature of his journey. But John looked thoughtful.

"Sam," he sighed, "come on, they don't matter: they are, maybe, what I was becoming."

At that Sam stared up at his father, and after a moment nodded. He didn't know how to put the thoughts racing through his mind into words, except he knew his father's words were true, but not anymore. He smiled. They retraced their steps to where they had slept and passed the remainder of the night restlessly.

The next morning they debated directions over coconuts.

"We don't know how far Dread City is," said John. "Suppose it is weeks, or months of walking, even of flying, the way the Flying Trapeze flies: think how long we sailed." He cast a doubtful glance at Lepanto's pile of coconuts. Furrows piled above one another on Lepanto's generous brow.

Sam felt instinctively his father was wrong.

"What makes you say so?" asked Lepanto. Sam shrugged. He stared blankly past the rim of the mesa, struggling to find words for his feeling: he knew they couldn't be far: how he knew was what he

found hard to explain.

"It's just, just…" He felt helpless—if only he had the Book here, he could draw a map and make the distance what he felt—and stopped himself. The Book! He thought of how he'd drawn the red land, and the boat, and the door over the stream. Of how each became an adventure, neatly recorded and illustrated in those pages. Of how he had dreamed about the Book when he'd at last fallen asleep.

"Just?" prodded his father.

"It's the Book," he breathed: "everything I've drawn has come true, and more: it's like… It's like we're inside the Book, turning pages, and now we've been at it a long time and…" They stared at him. "We not only have to get there, but find her, and then get back: so—so we must be close or there won't be room in the Book for all we have to do!"

"What an interesting idea," said Lepanto. "Everything is, after all, always a matter of timing." John rolled his eyes.

"Something like that," Sam agreed. "If I had the Book now I could draw the gates to the City, and we'd be there!" he added.

"Mm," said Lepanto.

"Don't make that sound," John said: "not after those heads." Lepanto nodded.

"It's all got something to do with my imagination," Sam blurted, remembering Lepanto's puzzling words, "that's how I imagine it, or something like that. I'm sure we're close."

John choked off his reply as he saw the Elephant nod. He took a breath.

"Well," he said, "which way, then?" They looked at him. "We shouldn't go back to the boat, even assuming it's still there. Those herders must be watching for us."

"Right," Lepanto said: "all that direction will be well watched, now. So—," and he pointed toward the red horizon where the mountain rose to a single, knobby, brooding peak. That meant risking the plains and herders, but there must be unguarded spots on the many mesas they could see receding across the plains towards the mountain where the Flying Trapeze could rest. And so, after another round of coconuts, they boarded the Flying Trapeze and set off in good spirits.

The plains stretched farther than they'd thought: a day's travel, with frequent rests for the Flying Trapeze, found them still among the mesas, with what seemed an equal number receding towards the mountain which steadily, if slowly, they thought grudgingly, grew ever more impressive.

They camped on another mesa that night, and again Lepanto heard voices. When they carefully searched out their origin, they found another pool of water surrounded by its own circle of philosophical heads, who yielded the same results when they tried to talk to them.

The next day passed the same way, flying mesa to mesa, resting, and flying again. They despaired of reaching an end to the plains, even though the mountain loomed on the horizon.

That night as they landed on a mesa they made no effort to trace the origin of the voices Lepanto heard again in the distance. Two philosophical dead-ends were enough! The next day their depressed spirits lifted: the mountain took up ever more of the sky before them, and that night they rested on the last mesa before the mountain's rise.

In the morning a last, broad stretch remained to cross before they reached the mountain, forcing the Flying Trapeze to rest on the plains on a spot free of the herders to regather its strength. The heat was unbearable. Lepanto thought he would turn into a coconut, he ate and drank so many, while their efforts to fan themselves only made them feel hotter.

"If only I had an umbrella," moaned Sam.

"How dumb of me! An umbrella!" Lepanto struck his brow, then reached into his vest and began emptying its pockets. He produced first a pile of coconuts that made them stare: how in the world had he gathered so many?

Next came a bottle of pills for seasickness which they hadn't used, a red-checked tablecloth, a packet of caravan tea he looked at fondly, a pair of pliers wrenched into a shape permitting an Elephant to use them, ivory polisher for his tusks, a set of Shakespeare, a set of Dryden, five Agatha Christie mysteries, a California field guide to wildlife, a dissecting kit with a bottle of formaldehyde, the strange globe that had lit the tent, his pipe kettle, a sun visor, the poetry of Senghor, a file for his nails, one rug to sit on, a collapsible table, two packets of dry lemonade, three packets of orange peel, and a collapsible umbrella.

Sam wondered how many new, strange items would come out of those pockets each time they were searched.

Lepanto stuffed all this but the umbrella back into his pockets, which belied its smallness by opening twelve feet in diameter: Sam and John sighed with relief, and Lepanto, and the Flying Trapeze. They had no sooner relaxed than a stubby-bodied stone person stomped into sight. It was Sam's size. It regarded them unblinkingly.

"Uh oh," Sam said, and in a rush they folded the umbrella and prepared to take off. Then another stone person appeared, smaller than the first. They immediately stood face to face.

"Pegmatite!" shouted the smaller.

"Shale!" growled the larger.

"Harder!" the smaller shrieked.

"Harder!" the larger growled.

"Not!"

They threw themselves against each other violently, and in a moment the smaller smashed the larger to bits. The three travelers suddenly felt much less sorry for the stony creatures they'd seen chased over the cliffs. The smaller jolted up to them.

"Pegmatite!" it shouted.

"Sam, John, and myself, an Elephant who likes to dance," replied Lepanto, holding the umbrella in front of him, letting his tusks catch the light.

"Pegmatite!" the intruder shouted, doubtfully. There were three of them, and the Elephant was large.

"We're so tough you shouldn't even be talking to us," said Sam, "We're going to Dread City."

"Never heard of it," the strange creature replied, unsure of himself. "Pegmatite," he added. "I'm tougher than you."

"I'm smarter," replied Sam.

"Pegmatite!" it shouted in fury, and flung himself forward.

"Up!" Lepanto ordered. The Flying Trapeze soared into the air as the stony creature rushed forward blindly and smashed into a larger creature that had come up behind them.

"All brains, and none," muttered John, referring to the heads on the mesas and stone persons being herded below.

"These are the Plains of Morons!" shouted Sam, laughing.

Lepanto smiled.

Below them they watched the drama play itself out. Now the larger stone person leapt forward and smashed the other to pieces.

"Har, har, har!" It's laugh receded behind them.

After that they risked only the shortest possible rests for the Flying Trapeze: fortunately they were at last in the foothills of the mountain, if seared by the heat. The Flying Trapeze required ever longer rests, gasping even though Lepanto kept the umbrella spread over them. They saw no life on the mountain's limbs or canyons, no snow on its head: it was just a jagged mass of red rock.

Exhausted though he was, the Flying Trapeze gritted nonexistent teeth and steadily swung up the mountain's face, for they were all determined to be as far above the plains as possible. They also hoped to get high enough to see some sign of where Dread City lay.

At last they halted in a steep little canyon near the mountain's crest where there was no sign of herders or argumentative boulders. They barely drank and ate from their store of coconuts before falling into an exhausted sleep.

"I never knew an adventure was such hard work!" Sam muttered as he lost consciousness. The others nodded as they too lost consciousness.

Heat woke them from dreams where they imagined they were being cooked. The violet sun blazed while the little canyon gathered and intensified its heat. Up went the umbrella again as they took stock.

"It all goes to show you the virtue of having head and body together," Lepanto was saying, "and in good balance, and looking about you and seeing what is to be seen, giving each thing its due."

"Sometimes I don't understand you at all," John snapped. "It's awful here!"

"Mmm," said Sam, then caught himself. "It sure is hot."

At that Lepanto brought out more of his endless supply of coconuts, and they sat there in the umbrella's hot shade sweating, drinking warm coconut milk and chewing white chunks of hot coconut flesh, too uncomfortable to say more. At last Lepanto put a final shattered coconut shell on the small mountain of shells before him, and leaned back with a sigh.

"It looks safe enough for now," he said. He stared up at the mountain's crest. "What can be beyond?"

"Something better than this. Anything would be better than this place," Sam added with real feeling.

"Even Dread City," he finished.

"I'm still too tired to fly," whined the Flying Trapeze, afraid Sam's words meant they had to start yet another exhausting day.

"Rest, rest," Lepanto murmured, but at those words the ground shook. They grabbed each other, alarmed, but saw nothing. The ground shook again.

"This is bad," said Sam.

"It's an awful place," agreed Lepanto, echoing John's words from a moment ago.

"SO YOU SAY," a cavernous voice replied from somewhere nearer the mountain's roots. When Lepanto reached for the Flying Trapeze they heard, "DON'T MOVE OR I WILL CLOSE THE CANYON ON YOU." Even as whoever spoke the canyon walls closed together, leaving just room for themselves.

"AWFUL," the voice echoed again. A rockslide fell near them.

"A talking mountain!" Sam shouted in glee, eyes gleaming.

"MOUNTAIN? MOUNTAIN? I AM THE GREATEST OF ALL!" the voice bellowed. Another rockslide fell nearer the travelers. "THE HARDEST OF HARD. THE TOUGHEST OF TOUGH. THE BIGGEST OF BIG!"

"You are indeed the hardest, toughest, biggest!" trumpeted Lepanto, staring around, hearing a rumbling they guessed was its laughter, which set avalanches rolling down its flanks. "It must be very dull for you," Lepanto added, making an inspired guess. "Awful, oh great stone giant."

"IT IS TERRIBLE TO HAVE NO ONE DECENT TO SMASH!" it groaned. "BUT GREAT STONE GIANT. I LIKE THAT!" And again it rumbled in laughter, setting off fresh avalanches.

"BUT IT IS AWFUL! AWFUL TOO!" it added. Just then the ground shuddered so badly they lost their footing and had to scramble to stand again. How will we get out of this, John wondered, frightened—as he could see Lepanto was, too. Only Sam looked unafraid, wide-eyed, fascinated by a stone person as huge as this mountain. To be his age again, John reflected: to find everything a wonder. But his thought was cut short as the Great Stone Giant bellowed "WHAT WAS THAT?"

"Wasn't it you," trumpeted Lepanto. There was no reply. Instead the mountain lifted to its full height, something that filled them with astonishment, as if they saw a mountain rise to its feet and survey its surroundings. Apparently it saw nothing, and settled down in a thunder of fresh rockslides and avalanches. After a time it spoke again.

"AWFUL BOREDOM WHEN THERE'S NOTHING LEFT WORTH SMASHING, THRASHING, CRASHING, ALTOGETHER CRUSHING INTO FRAGMENTS!" it moaned, and a thousand stony babbling bodies tumbled from its heights into the canyons. "I AM THE FATHER OF STONES!" it raved proudly. Then, sadly, "I CAN'T HELP IT. AND THEY ARE WORTHLESS. FIT ONLY FOR THOSE MISERABLE ANT-SIZED HERDERS TO DRIVE OFF CLIFFS."

"To have such power," Lepanto shouted, "and nothing to do!"

"AWFUL!" moaned the mountain again, shuddering to shake off the small babble of stony people it had shaken into existence. "SO DULL!" The ground shook again. "WHAT WAS THAT?"

"Perhaps an earthquake," Lepanto trumpeted.

"HMMM… HMMM…" Again it rose, again saw nothing, again settled in a roar and crash of rock, again shuddered to send the countless stone people cascading to its feet. WHAT ARE YOU?" the mountain asked.

"Flesh," replied Lepanto, guessing its meaning.

"FLESH? OH HARRRH HARRRH HARRRH."

When it finished laughing Sam said, "We're going to the Dread City."

"NEVER HEARD OF IT."

"The city where those no longer among the living go," John threw in.

"NEVER HEARD OF THEM!"

"He's never heard of anything!" Sam said.

"I HEARD THAT," the great stone giant growled. "YOU THINK I'M DUMB, HUH? I'M BIGGEST OF BIG, TOUGHEST OF TOUGH, HARDEST OF HARD!" The earth shook again. "WHAT IS DOING THAT?" the mountain cried.

Lepanto looked down the canyon towards the fragment of horizon visible in the distance. The mountain grew still, mumbling in its depths about how boring they were too, and that perhaps he should smash them. Flesh! That was a good one! He was about to squash the helpless travelers when again the ground trembled hard enough to fling them off their feet, thoroughly rattling the Great Stone Giant the mountain had revealed itself to be.

"WHAT WAS THAT WAS THAT!" it roared, and stood, tossing the travelers again off their feet. The canyon opened enough to let them have a good view of the horizon. "WHATISTHATISTHAT?" the stone giant roared with a new element in its voice they almost couldn't believe: fear. For on the horizon appeared a stone creature of even greater size.

"Your days of boredom are over," trumpeted Lepanto: "look there!"

Their mountainous giant stared as the greater stony giant narrowed the distance between them with great, earth-shaking strides. But instead of leaping with delight at the prospect of battle, their mountain flinched. The newcomer was so much larger his head was covered with storm clouds despite the heat of this region.

"OHHHH," their mountain quivered, sending fresh avalanches of stony people to the plains below.

"BIGGEST!" the oncoming roared, "TOUGHEST! HARDEST!"

"OHHHH," moaned the mountain. There was no mistaking that tone: fear! They felt the ground shake, and now great slabs of stone fell as the mountain seemed to forget their presence. They had to leap and dance to avoid being struck. In another moment they might be dead. Sam looked around desperately, but all he could see was the oncoming giant blocking out of sight everything ahead, while behind them stretched the long, hot miles back to the cliffs and the bay where they'd left their yacht, sure they'd find Dread City beyond those cliffs. Then Sam smiled.

"Oh Great Stone Giant! If you help us, I'll tell you how to win!"

"OHHHH…"

"Listen to me! I'll tell you how to WIN!" he shouted.

"OHHHH…" But the stone giant had heard. "WIN? TELL ME HOW TO WIN!"

"Take us back where we came from," Sam shouted, pointing.

"How can we go back?" demanded John.

"We can't go on where mountains run around," Sam answered. John rolled his eyes, but nodded with a sigh.

"No," agreed Lepanto, "but how can he defeat that?"

"Trust me! We have to go back to the boat and then to the other side. We should have gone left," Sam admitted. They all sighed.

"Hardest of HARD," Sam called. "To beat the other, this is what you must do." They felt the mountain tremble. Another moment and its giant enemy would be on it. "Make him follow you. He may be bigger, but you're smaller and faster. If you make him run after you,

147

he'll get tired!"

"MAYBE..."

"And when he's tired and not thinking, I show you what to do!"

"BIGGEST! HARDEST! TOUGHEST!" roared the oncoming giant. Their stone giant turned and fled as Sam had instructed.

"We'll prove him the dumbest!" Sam shouted. They felt a low rumble of laughter at that.

"DUMBEST!" roared the stone giant, and raced on.

The Greater Stone Giant was so enraged he tripped over a mesa and fell just as he was about to fling himself on them, giving them the smallest edge in the race across the plains. Herders and herds of small stone people scattered in wild disarray or disappeared under two sets of crushing feet as they raced across the plains that danced from their impact.

Their days of flying contracted into two hours of giant strides before a glint of water appeared on the horizon and swiftly grew into the bay, where their schooner still sat motionless, its sails sagging and still.

"Now," shouted Sam, "stop! Let him catch you! And just as he gets here step down the canyon and lay down next to the cliffs. He'll trip past you and for a moment be helpless: then jump on him. What could resist you then?"

"GOOD!" the monster roared, and opened the canyon where they had been trapped. They flung themselves onto the Flying Trapeze and soared upward and then, frighteningly, towards the oncoming, storm-crowned foe before the Flying Trapeze could swing forward out over the water towards the schooner. They gazed back. There on the ridge above the shore stood the mountainous Stone Giant.

"BIGGEST TOUGHEST HARDEST!" it screamed

in defiance.

"BIGGER TOUGHER HARDER!" came the reply of the onrushing colossus.

At the last moment their mountain stepped down onto the shore and lay against the cliffs, leaving a long ridge reaching above them that the other couldn't avoid. Unable to stop his momentum he tripped over that ridge and fell headlong into the water just as they landed on the deck. They watched a wall of water lift from the giant's impact.

"Oh no," muttered Sam.

"Grab something," shouted John, "anything!" Lepanto grabbed the mainmast and wrapped his trunk around Sam as John clung to a leathery leg whose elegant trousers were so dusty he sneezed despite himself.

"HARDEST! BIGGEST! TOUGHEST!" shouted the other as it rose and leaped on his enemy, fists hammering him apart, setting off a second, tumultuous wave that obscured the vision of collapsing canyons and ridges piling themselves into a heap in the water, creating a tall island where none had been before. Then the first wave lifted the boat and carried them headlong on its crest towards the other shore.

"OH NO!" cried Sam.

"OH NO!" cried the others.

X

Flesh to Stone

For a moment they feared they would smash into the swiftly approaching cliffs opposite as the wave carried them forward, but instead they were carried ever up towards the cliffs' crest. They hoped to ride the schooner to safety on high ground even as it twisted dangerously broadside when, with horror, they saw they were being carried towards a canyon-dividing wedge of rock.

"OHH" they cried, but even as they rushed towards the ridge the wave lost momentum.

"OHH" they cried again, but now at their precipitate drop.

Their stomachs heaved as though in an elevator that plummeted downwards as its floor fell away from their feet. They cried out a third time as the yacht grounded with a thud so they collapsed in a huddle of arms and legs, forcing even Lepanto to let go of the mast.

They staggered erect, grabbing whatever came to hand for safety as the yacht lurched, then slid down a steep ledge the water had deposited them on, grinding to a halt where the ledge leveled just before ending at a steep drop to the rocky shore far below.

They had only moments to take in their salvation, for drowning out the roar of the retreating wave was the great suck of water as the second wave drew that in as it soared in height. Then that wave tumbled over with a great roar and surged towards them. Helpless they watched it surge up the cliff and lift them up from the ledge and hurtle them again towards the wedge of rock.

"NOOO!" they cried as they struck and the schooner shattered and pitched them headlong into the frothing water.

"Dad!" cried Sam as the tumult carried him away.

"Sam!"

"Grab anything that floats!" Lepanto trumpeted.

The water snuffed out the others' voices as Sam went under, afraid any moment he would be dashed against a canyon wall. He spun blindly, struggling to hold his breath, a piece of submerged flotsam in a wild tumult. At last he could hold it no more and let go a desperate gurgle, twisting in terror as he took a gulp of water. Then he did strike stone and everything went dark.

Sam was sore and ached everywhere when he woke up, coughing water. His head felt almost too heavy to lift—long moments passed before he thought of his father or Lepanto, let alone of trying to stand. When he did he found himself in a narrow box canyon well below the cliff's edge where the high plains above ended.

In the other direction the canyon soon ended in a sheer drop to the distant beach. He balanced carefully on the canyon's lip and scanned the shore. There, straight below, was what was left of their schooner. It was split nearly in half, its masts snapped off at deck level and swept away, the remaining lines and halyards and shrouds tangled with broken planks and pieces of sail scattered along the shoreline. Whatever had been stored within it had been swept away too, for much of the deck was gone and the hollow remnants of the hull were bare to the eye.

Other waves must have come and gone while he lay unconscious, each a little smaller, he thought, because everything looked different from what they had glimpsed from the schooner.

Sam stepped back with a sigh. There were now two islands in the bay: their stone giant had destroyed the other, and the tidal waves set off by that conflict must have destroyed the victor. With another sigh he turned to explore the small box canyon for signs of his father or the Elephant, but they were nowhere to be seen.

He called their names but there was no reply, not even an echo in the leaden air. In the bay the water was unsettled, uneasily swirling in and around the two new islands, but here all was silent, hot, and steaming. He looked at the stone walls around him with more attention and saw no way out. Cautiously he looked over the sheer drop again for any sign of a path, and realized he was trapped as well as alone.

Desperately he called their names again, only to hear his cries die in the heavy air. He was completely alone. Worse, he was at fault for making them come and experience this disaster. What if they weren't just lost, but dead?

He stared at the seething bay: what if they had drowned? Guilt broke a new wave over him. His eyes watered: defiantly he brushed his tears away—then broke down and wept with deep heartfelt sobs. He looked suddenly like a little boy instead of the young man boldly leading Lepanto and his father.

Only as his hot tears and racking sobs wore down did he hear someone else crying, too. He raised his tear-stained face hopefully, but saw a strange creature beside him now in the canyon instead of Lepanto or his father.

His first impression was of a large teardrop: on a closer look he saw it was a pear-shaped, grief-stricken blob of a boy with spindly arms and legs and round, mournful eyes. After awhile the boy became aware of Sam's stare, tried to stop and wipe the tears from his eyes as Sam was doing, but broke down again.

"Everything's horrible!" the boy sobbed. "Horrible to be alone!" he moaned through his tears, and for a time Sam wept helplessly with him, overwhelmed by his own and the other's infectious grief. His tears burned. His throat grew raw.

"Everything's horrible!" wailed the other in a renewed torrent. But Sam fought for control. "It's all my fault!" wailed the strange boy, shaking and heaving. "How can you sit like that! As if you don't care!" he wailed further.

For a moment Sam nearly gave way to his grief again, but something in his mind said, "Don't." He stood up, silent as he fought with himself while the other wailed, slowly forcing down his grief and his fear in the hardest struggle he had ever faced, ship-wrecked, marooned, guilt-wracked, without those near him he loved and depended on, as helpless as he had ever been.

Silently he searched into himself and found an unexpected strength despite the ever greater fearful wailing from the strange boy. He would not give up, he thought, no, not now, not ever.

"How can you stand there silent? How can you bear to be alone? How?!" howled the blob of a boy from the ground. "How, when everything is your fault? When they're gone because of you! How?! Dead because of you! Horrible! Horrible! Horrible!" The boy gnashed his teeth, and shrieked. But Sam felt his anger stir.

"Maybe Dad and Lepanto are somewhere else and need my help," he asserted.

"No no no, all is lost, everything is over, finished, done!" sobbed the other.

"You're nothing but a stupid blob!" Sam said. "You don't know anything! Be quiet!" That only made the other cry more. "I'm going if you don't shut up," he warned. Renewed shrieks came from his companion. Sam walked as far into the canyon as he could.

"Don't leave me!" the other cried.

"Then stop it!" His anger broke. "STOP IT! Your stupid tears don't help anything!"

The other choked his tears back and followed Sam, throwing

fearful glances over his shoulder.

"Crying doesn't get anything done!" Sam snapped as the other began to weep again. He again choked himself silent.

The canyon wasn't as bleak as it had seemed at first glance. There

were corners of turf with more of the pink flowers he had seen before on the mesas, and in one place there was a slow trickle of water from a crevice. He licked thirstily at the water on the stone, ignoring its bitter mineral taste, but what there was only made him thirstier, and finally he leaned back, frustrated.

A soft cry drew his gaze: to his surprise gaily plumaged birds the size of ravens fluttered in place in the heavy air. At closer glance he saw their plumage was bedraggled, and their soft cries close to sobs. His companion looked after Sam and saw the birds, too.

"They're so sad," he whispered, great tears starting to roll down his cheeks.

"Don't do that!" shouted Sam. The other sniveled into silence. Sam continued to stare at the flutterbirds: something was not quite right. As he looked at the closest he realized its little face wasn't a bird's at all, but quite human. Its tiny eyes looked down at Sam in surprise.

"Who are you?" it tweeted.

"And where are you from?" tweeted another.

"Where are you going?" tweeted a third.

"Throw us something to eat! Please!" tweeted others. "We get so tired of fluttering."

"Why don't you land," asked Sam, "or fly somewhere else?"

"Why would we do that? Only a fool changes—"

"From place to place!" ended another.

"What will change get you but trouble?" tossed in a third.

"Well," Sam sighed, not wanting to get into another fruitless debate like he had with the thinking heads on the mesas, "I have to go to the Dread City, and find Dad and Lepanto: can you tell me how to get out of here so I can start looking?"

But his words scattered the flutterbirds like a sudden gust of wind, while his companion collapsed into terrified wails.

Sam's resolve hardened in the face of the other's wails. He didn't know what had happened to the Elephant, or his father, but he would try to find out. They may have been dropped somewhere like this canyon. But, if all else failed, he would not stop. Not after all that had happened. That would make it all worthless. No, he would go on, even if he had to go alone. If his father and Lepanto were lost, he'd find them and, he thought grimly, if gone he would make sure their sacrifice was worth it.

"Stop that or I will leave you!" he shouted at the newly wailing boy. His words had no effect now, and the other's wails rose to screams. Sam gritted his teeth, and, his face almost pressed against the rock wall, began to climb, searching out hand and toe holds in the sheer face visible only close up. Behind him the screams climbed up the vocal scale until he wanted to stuff his hands in his ears and scrunch his eyes shut, but he did neither.

He was going to get out.

He was not going to fall.

As he inched his way up the cliff's bare face he felt himself becoming a kind of moving extension of the stone wall. His entire world narrowed to the stone before his eyes, the crevices his fingers explored and his sneakers jammed into.

Time shrank to his moment by moment progress up the cliff—or did it lengthen into a taste of eternity made up of placing his fingers in this crevice, then pulling upwards as he jammed his toes into another crevice, and pushed?

He ignored the birds as he rose steadily above them. Even the boy's wails died away, or sounded as if coming from a great distance. He didn't look down. His eyes stayed fixed on the stone, on its seams and fissures, on his hands gripping now one crevice, then another, as his toes jammed into a lower lifted him a few more inches.

His concentration grew so intense he heard and saw nothing but his breath and the rock wall slowly sinking beneath him.

How long this went on he had no idea. Moments? A lifetime? He knew he couldn't stop or go back down, and didn't dare look down—or up. Inch by inch, his breath hot against the rock face, he ascended. Then his searching hand slid over the edge of the canyon's rim. He found an outcrop to hold onto while he pushed up from another narrow crevice, and now his eyes lifted over the canyon's edge.

He paused.

A rolling plain of brown grass confronted him. There were no mountains and, as far as he could see, no groups of herders or herded stone people. It was another red land, but altogether gentler than the previous. He sighed with relief, and carefully edged over the rim and lay at its edge.

But as he stared at the grass he had to amend his first impression. The grass was tall, taller than himself. He hadn't been able to see any details because he couldn't see over it, even when he stood. To go into it would mean immediately becoming lost. He had no way of knowing if Lepanto and his father had been carried here by the water. But a sudden hope rose in him: if he had survived, and gotten out of that trap of a canyon, then so might they!

"What should I do now?" he asked himself in frustration.

"Stand there forever," replied a flutterbird.

"How horrible," gasped his tearful companion as to Sam's surprise he crawled over the canyon's edge.

"Don't you even think about crying!" Sam said firmly. "Who are you, anyway?"

"No one," shuddered the creature, tears welling.

"No one is no one!" snapped Sam.

"I am."

"Then from now on you're someone. You're—you're George."

"George," George repeated, doubtfully.

"I could sure use Mr. Nicholas' mail truck now," Sam muttered, exasperated. He thought back to the Last House sadly, wondering if anyone had come by, like Mr. Nicholas, and missed them. George shook with repressed sobs. The flutterbird tweeted how it was best to do nothing.

Memory of the Last House opened a chink in his armor, and for a moment despair threatened to overwhelm Sam again: he was alone, or with a useless companion, had lost his father and the great Elephant, and had no idea what to do or where to go, assuming for a moment any direction made sense.

Dread City seemed infinitely far away, the Far Land of Fear impassable.

That was what all those signs at the bay's entrance had meant, he realized: Dread City was here, distant, everywhere, nowhere. He looked around heavily. A glint caught his eye—Lepanto's globe on the cliff's edge!

He picked it up, sadder, at first afraid Lepanto had met an awful end—how else explain the globe lying there outside one of Lepanto's bottomless pockets? Unless—unless Lepanto had been washed up onto the plain and was even now somewhere ahead of him.

"WAAAA," wailed George.

"Shut up, George!" snapped Sam. George looked at him in surprise, and choked back his sobs.

The globe was cool in his hands, and transparent. There was no trace of the bright light it had once shown.

"Stop hoping," tweeted a flutterbird.

"Give it up," moaned George.

But Sam remembered how Lepanto had put the globe in his hands in the tent, and how he had filled it with light. Not with Lepanto's blaze, but more than his father. Maybe the globe could show him where Lepanto and his father were!

He focused his thoughts and looked into its depths. Was it a trick of the light, or did he see something there? The moans of George dropped away, and the hopeless advice of the flutterbird. Something stirred in those depths. What, he wondered, and stared harder. There was at first only a small circle, something like a tiny head turned from him.

"Come closer," he muttered, "closer!" A thrill of excitement raced through him as he saw swirling brown hair with coppery highlights. When the head turned, it was his mother facing him. She said something he couldn't hear. "Louder!" he cried.

"Come and get me," sounded in his mind.

Energy and hope surged through him. He was the Sam who had drawn true adventures in the Book, then dared to start this journey, outwitted the sea-beast, challenged the herder, and saved them all from the Great Stone Giant: he would find Lepanto and his father. He would find his mother. He would find them all.

"Goin' my way?" asked someone behind him. Sam whirled, and stood stock still, thunderstruck. There stood Mr. Nicholas beside his truck, bales of newspapers in its bed. "Wondered how long ya were goin' ter stand there like a dummy lookin' inter tha' bauble." He reached for the globe. Sam drew it back. He had been so absorbed he had failed to hear Mr. Nicholas drive up.

"Just want ter see what's so all-fired interestin'," Mr. Nicholas said, reaching again.

"It's mine," said Sam, not willing to let him touch it.

Mr. Nicholas grabbed for it. Sam stumbled backwards, fell, and the globe flew up from his hands. There it spun a moment above their heads before it disappeared with a flash.

"Darn," growled Mr. Nicholas, struggling to smooth out his scowl. "Here, lemme help ya up," he said smiling with a strange menace. "I only wanted ter see. A very pertty bauble, thet." Sam got up on his own.

Mr. Nicholas towered over him. "Brave litter fella y'are ter come all tha' way here," he smiled. "Isn't ev'ryone sets off fer Dread City. Has its price though, don't it! Couldn't help but see ya crash from the roadside."

Sam wondered how he could have missed the road that now ran along the edge of the cliff. After his initial shock at seeing Mr.

Nicholas he felt as if he was walking underwater, and what was strange seemed less and less so. Something was wrong, Sam sensed, but he couldn't say what because his thoughts were too thick to come into focus.

"Can you help me?" he asked, thick-tongued.

"Didna think no one survived," Mr. Nicholas said, "'til I saw ya crawl up here with Georgie-porgy and ol' tweety head here." He tried to swat the bird. "So, sure, hop in. We'll see what we see," Mr. Nicholas added, his grin almost a snarl. Sam clumsily clambered into the truck and sat down as if pushed.

"Me too!" said George with tears in his eye and a catch in his throat.

"In!" Mr. Nicholas commanded, then stood on the seat and plucked a flutterbird from the air. "Ya may as well do some movin' aroun!" The flutterbird tweeted with terror from the rear of the truck.

"Les go," slurred Sam. Mr. Nicholas put the truck into gear and drove off with a loud back-fire from the engine. "Whas goin' on," lisped Sam, struggling to keep his eyes open. Mr. Nicholas' smile twisted his big purple nose to one side. Sam couldn't move. An alarm buzzed faintly in his head, ring-a-ring-a—.

"Stop thet!" growled Mr. Nicholas, as if reading his mind. Why can everyone always guess what I'm thinking? Sam wondered. Rinngg-a-rinngg-a-rinngg!

"I warned ya!" shouted Mr. Nicholas, and raised a hand to strike Sam. George wailed. The bird tweeted its fear. Sam groaned but couldn't move. Mr. Nicholas smiled with open malice.

"Goin' ter Dread City ter get yer mother, huh? Harr harr harr!"

"Rinngg-a-Rinngg-a-Rinngg!"

"Stop that!" Mr. Nicholas swung at him. The truck lurched, and he missed, his fist passing so close Sam felt its passage in the air next to his head. "Garn," Mr. Nicholas growled, grabbing the wheel and steering the truck away from the cliff's edge.

"I won't stop," whispered Sam. "I don't like you," he sighed.

"HARRH HARRH HARRH!" roared Mr. Nicholas.

"Rinngg-a—."

"STOP—"

"RINNGG!" a clock rang: or a creature much like one that now sat between Mr. Nicholas and Sam, crowding him against the astonished George. Its arms moved methodically around his round face on which were elegant Roman numerals from I-XII, while his stubby legs failed to reach the floor.

"RING RING RING!" the clock rang merrily.

"RING RING RING!" joined another from the back by the terrified flutterbird. They took turns ringing loudly, and letting their alarms fill the air.

"You dirty brat!" Mr. Nicholas roared in a rage, but then, "Oh no!" For now he sat in a large bathtub instead of his truck, crowded in with George, the flutterbird, and the two clocks. He found a sponge in his hand in place of a steering wheel.

"Drat!" he roared. Water slopped in the speeding tub. Sam felt his dullness drop away, and began to laugh. George didn't know whether he was laughing or crying. The flutterbird tweeted hysterically. The Clocks rang and rang: every moment another crowded in, its alarm sounding too. The noise drowned out Mr. Nicholas' curses whose twists and turns sent them careening into the tall grass, so that nothing was visible as it whipped past, the tub undiminished in speed.

A thought crept into Sam's mind: I was sad, and George appeared: I felt hopeless, and the flutterbirds showed up; I wished for Mr. Nicholas' truck, and there he was, so…. His hope surged.

"Clearing!" shouted Sam, inspired—and a broad clearing opened

161

in the midst of the grass.

"What are ya up ter—" began Mr. Nicholas.

"Cliffs!" shouted Sam.

"No!" shouted Mr. Nicholas—but now the road ran straight with steep drops on either side.

"Curves!" shouted Sam, convulsed with laughter at the craziness of it all, like being in a dream. Mr. Nicholas desperately lurched side to side to steer through a series of curves. The Clocks multiplied. The water slopped. George couldn't tell if he was laughing or sobbing. The flutterbird cried in terror.

"Tighter!" shouted Sam. The curves bunched together, and with a curse Mr. Nicholas lost control and they sailed out into the void.

"FALL APART!"

The bathtub cracked into pieces. The Clocks rang through the air. George sailed on with a thin scream, while the flutterbird hovered with a sigh of relief as the others plunged downwards—all but Mr. Nicholas, who disappeared as suddenly as he had appeared.

"Better a great height than none at all," breathed the bird.

Sam laughed as he flew downwards, blindly happy to be away from Mr. Nicholas. He watched the clocks by tens, then hundreds, then thousands soar through the air over and under him. Now they were just clocks, if round and tall as a man with little silvery knobs on each side for setting the time or alarm.

The clocks struck the ground first: glittering gears, wheels and springs bounced everywhere. Even as the ground grew dangerously close something stirred in Sam.

"It's one of our dreams," he breathed just before he landed squarely on a spring, felt it contract under him, then propel him upwards. He held on and again bounced, leaning forward to give the bouncing direction. He bounced into a grove trees where he half expected to see his father bounce by in turn, and three misshapen men playing cards, but all too soon he emerged into an empty land.

There he saw a small house: the gears, springs and wheels finally came to a stop before its gate, the spring dumping Sam roughly onto the ground. A moment later George landed laughing helplessly, tears streaming down his eyes.

"Stop that!" Sam commanded, and George caught his breath, then burst into laughter again. Sam felt it well up in himself, and, desperate not to lose control again, shook George. Tears steamed silently down George's cheeks.

"Sorry," said Sam, who suddenly felt awful, "but you have to stop!" George nodded, miserable. "Phew," Sam breathed, looking around at the wreckage of clocks, "what a waste of time!" He looked longer. "I guess some people live and die by time," he added at last. He looked in the sky where two violet suns shone. With a start he realized there were five, not two. A moment later there were ten. He looked away.

"How horrible," George began to sob.

"Just be quiet!" Sam ordered, and at his tone George gulped down a sob and lapsed into a quivering silence. Sam took in the house—it looked like a small version of his own, so far away. It too was painted in many faded, often peeling colors, and covered with Victorian woodwork. Then he stiffened.

There were voices inside.

He stood irresolute, not sure whether to run or look. But he edged nearer cautiously until he could make out what the voices were saying, gesturing at George to be still and stay behind him.

"I'll have her," one voice said.

"No! She's mine!" said another.

"Mine!"

"No, mine!"

Sam crept to a window and peered in. A kindly-seeming old woman was arguing with someone seated on the floor, hidden under a shawl. But a thrill raced through Sam when he saw a lock of brown hair with coppery highlights dangle in front of the shawl. On the table in the middle of the room lay a little girl some years younger than himself, bound head and foot.

Across the room was an oven that took up the entire wall. "FLESH TO STONE" was neatly stenciled on the wall above. So there was more than one way for someone to turn to stone, Sam thought. As he watched the old lady opened the oven door and removed a rather small stony figure with tongs. Even outside Sam imagined he could feel the blast of heat.

"Sandstone," murmured the old woman. She went to the door and handed it to someone he couldn't see. Sam heard the roar of a truck that sounded like Mr. Nicholas' race into the distance. Then the old woman turned to the girl.

"She'll make a lovely little mica-girl," the old lady murmured sweetly, and headed towards the oven with her.

"No, please," wept the figure covered with a shawl.

"You can never have her," the old woman cried scornfully. "She's been taken from you, like everything else," she cackled. The woman covered with a shawl rose to her knees before the old woman.

"Please," she breathed, while the woman laughed.

"We have to do something!" Sam whispered to George.

"No, we can't," he sniffled.

"Follow me," Sam ordered, thrusting some rocks into George's hands, and taking some for himself: "we'll break in and surprise her." All the boyishness had vanished from his face. He crept around the other side, only to make a complete circuit of the house without finding

the door he had seen the old lady open.

"We'll jump in," he said, desperate as he saw through the window the old woman open the oven door with one hand, the bound child in her other as the woman on her knees begged helplessly. He backed up, took a running start, and leapt through the window with a crash, hands in front of his face. Even as he rolled forward on the floor he heard George land behind him, surprised he'd actually followed. But he gave him no thought as the old woman shrieked, dropped the girl, and dashed out the door they had somehow missed.

Sam ignored her and the little girl as the figure in the shawl stood. Her shawl fell back from her head and slid to the floor. Her sad face was unmistakable, her level brown eyes, her swirl of brown hair with its coppery highlights, her warm, balanced features.

"Sam," she murmured.

"Mother," he cried, astonished. She opened her arms with a smile that transformed her face. Blinded by tears of joy he hurried into them, but even as his arms closed around her hungrily she faded from sight.

"Don't go, please don't go!" he cried.

"Come for me," she whispered, and then there was only her voice in his mind.

"Mm mm mm," groaned the little girl on the floor.

Sam stared where his mother had been another moment, then turned to where the girl struggled against her knots on the floor, and pulled off her gag as he bent to help her.

"Dummy," was the first thing she said: "why were you embracing the air?"

"Because my mother was there!"

"I didn't see anyone. Boy, are you dumb. Boys! You almost let that old witch bake me!"

She was perhaps seven, maybe eight, with pale blue eyes and intensely blonde hair framing a pert face. Her lips curled in disdain as she shrugged off her loosened knots and stood up, eyeing him from head to foot, then turning to George.

"I just saved you!" he blurted. She ignored him, her look of disdain deepening as she took in George.

"Who's fatty?" she exclaimed cruelly, pointing at George. Big tears welled in his eyes. "I said I just saved you! He helped! You're a—a—"

"What am I?" she demanded, hands on hips. He thought better of calling her the name on the tip of his tongue.

"How about saying, 'Thank you'?"

"You were slow enough!" she said. Then her fear overwhelmed her anger and she burst into tears. George burst into tears. Sam was astonished.

"Girls," he muttered, but to himself. Louder, "Both of you stop it! Now!" demanded Sam.

They sniveled to a stop. He thought for a moment about embracing the girl to reassure her, then dismissed the idea.

"We have to get out of here," was all he said. They dumbly followed him out the same door the old woman had used.

"Well hello," a sweet voice, greeted them. She was waiting for them outside. "You gave me quite a shock," she added. Sam's head whirled. "I think we should get to know each other better."

How sweet her voice was, full of the warmth of a long summer's afternoon, or the croon of a mother to her infant, the hope of every little boy. Sam swayed. She couldn't really have been doing what I saw her doing, opening the oven to bake that girl, Sam thought.

"What a lovely child you are," she crooned to Sam, then repeated herself to the girl, who also stood in sudden silence, and then to George, who smiled helplessly and took a step forward. Instinctively Sam threw an arm across his chest, stopping him.

"Don't be afraid," the old woman murmured with the murmur of bees gathering honey from a flowering tree. "All will be well. Let's go back into the house and I'll give you all some lemonade and cookies." George beamed, even the girl smiled, if a little uncertainly. Sam felt himself weaken: how he longed to be talked to by a woman in just such a voice.

"You're not my moth—moth—mother," he slurred. The old woman smiled and stepped forward to take his hand. Sam gasped: suddenly there were two old women. All three children stepped back. Where one stepped flowers sprang up which the other stepped on and froze. Then there were three old women.

"Pull yourself together," the old woman snapped at Sam, her voice for a moment harsh, her features ugly and distorted before she smoothed them out, and sweetness filled her voice again.

"I don't know what you're afraid of," she murmured, "surely

three grandmothers are better than one!" She lunged forward abruptly for Sam. But her momentary lapse was all Sam needed to regain his senses, and he easily evaded her, knocking the others aside too. That brought George and the girl fully awake, too. Then he saw Mr. Nicholas driving up.

"Run!" he shouted at George, "run!" at the girl, and gave them both another push as he took to his heels. They easily distanced themselves from the old women, but Mr. Nicholas saw what was happening and swerved to join the pursuit. It looked like all three would end up inside the "FLESH TO STONE" oven for Sam could see no cover or escape in this wide, flat land: Mr. Nicholas would get them easily. He saw a little hill rising to one side and pointed.

"There!" he shouted at the girl; "there!" at George. They nodded and the three reached its slope and raced up towards its crest where they knew they would have to turn and fight.

XI

John Finds His Courage—

Grimly Lepanto grasped John again as first the yacht then Sam was torn away in the tumult. Together they somersaulted helplessly underwater until Lepanto's blood drummed and his lungs felt as though they must burst. Water flooded his ears, gurgled into his throat and snaked up his trunk. His vision dimmed and he felt his hold on John slip, sure he must drown or both be dashed senseless against the canyon wall.

Then he was dumped roughly on a ledge jutting from the canyon wall as the water fell away abruptly, his trunk dangling over the edge of an abyss with John hanging from its tip.

Groaning, Lepanto lifted John beside him. Both gasped for air, John on his knees, head down, vomiting water. Stunned they saw the wave recede until swallowed in another that rose and broke against the cliffs where they lay, but this time barely lapped its edge before it sank back, each one following lower.

At length the breathing of first one, then the other, calmed. They took in their good and bad fortune: they had survived, but were stranded on a lip of rock far above the canyon floor yet still well below its rim and the plains above. There was nothing but sheer rock above and below.

Sam was nowhere to be seen.

Fear spread its wings in their hearts.

"Sam," croaked John. Then more strongly, "SAM!"

"SAM!" trumpeted Lepanto. Their calls hung and died in

the heavy air.

"What's happened to my boy," John groaned. "Why did I ever let myself be talked into this! SAM!"

Not even an echo replied in that air, and John sank to his knees with a sob.

"We don't know what's happened," Lepanto said: "he may be safe just out of sight or hearing." John shook his head, looking bleakly at their impossible situation.

"Even if he is, what can we do? We are trapped here!" Then a thought hit him, and he rose to his feet and turned to Lepanto eagerly. "The Flying Trapeze!"

Lepanto nodded, and fumbled in his pockets, but when he drew out the Flying Trapeze they saw it had been shattered in their tumultuous crash. John groaned in despair and sank down again.

The Elephant saw how faded, how gray John looked again, but said nothing. He wrung his clothes out in silence and put them back on with a shudder, patting his pockets, then hesitating.

"What I need just now," Lepanto said at last, "is a good smoke." He drew out his pipe kettle and a small traveling burner, set the kettle up with a wad of soggy caravan tea, and ordered: "Light!" The burner sputtered, sputtered, and...caught: soon the kettle was steaming, and Lepanto picked up the pipe and drew in deep puffs, blowing out shapeless clouds.

"How can you," John said, "after what's happened! Instead of a pipe, why don't you pull out a Magic Carpet? How about a ladder that just keeps going up and up no matter how many rungs we climb to scale that cliff? For that matter, why not a Flying Saucer we could ride wherever we want?!"

There was an edge of hysteria in his voice. At the same time he knew Lepanto was Sam's doing, somehow: what did he know about

magic elephants? Of any kind of elephant? Crazy laughter threatened
to engulf him, but he fought it down, and ended by staring unhappily
into Lepanto's fire.

Lepanto took a deep drag on his pipe and blew out a long spear
of smoke that sailed out of sight above the distant rim's edge.

"Ahhh…" Clouds of vapor rose from the drying canyon as the
oppressive heat resumed. He said nothing as John withdrew into
himself. The moments dragged, marked only by Lepanto's steady
puffs as though he had not a care in the world. At last John burst out.

"How can you just sit there? Don't you even feel Sam's loss?"

Lepanto gave him a long look, surveyed their hopeless situation
again, and took another puff.

"We can't stay here forever."

"Use your ingenuity. I'm just an elephant," came his disconcerting
reply. His brown and amber eyes fixed on John.

"You're a Magic Elephant."

"You don't really believe that."

"Let's not start that again!" John groaned.

"You only pushed your doubt aside—you never believed. You've been a sleepwalker this entire time, as gray around the gills as a hooked flounder." Lepanto breathed out another long spear of smoke that this time sailed out into the abyss.

"Sleepwalker? Gray? Flounder?!?!" That seemed very unfair, especially with Sam missing.

"Sam got us going, Sam saved us at sea. Sam's daring alerted us to the herders. Sam saved us from Great Stone Giant. You've come this far because of Sam. You're alive because of Sam, as far as anyone would say you're alive."

John jumped up. He nearly hopped in anger, but couldn't think of anything to say in response to Lepanto's unexpected attack.

"You're gray even when you're angry," Lepanto observed unkindly. John remembered how he had saved them after the Elephant had danced through the deck in the Sea of Faces, and blurted that out.

"Ah, yes, that one time you showed some fire."

John was mad because he knew Lepanto was right. He lost Madelyn, and faded in those quiet years afterward with Sam before this adventure. And here they were now, or he was, he amended his thought, caught permanently between belief and disbelief, believing in the canyon where they were trapped, yet also, somehow, expecting to wake from this as though from a bad dream in his bedroom in the Last House. Sam would be upstairs in his bedroom where an elephant, dragon, and yacht hung from the ceiling, each turning in the room's slow air currents.

"This is some sort of test, isn't it? And you know where Sam is, and how to leave here. That's why you're not upset."

"I don't know where he is, no, but yes, I can leave whenever I choose. That's not the issue."

"What is?" John took in their situation again, the hopeless fall over the edge of the cliff, the sheer rock face rising above them.

"You don't think we're ever going to get to Dread City, ever going to find Madelyn and find a way for all of us to escape, do you, with you dragging along like this? If we can't get some good, robust life into you, you might just as well go to Dread City—if that's your destination—the short way." John was stunned.

"What! How?!"

Lepanto gestured at the jagged landing far below.

"Jump."

John stared at the Elephant, dumbfounded.

"Why do you think the forces of the Far Land of Fear were able to come to your home if you weren't already more than meeting them half way?"

"So what," John said finally. "I had cause."

"Really?" The look on Lepanto's face made him madder.

"First Madelyn was taken from me. Now Sam! And things like this—" he waved his hands about taking in the Elephant, and the cliffs—"they don't happen!"

He would have flung himself at Lepanto except even in a rage he knew better than to assault an elephant, let alone one as large as Lepanto, and, infuriatingly, so well tusked and dressed! He hopped from one foot to the other and waved a futile fist at the Elephant who, in response, took several delicious puffs of his aromatic tea.

"Then there's little to hold you here." He gestured again towards the edge of the ledge. John stood in deep confusion. Lepanto was right, now that he had finally admitted his despair and disbelief—and his absurd sense of grievance!

"You even made Sam 'live' in the same way as yourself,"

murmured the Elephant.

Yes, John thought, I gave up, I ran, I hid, I slept…and I made Sam echo me. He stepped to the edge of their ledge as Lepanto watched. The descent was dizzying. One more step, he thought, and what an easy end to all doubt, all confusion, all guilt.

But he thought instead of Sam, and his impossible quest. He lifted his hands and remembered the pain of his rope burns and torn flesh as he flexed them. He had been on that yacht. He had hurt himself.

That was real.

He stepped back, and faced Lepanto. There was no doubt about the Elephant's bulk, or the maddening tinge of cologne that wafted from his neat suit, or the spear of vapor he shot over John's shoulder into the abyss, or the itchiness of his own drying clothes. There was no denying the depths of those dark brown amber-flecked eyes meeting his.

"Sam may have been washed all the way over the rim," John said. Lepanto shaped his puffs into air balloons carrying gondolas steadily upward. "I think…" John's voice trailed off. "I think I'd know it if he was dead." Another silence. "I'd feel it here." John touched his chest. "In whatever is left in there."

The Elephant finally reacted with a nod.

"Sam and I have come so far, far in miles, far in imagination, farther than I can measure in emotion, farther in resolve and yes, farther in daring," he added.

Lepanto nodded again, and said, "What about Madelyn? How was she at the end? I doubt anything has been taken from you unjustly."

John was staggered.

"How can you live without hope?"

"I'll tell you how she was at the end," John blurted, "she faded

174

away—."

"What did you do?" Lepanto had brought John this far before—now he was relentless.

"I didn't do anything!" John answered, emphasizing 'do'. Then, lower, before the Elephant's look: "I stopped giving." Those amber-flecked eyes held his, unblinking.

"Even when she needed you?"

John nodded, miserable. "I failed her." He had loved her, and he had taken her for granted…. He had lived in her but been bewildered when she withdrew and became ill….

"Go on," said Lepanto, as though reading his mind. John nodded without protest.

"I was confused—I was angry at losing her…and I didn't help when I, when I—…"

"Should have because—…" Lepanto left that "because" hang between them.

John made no effort to brush away the tears that rolled down his cheeks.

"Because I was only thinking of myself. As if my loss amounted to anything compared to hers!"

"Yes."

He took a deep breath.

"She died from love's neglect."

"Yes, exactly."

John felt as bleak as their surroundings. That, somehow, was right. He stooped down and picked up a stone, and squeezed it in his palm until it hurt.

He was here.

"I'd give anything to see her again, beg her forgiveness."

"How can so many wonderful things happen to you, without your hoping for the most wonderful of all?" Lepanto said, again astonishing John. "Life is given, but nothing else—we hope, we desire, we love in defiance of all the damage the world causes and make something good and warm and beyond price despite that, something that couldn't otherwise exist."

Lepanto was right. It was that oh so ordinary wonderful thing he had shared blindly with Madelyn and whose loss that had broken him. The last days and weeks ran through his mind again with the bright face of Sam woven into them, and his shoulders shook.

Then he cried with a grown man's pain and shame, and a grown man's relief at releasing long dammed-up guilt. He cried until the great weight of his mingled guilt and regret slid from his shoulders. "Sam!" he croaked at last, then, "Madelyn!"

In the silence a resolve as hard as the stone in his hands took shape. He brushed his tears away and confronted the Elephant.

"Very well, Lepanto," he said, "we'll go to Dread City. We'll go somewhere worse, if need be. And one way or another we'll find them both and bring them home. No matter what the odds. Or opposition. Or how this is possible."

The Elephant approved of John's color. He liked the new, straighter set of his shoulders. He blew out more elegant hot air balloons that drifted up and out of the canyon, then interlocking circles of smoke.

"How can we get out of here?" John chafed his knuckles against the canyon wall, ignoring Lepanto's feats of smoke.

"Well," breathed Lepanto. He disassembled his pipe kettle, extinguished the flame, and patiently blew on the kettle until it was cool enough to put away in a vest pocket. "It's time to leave."

"What do you mean, leave?" John stared around at their impossible setting. The Elephant gave him a long look, and then a disconcerting smile.

"I am going to concentrate on the top of this cliff, and—" matching action to word, "when I see it clearly in my mind, I—am—going—..." John watched the Elephant grow translucent and then, before his astonished eyes, fade from sight. Incredulous, he walked to where Lepanto was a moment ago and thrust his hands through the empty air.

"Going, going, gone," he heard the Elephant sigh in the empty air, his tusks the last to fade.

He looked up at the distant rim of the canyon, expecting to see Lepanto lean over and wave, but nothing broke its clear line against the sky. He got down on his hands and knees and crept to the ledge's edge, but the drop was sheer, offering no handholds down that he could see, nor was there any sign of Lepanto below, in case he had miscalculated.

For a moment rage filled him and he almost danced in fury.

"I—am—going—going going gone! Hahahaha! I get it! It's another test! Okay. Okay!"

But there was no answer from the air, no sign of Lepanto, and John found himself in the center of the ledge, quite alone. He took a deep breath.

"Okay. I am here. On my own. Very well!"

He examined the cliff wall. Close up it was fissured and cracked in many places, and with a sigh he began to climb. After six careful feet his searching fingers found nothing more to grasp. Carefully he climbed back down. He was stumped. He remembered Lepanto saying,

"I am going to concentrate on the top of this cliff, and when I see it clearly in my mind, I am—going—."

He sat like the Elephant had.

"Okay," he muttered, "anything you can do I can do better!" He closed his eyes, and struggled to clear his mind.

"I am going to concentrate on the top of the cliff and when I see it clearly in my mind, I—am—going—." But hard as he tried to blot them out, images of Madelyn or fragments their adventures with Sam crowded into his mind and prevented his imagining the top of the cliff clearly.

He took a deep breath and imagined the canyon wall crevice by crevice, imagined himself edging up as though actually climbing. Long before he reached the top he remembered the surge of water overwhelming their yacht and how he, Lepanto and Sam were pitched overboard, water enveloping them, and forgot his imaginary climb. He opened his eyes, still sitting on the ledge.

Determined, he shut them again and now tried to imagine the land just beyond canyon's rim. He imagined a stretch of plain like the one they had fled, a plain filled with loose rocks and brown blades of grass but without three-headed centaurs or stony people. A breeze a touch too warm blew, and the air did not smell fresh. He imagined it ruffling his hair as he sat on a stone that grew very uncomfortable.

It was so real his confidence surged and he felt his hand touch the brown earth beside him and opened his eyes in triumph—and saw he was still on the ledge.

For a time he danced and hopped about and shouted at the cliff in fury. Then an irreverent thought filtered through his rage, and he calmed.

"I'm not an Elephant, not a magical one or any other kind! I can do this, but it has to be my way," he said aloud.

He examined the canyon wall above him again as his words hung in the heavy air. This time he searched its edges overlooking the drop below: nothing met his eyes on one side, so he moved to the other. There a small ledge hardly big enough to hold a man caught his eye a few yards away. He stared at what at first seemed a rock on the ledge, then realized it was his satchel with the ropes and bola and, who knows, maybe the mysterious Book in its depths.

He eyed the gap to the ledge uncomfortably.

"One misstep and I get to Dread City the quick way," he muttered.

The rock face between himself and the ledge was fissured and cracked, and he thought he could see toe and finger holds across it. He took a deep breath, and slowly edged out onto the rock face. Hold by hold he inched towards the ledge. He tasted his sweat, and smelled and tasted the bitter minerals in the rock face.

Half way....

A rivulet of salty sweat ran into one eye, then the other. He didn't dare shake his head as he inched on, half blind.

Three quarters of the way....

His sweat was so bad he simply shut his eyes and held fast to the wall, motionless. After a time he felt rather than saw his way the remaining distance. Ever so carefully he maneuvered himself onto the ledge with the satchel.

He sighed with relief and wiped the sweat from his eyes. There was only room to kneel and search the satchel. The Book was not in its depths, but the ropes and bola were there. He pulled out a rope, and searched the height above him for something to try to reach, but saw nothing except a dark smear against the sky at the very top that indicated a tree limb or stone outcropping. He sagged. But as he looked down towards the beach he saw nothing to lift his spirits or provide an alternative.

He looked up at the outcropping again.

"At least try," he muttered to himself.

He looked at the rope: it was long, but he doubted long enough.

Besides, what would hold it there even if he succeeded in tossing it around whatever outcrop seemed outlined against the sky? After a moment he pulled out the bola, and looked from it to the outcropping. Then he tied it to the rope and, positioning himself carefully, swung the bola, letting its weights carry the rope farther upward than he could have thrown it.

Up it soared, only to waver and fall back a good way from the outcrop. Hope flooded him nonetheless—the rope went higher than he had thought possible.

"I never believe," he muttered, nodding his head, remembering Lepanto's reproaches. Carefully he gathered the rope together, repositioned himself, swung the bola with determination, and sent it soaring upward.

"Fly rope! Fly!" he cried, urging it on as he watched. Up it flew, the bola spinning at its apogee about the outcrop.

"Yes! Yes yes!" he shouted, punching the air with a fist, then pressing back against the rock face when the drop down loomed too close. He pulled gingerly at the rope, then hard: it held firm. He slung the satchel over his shoulder, then pulled himself up, a stretch of slack rope sliding between his feet until, knees bent, he tightened his feet on the rope and stood, gaining a few feet.

Steadily he half lifted half pulled himself up, never daring to look down, until he felt the edge of the cliff meet his searching hand.

He kept his eyes firmly on the rock face before him and edged beside the outcrop, swung a leg over the cliff's edge, then forced himself onto the level ground beyond. There he squirmed carefully farther onto the flat ground before rolling over and standing, breathing hard. A quiet pride filled him.

He expected to see Lepanto and to get a hearty slap on the back for a job well done. But Lepanto was nowhere to be seen. John stared in either direction along the cliff's rim, then along the edge of a forest that blocked the view inland. He searched the ground in each direction for tracks leading into the forest. Finally he went back to the outcrop and recovered his rope and bola.

He turned and faced the forest.

XII

And Runs From His Dream

The trees were old and tall, the ground largely clear at their feet beyond an initial wall of brush. John took a breath, settled his satchel on his shoulder, and pushed through. When he looked back the brush formed an impenetrable wall of thorns.

I'm not in control of where I go then, he realized. If anything, his determination hardened.

He turned and walked resolutely into the forest. After a time he found something of a path that looked like one made by animals, and although he had no wish to see what might be roaming here, followed it for lack of a better alternative.

To his surprise there were flowers everywhere: thickets of red and purple bougainvillea, frangipani, roses, and dark-hued birds-of-paradise; carnations in thick, red clumps and geraniums up to his waist forced the path's meander. Rich fragrances threaded the air. The thick canopy held out the sun except for a stray beam here and there, while the deeper he penetrated into the trees the sultrier the air became.

Soon John wiped sweat from his brow and his shirt clung to his skin. His eyelids grew heavy from the rich air and the humidity. Periodically his pace slackened until he shook his head to clear its heaviness, and forced himself to walk again briskly. After a time he yawned.

His pace slowed almost to a stop.

In his daze he felt as if some of the flowers had faces—silent faces—numbly shuddering at his passage.

"Gotcha!" a harsh voice grunted as a heavy body landed on John's with a painful thump and knocked him to the ground. But the shock galvanized John who twisted, swinging a fist that struck the man in the jaw and knocked him off. He sprang to his feet.

"A little hasty, aren't you?" The man was the color of a beet, with red eyes, and a purple nose too large for his face. He lunged forward again, but John rocked back on his heels and then put his full weight into another blow to the man's jaw.

"Gnarrfff!" cried the man, and crumpled. John held his place, ready for another assault, but after one look at his determined face the man backed off, then ran down the path. John grabbed his bola from the satchel, twirled and launched it after him: the man fell with a cry as it wrapped itself around his legs. John hurried up ready to bind the man with his rope and get some answers to the questions racing through his mind when the man faded from sight and the bola fell in a tangle on the ground.

"It must be catching," he muttered, thinking of how Lepanto had disappeared. He rewound the bola and started down the path again, fighting off the heat and fragrance. The path wound deeper into the forest, never varying. Whenever he looked back he found it closed thornily against him.

After a time John's pace slowed and his mind began to drift, his wary watchfulness against another assault fading in the sultry heat. His eyelids sagged. Once he thought he saw shapes to one side, hiding behind a thicket of bougainvillea, and shook himself alert: nothing more was seen.

After that even though he felt eyes on himself constantly there were no more sightings. The miles wore on. The sultry, fragrant heat made movement ever harder. He grew thirsty. Surely there must be streams or ponds somewhere in woods like these, he thought, but none appeared.

"On," he muttered, to encourage himself, and stumbled.

"Gotcha!" cried a rough voice as another man with a too-large purple nose launched himself on him. But John snapped awake and turned swinging. He connected solidly. The man crumpled in wordless surprise.

"Gotcha!" cried another rough voice. John whirled, but was grappled by a big man with a mane of flaming red hair.

"Gotcha!" shouted a third, flinging himself on the other two so John fell backwards. He fought desperately, but now the man he had flattened joined in and soon they had him spread-eagled on the ground, pummeling him. He groaned under the assault, shook an arm loose and punched one man in the eye, then lost consciousness as another raised a club and struck him.

He woke in a dim cavern. A dilapidated bar was to one side with dirty bottles on its shelves. Some were broken, some opened and empty, some full of an ugly, purple-brown liquid.

"Have some," a rough voice said, and the man with the flaming mane poured a foul drink into his throat. John gasped.

"Water," he asked, for the drink made him thirstier. The man slapped him hard with a malicious laugh.

"C'mon," shouted the beet colored man to the other with the flaming hair that dominated his face: somehow his head did not fit his body properly.

"Leave him for later. He'll be here soon enough." Whom 'he' was they left menacingly unexplained.

The men settled around a splintered table with four rickety chairs and started a game of poker with well-worn cards. John now made out the third, beet-hued one, red-haired like the other, and something odder: one arm was noticeably shorter than the other. They were all misshapen.

Instead of chips they used eyes like those he had seen on the beach outside Lepanto's tent so long ago. Something stirred in memory, and he remembered how in one of his dreams he shared with Sam three men played in a similar way, although they were in a tree.

The Watchers rolled around the table, touching off disputes about which belonged to whom, while they constantly gave away each player's hand. But instead of getting mad at the Watchers the men turned on each other until carried away by anger knives flashed and chairs fell backward as the men lunged at each other.

"Wait until he comes," filled their minds. John realized the thought came from the Watchers. The men straightened. After a tense moment they sheathed their knives, set the chairs upright, and resumed their game.

"Where's Sam?" John asked painfully. "Do you have him?"

"What?"

"Who?"

"Sam? Ha haha!"

"Lepanto will be after you," he threw out.

"Lepanto who?" asked the man with the flaming mane, who seemed to be the leader.

"The Elephant!"

"Elephant?"

"Elephant he said!"

"There are no Elephants here!"

They roared with laughter; then the leader got up and forced John to take another drink of the purple liquid, who spluttered and spilled it over his clothes. He felt an agony of thirst. If I don't get out of here soon it won't matter who 'he' is, John thought: I'll go mad of thirst. That would be a horrible way to get to Dread City! He wriggled his

187

hands: they were bound behind him so tightly he had lost sensation in them as well as in his feet. The game degenerated into another brawl.

"This is so stupid," he sighed as they fought.

"Am not stupid!" said one, swinging at another.

"You are," said the second to the third.

"No, you are!" shouted the third beside himself. John laughed to himself.

"Liar!" he flung into the tumult.

"Not me!" cried one.

"Are so!" said another.

"You!" shouted a third. The leader in blind fury slashed the other across his chest.

"You were always a worthless piece of flesh!" he roared.

This time it didn't matter when the Watchers tried to intervene with another, "Wait. He will soon be here." Any thought of restraint only deepened their fury. They overturned the table, smashed chairs against one another, and stomped on each other as now one, then

another, fell. The pandemonium was terrible.

"Coward!" shouted John into the pandemonium.

A fury of denials and accusations followed from the men. There was a cry as one failed to avoid another's club, and lay motionless. That left the leader, with his misshapen, flaming head, and the man with the great purple nose. They squared off, paused, and flung themselves forward, knives flashing.

The leader spun out of the way of the other's charge at the last moment and plunged his knife into the other's throat—but laughed too soon, as the other thrust up from his knees into his heart before toppling over. With a maddened cry the leader collapsed on him. Silence fell in the room.

John stared at the ropes binding his legs: his own, he recognized with an ironic smile. He lay back. The men were done for, but he was still a prisoner. He shut his eyes for a moment and, unbidden, an image of himself watching his rope fly upward towards the canyon's rim at his command filled his mind. For a moment he balked at the thought, then, staring at his legs, commanded, "Loosen!"

Nothing happened at first: then the knots slithered like snakes, freeing themselves from one another, and fell from his legs. A moment later his hands were free. He leaned forward and rubbed the circulation back into his hands and feet with a groan until he was able to force himself upright. He repacked the satchel, and edged out of the cavern.

"Just you wait," filled his mind as he left that room.…

A narrow path led into the tall trees and pungent masses of flowers. He hurried into it and raced ahead before the mysterious 'he' arrived. Soon he reached a crossing, and stopped. There stood a narrow sign with "Dread City" carved on it, and an arrow pointing down his path.

He took a long look at that sign. It was a simple square of brown

wood nailed to a rough post in the ground. The nailheads were rusted, while the red paint in the engraved lettering was faded. He sighed, and continued down the path.

Slowly his fear of pursuit lessened as he found himself fighting off sleepiness instead of renewed attacks. Just as he entirely relaxed there was a raucous laugh behind him. He whirled. There was the man whose face was like a beet, none the worse for his wounds. Behind him were his other two captors.

"The joke's on you, dummy!" the nearest shouted, but even as he charged John had turned on his heels and was already in flight, heedless of whipping branches or thorns from stray shoots of bougainvillea. He heard their laughter change to curses and fade.

He continued to race down the path until his breath seared his throat; he flogged himself farther on before finally stopping with a groan. He looked around as he caught his breath for any sign of pursuit, but there was a dead stillness in every direction except for his own breathing.

"Gotcha!" a voice cried, but John whirled, his fist connecting cleanly with the jaw of a man with uneven arms. He dropped instantly.

"Gotcha! Gotcha!" shouted the others. Desperately he eluded their grasp and fled again down the path. This time though he outran them he could not leave them entirely behind, and when he risked a quick glance over his shoulder saw there were now two of each. A movement to his left caught his eye, and he saw additional 'triplets' of his pursuers climbing down from a tree.

Grimly he ran on, searching in the satchel for his bola. Even as he readied it he saw other 'triplets' racing through the trees trying to cut him off from the other side of the path. One by one they drew their knives. He didn't need to look to know those behind him had done the same.

He swung the bola over his head without breaking stride and let it fly as the first of the triplets angling to cut him off jumped into the path ahead of him. The man threw up his arms with a cry as the bola wrapped itself around him, binding his arms to his head; he twisted with surprise and fell backward into his companions who reached fruitlessly for John as he leaped over their fallen comrade and raced on.

He had gained a clear lead! But now his breath came in pants, and he knew from the shouts all around him that even more had joined the race, while his one bola was gone.

The image of Lepanto disappearing before him on the ledge as he said, "I am going to concentrate on the top of this cliff, and when I see it clearly in my mind, I—am—going—" slipped into his mind again. He tried to shake the image away. He had only his own resources here. But the image refused to go. "You just put your doubt aside, you never believed. You've been a sleepwalker this entire time as gray around the gills as a hooked flounder," echoed now in his mind, too.

Well, he thought, so much for not believing! Look at me now! He shook his head, gasping for air, keeping his eye out for more misshapen men trying to cut him off, but the image and words stayed. He took a ragged breath, and realized he wouldn't be able to go on much longer.

He stopped as pain in his side doubled him over. A howl of triumph went up from his pursuers who swiftly closed in. John sat in the path.

"Very well," he gasped, "fool that I am... 'I am going to concentrate.' Ha!" But concentrate he did.

At first he saw only the image of Lepanto disappearing on his ledge, but John shook his head and fought to think beyond his gasps as his pursuers closed in. The ledge was the one place he didn't want to get back to. For a moment he was blank. Then he thought how much better off he would be in a desert where there were no trees and he'd be able to see in all directions, and choose the safest. That was good enough!

Desert, he thought, inspired. Sand…. Dunes…. He remembered pictures he'd seen of the Sahara, of its endless vistas of dunes receding to the horizon under a beating sun, just—sand…. He could lean down and touch it in his desire; he could scoop a handful of grains in his hands, feel the grains run through his fingers. Bemused, he watched the last grains trickle between his fingers, and stood up in the desert, flat ahead of him as far as he could see except for a single dune in the distance.

He wiped his hand against his trousers with a laugh. "I am going to concentrate…and…I—am—going." Gone, he amended the thought, and laughed again.

He was on the desert's edge, the thinning forest behind him. There was no sign of his pursuers. He wished Lepanto was here; there was a conversation he'd like to have with him now! Just where was he, for that matter? A thought stole into his mind: he saw himself sitting again, eyes closed, thinking very hard, Lepanto, and then opening his eyes to find them together: and, with greater excitement, repeating this to find: Sam.

But just as he sat and tried to concentrate a faint sound distracted him. He looked back into the forest towards where the trees thickened and the clumps of flowers grew, but saw nothing. Then it seemed a wall of bushes moved towards him, a wall that resolved into a myriad of small shapes, men with faces like a beet and huge purple noses, men with flaming manes, and men with arms of different lengths.

Without thinking he stood and dashed into the desert. He would find some nook, some twist of sand or dune where he would be out of sight and could sit down and clear his mind. But somehow he knew it would be harder this time for a sense of panic he could barely master seemed to catch up with him from the men racing in pursuit.

How could there be so many? How could they have found him so easily? If this had something to do with the dream he used to share with Sam, it had been swallowed in its own malice and run to such an extreme he felt despair like weights on his feet. They were not going to let him clear his mind again if they could help it.

Ahead and to the right was the dune he had seen at first, and he changed direction and raced towards it, flinging himself forward with renewed speed, hoping to disappear over its ridge and have enough time, out of sight, to try and imagine a safer place.

XIII

The Voice of Doom

Lepanto opened his eyes to find himself not on the cliff above John as he had intended but gliding through a world of shifting colors and forms with no up or down. No sooner did he sort out a definite shape or color than everything shifted again. He was trapped in a three-dimensional kaleidoscope someone constantly shook and reset.

It took a great act of will to keep the contents of his stomach where they belonged. After a time he stopped worrying about his stomach as his mind moved from bewildered to helpless among the flow of shapes and colors that seemed without limit.

It didn't help to close his eyes: vague blurs of light and outlines of shapes almost but not quite defined moved across his eyelids like the images of a blurred film. It was better to stare at the shifting shapes themselves.

Bit by bit he fought down dizziness and bewilderment until he was at least able to endure his helplessness without panic.

Then an ordinary doorway floated past, at once steady in shape yet out of reach. After a time another drifted towards him: he reached out and the door swung open. He tried to grasp the frame to steady himself, but it slid from his hand as though greased. Once through the door everything was different. When he turned, the door had vanished.

"Mmm," he murmured, shaking his head. He felt he was in a room, and realized he was seated. He felt floor underfoot but couldn't make out the distant walls. There was barely enough light to make out his own hands.

"Mmm," he murmured again, and stood, glad at least the shifting shapes were gone and something firm was underfoot. But to his shock that simple act put him in another room altogether. If better lit, the walls, floors, and ceilings broke apart and mixed together as he watched so he had no idea if he was upright or sitting upside down, feet weirdly waving overhead or steady beneath him. Everything was on an immense scale.

The harder he tried to make sense of what he saw the queasier he felt. That queasiness didn't climax but just kept deepening. He took a deep breath and forced himself again to clear his mind, allowing the fractured room to assemble and reassemble as though he was back in the kaleidoscope.

He even began to develop an appreciation of the odd combinations that took shape. Just as he sighed in relief a new door formed before him and he sailed through alarmed at what he would find next.

"Poor John," he said sadly to himself, just to hear the sound of a voice. "What has happened to you? To your new courage? Will you ever get out of that canyon? And Sam! What has become of you!? Ah my, all is lost, lost!"

His fear for the others now filled his mind with a sense of despair, for the new place he found himself in was pitch black. He saw nothing, felt nothing, knew only he spun slowly in total isolation.

Worse, his fears for the others clouded his mind and kept him from getting a grasp on his present dilemma. His confusion deepened, and he realized with a start he could not tell how long he had been fighting it: a minute? For hours? He spun in darkness, and spun, and spun.

"HOW LONG HAVE I BEEN LIKE THIS!?" he trumpeted in rage. It couldn't be that this shapeless drifting was all that was real, and that Sam, John, and all their adventures were only dreams he had now woken from into this darkness.

That way lay madness.

That way lay self-destruction!

Who could bear to find all he had known and done were delusions?

Then he thought Sam hadn't just imagined him as an elephant: maybe he really was an elephant, and since when did an elephant go on adventures? Hopelessness as black as the place he was in choked him. He might have broken at that moment, given in to the desire to erase himself, like words on a page—but a dot of color in the distance caught his attention.

Suddenly it moved towards him. At length, astonished, he saw an ugly, haggard old witch, all greens and reds and splotches of dirty yellows sitting on a broom, equally surprised to see Lepanto. She glowed like a neon sign in the night, providing the only light.

She flew around him, taking in every detail of his appearance, and then began to shake. Lepanto thought she was having a convulsion until a cascade of increasingly loud cackles broke from her and nearly shook her off her broom.

Those were loud enough to summon another dot of color: it zoomed towards Lepanto and resolved into a hobgoblin with icily blue flesh. He too examined Lepanto closely, began to shake, and finally let out a series of screeches Lepanto realized were his laughs.

Now the darkness filled with dots of neon-bright color that turned into witches, wizards, warlocks, sprites, ghosts, goblins, hobgoblins, gnomes, ghouls, imps, dwarves with golden eyes, dragons, hippogriffs, and griffons, all figures from nightmare or frightening fairy tales.

What were they doing here? Where was "here?" Around and around Lepanto they swung laughing, cackling, shrieking, moaning, groaning, crying, shouting, cursing, mocking, hissing, and roaring.

They pulled out their cauldrons, their forges and hammers, recited incantations and summoned all the creatures possible from a nightmare bestiary. They howled in mockery, convulsed by the sight of Lepanto and his helplessness, while the wizards and witches and warlocks tried to excel one another in turning the Elephant now into a heap of mice, then into a pack of rats lost in a maze, starving, turning on one another, next into snakes knotted together, then spiders frantically climbing over one another, and last into creatures just like those circling him, howling, tearing, roaring!

He flailed at them, but they avoided him with mocking sneers and roars and hisses and groans until in his despair Lepanto thought it was himself who shrieked and roared and groaned and hissed. On they all went until their sound was deafening. They spun around ever faster until he was in a sphere of witches and warlocks, brooms, beasts, wands, flashing robes, and curses.

Abruptly they stopped spinning around him, stopped making any sound: his ears rang in the silence. They gave an abrupt shriek that had him fling his hands over his great ears helplessly, and closed in on him with one will.

He shut his eyes, expecting to feel them tear him apart but nothing happened. He kept his eyes shut. He heard their angry, frustrated cries and shrieks fade into a silence that turned absolute. Cautiously he lifted first one hand, then the other, from his ears: silence....

But something was different—yes—he wasn't moving any longer. In fact, he was seated.

He heaved his bottom side to side: yes, definitely, seated. Cautiously he opened first one, then his other eye.

He was on a raised dais on a throne so large that despite his bulk he felt like a small child in an adult's chair. A long, wide hall confronted him. Its ceiling was high overhead, held up at distant corners by four great pillars. There were no walls.

People and animals pressed towards the foot of his throne with more ranks of people and animals beyond the hall pressing in turn as far as he could see. They shuffled and moaned, turned on those behind them, and stopped only at the stairs at the foot of his throne and there implored him with out-stretched arms in waves of sound rolling in from the horizon.

"Judge us! Judge us!" they cried in words and howls and bays and roars and hisses and chirps and hoots.

"Quiet!" he begged, unable to hear his thoughts for the din.

"Judge us! Judge us!" they cried without cease.

"QUIET!" Lepanto trumpeted. Stillness spread slowly outward from where he found himself standing on the dais until it reached even the horizon. Instead their low shuffling and occasional crushed moan filled the great hall like the waves of the sea.

"Stop! STOP!" he bellowed, pleased they obeyed. Slowly the shuffling and moans stopped too, receding over horizon. Lepanto took in the numbers before him and wished he was back in the nightmare darkness about to be torn apart.

"How can I judge all of you?"

"JUDGE US!" they demanded in renewed waves of cries and howls and roars and hisses and...that receded to the horizon, holding out their hands or paws or wings imploringly until he held his ears again and trumpeted,

"QUIET!"

Silence spread in waves again down the great hall and beyond.

"I may be the wisest of Elephants," he sighed, "but wisdom knows its limits! There are too many of you. It would take a lifetime, no, many lifetimes, to judge all of you. And who am I to do so?" he added, desperately.

But the men shouted and the women wailed and the children cried and the beasts bleated and howled and roared for judgment drowning his words, for any judgment that would relieve them of their endless waiting for judgment.

Lepanto's head sank slowly, and his shoulders sagged with the burden of their hunger for judgment. At first he thought the sheer weight of their suffering would break him, then he felt anger surface at being so pressured. He didn't want to do this! Yet they wouldn't give him any peace unless he did. His anger grew when they ignored his cries to be "Quiet!" now, grew as they clamored at him, grew until he shook with fury.

"Miserable creatures," he said angrily, "miserable one and all! You want to be judged? Really? That's what it will take to shut you up?" They pleaded and roared and hissed and....

"Very well!" A shiver and a groan ran through the crowd.

He found a silver scale in his hands, one scale just large enough to hold a heart, the other, a feather, and understood doom would follow if a heart, heavy with its wrongs, outweighed the feather. As he watched stunned each supplicant placed his or her heart on the scale, and always the heart sank and the feather rose.

"Doom!" a voice pronounced each time, "Doom!" the voice went on, until in a daze Lepanto recognized the voice was his own, with a life of its own.

"Doom!" he pronounced again and again against man after woman after child after beast without a pause. Each individual so

judged faded into a pale gray and then collapsed with a thin cry into a heap of ashes at his feet which a steady wind blew away. He felt more certain with each "Doom!" that they were getting what they deserved, and his gnawing doubt and reluctance faded.

Yet he tried to hold onto mercy and compassion, and looked everywhere for more feathers so that their hearts would not be heavier and he could spare them. Feathers sprouted from his head, rustled and tickled under his clothes so that he tore them off and plucked himself like a chicken. But as fast as he placed feathers on the scale the hearts grew heavier. No one was saved.

Exhausted, he sat on the throne. When a gust of wind blew all his feathers in a tumbling cloud from the scale he made no effort to replace them. He made no effort to weigh their offered hearts. No one seemed to care, accepting his shouted or muttered "Doom!" as if doom was a foregone conclusion. How dumb they are, he thought, how weak, how hopeless.

That dumb weakness infuriated him. He thought of how Sam was so resourceful in a fight, yet these lacked even a child's spunk. His contempt broke in a great wave over and through him. He rose to his feet again and stepped to the edge of the dais. He flung the scale aside.

"DOOM! DOOM!" he bellowed, "DOOM!" again and again until he grew hoarse, "DOOM! DOOM!" waving his arms over them, "DOOM! YOU ARE ALL DOOMED!" he raged, "DOOM! DOOM! DOOM!" he pronounced until his hoarse voice was only a whisper. "DOOMED!"

A single family was left. They fell on their knees before him, staring into his red, maddened eyes with hopeless looks. It was John, Madelyn, and Sam. Lepanto stared at them: how gray they were, how hopeless, how dumb he thought in his madness. He found his voice a last time.

202

"DOOM!" he cried, "DOOM! YOU ARE DOOMED!"

"Lepanto," they wailed as they faded and turned to ashes scattered by a gust of wind. The hall was empty. The Elephant sat down, shuddering at the enormity of his betrayal. The madness drained from his eyes, where now, at last, and very much too late, tears welled.

"Even I," he sobbed, "even I betrayed them," he cried bitterly. His shoulders shook, then tears ran down his long face onto his trunk. He rose with a shuddering cry, placed his own heart in the scales, and shrieked, "DOOM!"

He expected to fade and fall into ashes and be blown from existence with a thinning cry.

Nothing happened.

That was the worst thing that could have happened.

"Judge me!" he demanded of the empty room, the empty horizon. "Judge me!" A weight of guilt crushed him to his knees, then to the floor.

"Judge me," he sobbed, digging his hands into his eyes.

Nothing happened. He drew into himself, quaking, eyes shut, moaning at the foot of the high throne, overwhelmed by his cruelty and guilt.

The ground disappeared. A joyous emotion surged through him—"I am judged!"—but when he opened his eyes and tried to sit up he discovered he was floating through the air over an open savanna on the edge of a wide river.

Groves of trees clumped here and there. Beyond these there was nothing else to be seen. After a time as he floated along Lepanto saw an animal laying on its side near the river. He strained to see better, but could not change his direction. Men swarmed around it, although he could not make out who they were.

He floated by another such group, nearer. Now he saw an

elephant being cut to pieces by a swarm of sweating men who kept their faces averted. He groaned. They took no notice. He passed one group after another cutting elephants to pieces.

He trumpeted in horror and fury, but no one paid any attention. Once he floated past a herd of elephants being pursued by men as tall as the elephants who, once they caught up with one, drove a spear though its heart, and raced on to the next as the beast collapsed.

Men swarmed over each and began to pull straw from what had been a living animal a moment before. Lepanto's horror gave way to a different sentiment, then: this was just what he wanted.

"Judge me," he cried, "reduce me to stuffing and pull it all out!" He went on shouting and gesturing and trumpeting but was ignored.

Am I invisible, he wondered?

Won't anyone release me from my suffering?

He remembered how he had doomed Sam and John and Madelyn, and cried out again to get their attention.

"Righto!" said a thick voice. There standing in his path was one who was a giant to the giants. Lepanto saw his face. This great figure confronting him was none other than Mr. Nicholas!

Lepanto recognized now the smaller giants and smaller men all had Mr. Nicholas' thatch of red hair, or his beet-colored face and his purple misshapen nose, or had one arm shorter than another, just like Mr. Nicholas. Then Lepanto realized he was standing too and had to crane his neck to face a towering Mr. Nicholas.

Mr. Nicholas laughed and raised hands big as boulders—or were they clouds that darkened as he raised them, rolling with thunder, flashing with lightning?

"You don't even know who you are!" he roared with laughter. "This is too easy! But what pleasure it is to destroy the most foolish of Elephants! Let's get on with it!" He spoke with no trace of his usual accent.

Lepanto was mesmerized. Not know who he was? Be so easy to destroy? For he had no doubt this great Mr. Nicholas could swat him like a fly.

"At least I know I'm not you! Not one of your look-alikes! I am Lepanto, the Elephant Who Dances!" he said.

Mr. Nicholas doubled over with laughter. Lepanto shook his head sharply. He remembered how he had thought himself dreaming when his eyes first opened in the kaleidoscopic world instead of on the cliff's top. He remembered he went through a door and found witches, warlocks, dragons, whatever! He had sat on the Throne of Doom and judged everyone. Everyone? Really? Even Sam and John and Madelyn? Now here was Mr. Nicholas tall as a building?

His thoughts were like fish who tried to swim in water thick as syrup. What was going on? He tried to move his feet. They felt stuck in mud. He tried to avert his head. It felt stiff as thick wire. He stuck his hands in his vest, but he had thrown away his clothes. He clutched at himself. When, he wondered, did I do that? After I doomed everyone? He felt exposed and vulnerable.

Mr. Nicholas laughed more at his confusion. A look of pure joy filled his face as he closed in on Lepanto and his followers cheered him on, eager to see Mr. Nicholas finish him off.

Lepanto made a last desperate grab towards his missing pockets before stopping the gesture. Yet there was something in his hands that had not been there before: he held it up. Mr. Nicholas stopped in his tracks, his followers crowding into him from behind. Lepanto held the Book.

He opened it in wonder. He didn't understand the picture that met his eyes of Sam running with a fearful look in his eyes as he gazed backwards at—he couldn't see his enemies. The next page fluttered open. It was John running in terror with a backward gaze at—but Lepanto again couldn't see his enemies. A terrible thought hit him and he trumpeted in rage. Mr. Nicholas recoiled a step involuntarily as Lepanto's tusks burst into white flames.

"Out of my way!" he trumpeted at Mr. Nicholas. Lepanto felt invisible bonds snapping. He stamped his feet. He was on firm ground. He could move. And Mr. Nicholas did not seem so tall. The thunder and lightning in his fists stalled. Or was it Lepanto who was large, Lepanto whose tusks were lightning? He did not take the time to sort out any of this, but charged!

Mr. Nicholas leapt aside, surprised by this turn of events, and his followers scattered from that mad charge. Then with an angry cry he jumped after the Elephant. The other giants closed in behind him, but now Lepanto was ahead of them. The pictures in the Book he clutched could mean only one thing: Sam was alive and in trouble, pursued by an unknown menace. And so was John! He had doomed no one!

They needed his help!

Lepanto raced on until he realized he had no idea where to run to. He faltered, and looked back: there was Mr. Nicholas and his pack of giants. He began to run again. The savanna dried, the river sank into a mud-caked riverbed, then into sand while the temperature seemed to climb without relief. Soon his lungs burned with the heat.

But his pursuers showed no signs of weakening; if not gaining, they certainly were not falling farther behind. He knew he couldn't keep this pace up forever, though: he was flesh, he would weaken, dancing elephant or not! They would see that, redouble their efforts, and close in on him after all.

Am I going to fail after all, he wondered, and not find John and Sam? Are Mr. Nicholas and the others going to run me down? Bitterness and failure were rare tastes on the Elephant's tongue, if frequent today, yet never worse than now. He couldn't fight them all. He couldn't keep running much longer, after he flogged himself forward for another burning hour. He saw a little hill off to one side, and turned towards it.

Better to make a last stand there, he thought grimly, one I will make sure they will never forget. A howl went up behind him as he changed direction.

XIV

The Way to Dread City

The hill was steeper than it looked.

Lepanto struggled to heave his bulk upwards, slowing steadily even as Mr. Nicholas and the giants began scrambling up behind him. With a last heave he threw himself onto the summit. There, before he could turn to fight his pursuers, astonished, he saw Sam scrambling up another side, and from a third John clawed onto the summit as though pursued by an army of terrors.

"Lepanto!"

"Sam!"

"Dad!"

"Sam!"

"John!"

"Lepanto!"

"It's good we're together before the end," cried John, embracing Sam as Lepanto embraced them both. "Get ready to fight the deformed men," John added, pointing down the hill where he saw them leaping upwards.

"Yes!" shouted Sam, hugging his father, "let's give those witches and Mr. Nicholas a good fight!"

"Hurry!" yelled Lepanto. "We'll give those elephant killers something to remember!" Then, puzzled, "Mr. Nicholas? He's behind me!"

"Where?" asked Sam, looking past Lepanto

"Who?" asked John, looking past Sam.

"What deformed men?" cried Lepanto, looking past John.

They couldn't see each other's pursuers.

Their words jumbled together.

"There's no one behind you," shouted Sam at Lepanto.

"There's no one behind you," shouted John at Sam.

"There's no one behind you!" shouted Lepanto at John.

Lepanto remembered the images in the Book: their enemies hadn't been left off the page—the page was blank except for their fleeing figures because no one was there.

"They aren't there!" trumpeted Lepanto. "Stare them down! NO—ONE—IS—THERE!"

They turned and stared back in the direction from which they had fled, Lepanto's words echoing in their minds. Lepanto felt his self-control flood back, his eyes return to his use, his limbs to his commands that he realized with growing astonishment had not been at his command since—since they had sailed into the bay.

He stared as Mr. Nicholas and his troop of giants melted away like a dab of butter in a hot pan. Sam was next to regain his self-control. At first the witches raced on, climbing the hill like athletes.

"You aren't there," Sam said firmly. They hesitated.

"Think of Madelyn," the Elephant suggested.

"Mother," Sam sighed. He concentrated on her image. "Oooh," he said as the old women shriveled with forlorn cries and disappeared.

But John kicked and struck out at the clear air until Lepanto seized and shook him so his head snapped back and forth.

"Lepanto?" John whispered, when the Elephant stopped. He stared around. "Where are they?"

"They were never here."

John stood dazed: then he too felt the same self-control reassert itself that Sam and Lepanto had. He nodded.

"I think you'd better look now at what's really here," Lepanto said to John and Sam. They turned at Lepanto's words to stare down the hill that was much smaller than the one they had climbed. John gasped.

"Ugh," breathed Sam.

On all sides as far as they could see the beach was filled with posts at different heights and small pyramids, some larger than others, but none taller than a man. On each post rested a Watcher, while others were encased in the pyramids' clear tips, lidded unlike the naked eyes on the posts, each pyramid tip floating above its base. They were guardians of the Far Land of Fear, able to read their inmost thoughts and play with their minds.

"We have been fools," Lepanto said. "We have been in their power since we entered the bay." They looked across the bay to where the remnants of the stone giants should have been, but the water was flat to the other shore which was much closer than they had thought when the monster's breath blew them in.

Nor had they crashed against a cliff in a great wave. There lay their ruined, hump-backed yacht on the beach. They had not run out of wind in the middle of the bay, but sailed up onto rocks jutting out from the beach, and broken the keel. The masts had broken from the impact and lay in a welter of sails and rigging.

"We have been their toys," Lepanto went on, shaking his head as he realized the extent of their delusions. "If luck hadn't brought us to this same place, too desperate any longer to be controlled except in our terrors, we would have met terrible, self-inflicted ends: if they had been wiser and made us see only our hearts' desires, we would have been lost in fantasy, and never have come to ourselves."

The three sensed the Watchers' thoughts now, too, in response to Lepanto's words: angry thoughts, mocking thoughts.

"Mock as you like," Lepanto trumpeted, "you have failed."

"Like anyone else who tries to beat us!" shouted Sam.

"I am past your power," John said more grimly. "Don't think of me again."

A wave of hatred filled their minds.

"YOU ARE LOST," echoed in their minds, but fruitlessly, now.

"No," the three replied, "You are."

"I'm going to Dread City and I am going to save my mother," Sam said firmly.

"And I'm going with him to make sure he does," added Lepanto.

"Nothing will ever make me doubt again," said John.

The wave of hatred weakened.

"To see so much, and understand so little," Lepanto said. With that they felt a confusion under the malice. The three travelers resolutely turned their backs on the Watchers and clambered up the mild height that had seemed impossibly steep in what they felt sure was the right direction for Dread City. Sam stopped.

"Where's George? And the girl?"

"Who?" asked John. Sam explained about George and the girl they had so daringly rescued from the old hag.

"Hmmm," Lepanto breathed. "Neither the boy nor the girl were real. Not yet, anyway," he added obscurely.

Sam shook his head a little sadly. He wasn't so sure. There had been something about them—about the girl's anger and rudeness especially which he actually found himself recalling with unexpected warmth. And George...George the Dependent. He had been like having a younger brother ready to follow him no matter what.

But Lepanto was right. They were gone with the rest of their fantasies. Sam only sighed in response to Lepanto's words, and went on climbing. John told his story in turn. He was proud of the admiration in Sam's eyes. When he finished, Lepanto reluctantly told his.

211

"But you wouldn't do that!" said Sam when the Elephant told how he had doomed even them.

"But I did," Lepanto said.

"There are parts of all of us we've needed to discover," John said calmly, "some to reclaim, some to abandon forever." Lepanto gave him a level look.

"Do you still have the Book?" asked Sam. The Elephant hesitated: he searched his pockets, suddenly aware he had pockets, and had never, in fact, lost his clothes. Another part of the Watchers' effect on him, he reflected. But the Book was not there: he half expected to find feathers and was relieved there were none.

"At least I've still got my satchel," smiled John, holding it up with the useful ropes and bola. They walked on in silence.

"Why don't we fly?" said Sam, suddenly, and Lepanto nodded. But when he drew out the Flying Trapeze it was in fractured parts.

"It must have happened when we ran aground," Lepanto sighed.

"So it wasn't all just imagined," Sam said at last with a frown. Then his frown deepened. "Even the imagined bits were real," he added. They looked at him. "It was like living in myself. And that's real in its own way," he explained.

"From the mouths of children," laughed Lepanto as he stuffed away the broken Flying Trapeze.

"I'm not a child!"

"No," smiled John, "At least, less and less!"

"We lived ourselves, our fears, our desires, our wildest imaginings," agreed Lepanto.

They walked in silence for some time. "I've learned one thing," John said. His companions looked at him. "A life lived without love, without even the desire for love, is a life without meaning."

"I've learned something too," Sam added with a mischievous

smile. They looked at him. "Real or not I'll never eat a coconut again!"

They laughed, and walked on silently. They reached the top of the rise and found themselves faced with a somber, featureless expanse with few rocks and only occasional low, shrub-like growths that were no obstacle to walk around or through. At least it wasn't a desert, or full of strange creatures.

They took a breath, and set off resolutely with their backs to the bay and defeated Watchers, each turning their adventures over in their minds as they walked on.

Here and there were short stretches of what looked like a path. At times it disappeared, but always reappeared farther on. Once they found a plain sign like the one in John's adventure. Its arrow pointed straight down their path.

"Yes, that's it" was painted in fading letters beneath the arrow. John shook his head, Lepanto gave an impressive snort, but Sam laughed and strode ahead, eager to get to Dread City. The others hurried after him.

After a few hours the plains began to lift into rolling hills that slowly covered themselves with brown grass and pygmy trees. Dark, near-earth colored flowers appeared, and here and there tepid pools of water where they relieved their thirst, though the water was at once flat and mineral with an unpleasant metallic tang.

The sun ebbed slowly from violet to red as they walked on without giving any thought to stopping. After what had passed they were not as frightened as they might have been over what adventure they might stumble into.

Down they plodded into a little valley then up its facing hill, noticing, still in silence, how the hills were growing steeper. They began to puff, to feel hunger and thirst and an ache in their muscles when they reached the top of another hill sometime later, the steepest

they had encountered so far.

Sam was on the point of demanding Lepanto search his vest even for coconuts or whatever might still be there when he stopped in his tracks. Two fading signs confronted the three travelers.

"One More Ridge," and "Dread City." They exchanged startled glances, hunger and thirst forgotten, then looked around to see if there was anything else or a sign of threat. But there was only a steep descent, then a narrow valley to cross to a hill that ended in a ridge of stone.

"Who put them there?" John asked.

"And what will we find after one more ridge?" added Lepanto.

"Dread City!" Sam said impatiently. Their words sounded odd in the air after so long a silence.

"It doesn't say that," Lepanto replied, "although I grant you it's hard to imagine what else it could mean."

"Should we just march up to whatever it is?" asked John.

"Why not," answered Lepanto. "We're going where very few choose to come. And those all left empty-handed."

"Until now!"

Lepanto smiled at Sam. "Until now." He shook his head, half amused, half in wonder.

The reverse side of the hill going down had them scrabbling and grabbing at handholds, sliding despite themselves for stretches until they sat and slid down over a rough scree to the foot of the hill, wincing. The ridge now confronting them across the narrow canyon looked just this side of sheer. For a moment they were daunted, then Sam shouted,

"Look!"

He pointed where a clear path zigzagged conveniently up its slope, making their ascent bearable. It was as though having come this far no effort was made any longer to resist them: instead, they felt they were now, at last, being encouraged. Whoever made this path obviously assumed anyone traveling here should be here and could only be going to one place!

And just when their mouths were driest they found a small rivulet of flat, mineral rich but bitter water to relieve their thirst.

Their relief was short-lived, for as they caught their breath it hit them how still everything was. Then they felt it: there was a heaviness on their shoulders they couldn't shake off: a sense of dread. They exchanged glances, and nodded.

"Very well," said Lepanto after a time, "onward," sure now Sam must be right and Dread City lie just over the summit. The zigzags steepened as they neared the sharp ridge top so that each step became ever more of an effort. No one said anything, or paused, even as their sense of dread thickened. The thought they were near their goal kept them going until they stood on the rock-ribbed summit of the ridge and stared down the other side.

"I'll be," said John.

A wide valley spread below them, then a range of mountains rose to snowless, ragged peaks in the far distance. Running straight down the middle of the valley was a wide, empty highway. Across its eight lanes opposite them was a rest area with a roof built over it and a bench within. A pole with a sign stood beside the rest area.

"I'll bet that says 'Bus Stop,'" grinned Sam. They exchanged glances: why not?

Going down proved harder than going up—back and forth they went until it felt endless. Now they zigged, now zagged down the ridge's side eager to be down, but by the time they reached its foot found their thigh muscles trembling like water. They paused to let them still, and took more than one deep breath.

"Ready?" said Sam at last. The others nodded, and they set off across the valley in easy strides until they reached the highway they had seen from the ridge. They paused on its edge: it looked, well, if not new, hardly used, a fine eight-lane highway stretching farther than they could see in either direction.

They still saw no traffic, and half expected the pavement to disappear underfoot when they stepped on it. But the pavement was firm, and their steps fell eerily flat in the heavy silence until they reached the rest stop, for the weight on their shoulders did not lessen.

Sam was right when they reached the rest area: its sign read "Bus Stop," and it was clearly designed for travelers to sit and wait for the next bus. At one end was a map behind a plastic cover. They crowded around it. The map showed Bus Route #1 running into Dread City. There were no other routes.

"We're here," Sam said and pointed to a red arrow on the map above a neat logo, "You are here." The route ended in a complex web of streets.

"We're almost there," Lepanto observed needlessly.

"All we have to do is wait for the bus," Sam added with a grin. John shook his head.

"When's the next one?"

John searched fruitlessly for a timetable, but there was none posted beneath the map or anywhere else in the little shelter.

"Should we wait?" John asked, doubtfully.

"Why not!" Sam answered with a brightness that lifted the others' spirits: "let them give us a ride the last few miles!" He laughed as the others exchanged glances wondering who "them" might turn out to be.

"We don't know when the next is," murmured Lepanto doubtfully.

"I bet with us here it will come pretty soon!" Sam answered, just as confidently. Lepanto and John both laughed now and sat down, deciding to make the best of it. After a few idle minutes Sam got up to explore.

At the end opposite the side with the bus route were some empty shelves that must once have held literature of some kind. He got down on his knees to see what he could find under the lowest. There was something wedged in. Carefully he pried it out and turned to the others holding it. They stared at the Book in his hands.

"Let's have that here," ordered Lepanto. Sam handed it over and sat down next to him. He and John peered into the Book as Lepanto turned its pages full of their adventures while they waited for the most unlikely of buses in the most unlikely of bus stops.

The Book was almost filled.

XV

Dancing From A Dangerous Bench!

S lowly they turned the pages back from Lepanto on the Throne of Doom. There was John's struggle in the cave, and Sam's in Mr. Nicholas' truck and bathtub with the multiplying clocks and George, and then the dangerous old woman and the girl he and George rescued.

There were the three-headed centaurs and the Great Stone Giant, the quiet days at sea after the adventure with the sea monster when its breath filled their sails, and the storm-wracked Sea of Faces. They looked to the beginning where "No dreams" was written, and shook their heads.

"I feel like I've lived through one dream after another," said John, and then, with a bemused shake of his head, "but nothing has ever felt more real, and I can't remember when I last felt so alive."

Lepanto's trunk curled in approval, and Sam nodded.

"If I pinch myself it just hurts," he laughed, giving himself a good pinch. "Ouch!" The others laughed too, then turned their attention back to the Book. There were enough blank pages left for some serious adventures, still.

They weren't done—as their eyes met they shared the unspoken thought that the hardest task was still ahead. Sam felt a sudden panic.

"We don't have our boat anymore, or the Flying Trapeze—once we find Madelyn," he said bravely, "how do we get her home?" A frown deepened on John's face and Lepanto sat, silent.

"Even if we can get away?"

Sam's mind raced with all the strange enemies they had overcome so far, real or imagined real: there must be more. And worse. "From whoever has her?"

John groaned as Sam's words struck home. In a flash all the hopelessness he had disavowed rose up again and buried his moment of self-confidence. How foolish he was ever to think they could actually pull off this stunt! Being here was no place for anyone in their right minds to be! He said so.

"We've been fools! What an idiot I am even to toy with the idea there are second chances! We must be madmen in an asylum sharing the same fantasies, not a man and a boy and an Elephant. An Elephant! Really!" he spluttered. "Even mad, how could we think we could find Madelyn in Dread City after she died," said John brutally, "and bring her back? We'll be hard put to save ourselves, if we go down that road." He shrank into himself, sightless.

Sam hunched over while Lepanto's eyes took on a distant look. Their silence drew out in the still landscape where nothing moved and nothing appeared in either direction on the road.

I've been so hasty, rushing from one thing to another, Sam thought now. He at least didn't doubt what they had been through, or that he was close to finding his mother, but now it seemed really pointless to find her when they had no way out. All they would be able to do was run around Dread City or the Far Land of Fear, always pursued. He shuddered. Sam stared at the blank pages remaining in the Book with eyes as blank as those pages. He leaned against Lepanto, hopeless.

For once Lepanto couldn't find the words to reassure. He had danced in the Sea of Faces, charged Mr. Nicholas on the Elephant Slaughter Plains, rescued the others time and again, but now? He stared at the blank pages remaining, just as blank as Sam. He was not full of hidden resources, dangerous when aroused, full of magic or what was often much the same, wisdom.

An animal denseness dulled his mind so that now as the pages fluttered their images and words made no sense to him at all. Each in his own way felt heavy with despair.

So they did not see the beet-faced man with a great purple nose in a policeman's uniform peer in at them from behind the shelter, smile maliciously at their still forms, and disappear.

A single tear at length fell from Sam's eye, rolled down his cheek and plopped onto the Book. Even that slight sound was loud in the deep silence they had fallen into. Sam slowly lifted a hand to his face as the Book slid from Lepanto's senseless hands to the ground.

Sam felt as though he was in a waking dream, doer and watcher at once, as he saw himself grab—in slow motion—for the Book, bending over and down like a sleepwalker, until he saw himself lose his balance and lose contact with the bench—and tumble abruptly to the ground, his head only partly shielded by his arm from the pavement.

"Ow," he muttered. Then more strongly, "Ouch!" He sat up, rubbing his head where it had hit, then stood, momentarily dizzy. His despair and drowsiness disappeared as he steadied: life blazed up in him, and anger.

"Look at all we've done!" he said to John and Lepanto's still bodies. "Look how far we've come! We're almost there! And as far as getting home—well," his jaw clenched in determination, "I'll find a way! Like I always have! Like we have!"

But the others didn't stir. They were sunk into themselves, hardly breathing. They hadn't even noticed Sam's fall or heard him cry out as he hit the pavement or a word he'd shouted at them. Alarm swept through him. This wasn't right at all.

"Get up," he told his father. John didn't move. "Lepanto, get up!"

The Elephant stared straight ahead sightless. Both looked grayer than Sam had ever seen them. He must have looked like them a moment ago. Suddenly he understood: it was the bench!

"Get up!" he shouted. "That bench is making us give up. It wants us to sit there forever!"

"Shush," sighed John, as if from a great distance. But Sam grabbed him and with an effort toppled him heavily onto the ground.

"Ow," John muttered. Then more strongly, "Ouch!" He sat up, dizzy. "What's going on?" He let Sam help pull him to his feet, where he swayed a moment uncertainly.

"It's that bench! It's making us give up!" Sam shouted, giving him a push away when John started to sit down again. Energy flowed back into John now, too, and his hopelessness and disbelief faded as swiftly as Sam's had now he was free of the bench.

"That's a Bench of Forgetting," John said, emphasizing the words, alert again and taking in what had happened. His resolve flooded back, and his anger at being so easily thrown back into his gray, doubting self.

"We have to get Lepanto off," Sam said. That was easier said than done. They took in the massive Elephant, looked at each other, took deep breaths, grabbed an arm each, and at a nod from John, tugged. Nothing happened. They took deeper breaths and at another nod put their hearts and souls into pulling Lepanto free. Nothing happened.

"This is bad, very bad," John breathed heavily, standing back. "We'll never move him," Sam panted. John stared at the frozen Elephant, and suddenly smiled, if a little grimly. "I know how to get him up."

John brushed back one of Lepanto's fan-like ears and stood as close to him as possible as he said, "Lepanto. Lepanto! Get up... You're on the Throne of Doom!"

"Ohh," groaned the Elephant. "Ohhh nooo…" The Elephant shuddered. He lurched side to side.

"Doom! Doomdoom!" shouted John.

"Ohhh nooo!" Lepanto groaned again, and heaved himself forward while John and Sam grabbed an arm each and pulled for all they were worth, letting go his arms and jumping aside at the last moment to avoid being crushed as the Elephant fell heavily, his tusks hitting the ground with a crack. "NNNOOO!" he trumpeted in abrupt pain and fury, getting up to charge the figures before him, blind rage in his eyes. "Not again!" Sam dashed behind him as Lepanto towered over John.

"Lepanto!" shouted Sam, "LEPANTO!" And he kicked him in the leg to get his attention.

"Ouch!" he bellowed as he turned on Sam. But there was confusion in his eyes. Then John slapped him from behind as hard as he could in turn.

"OW!" he roared, and turned towards John.

"LEPANTO!" Sam called, distracting him.

"LEPANTO!" John yelled as he turned towards Sam. The Elephant stopped.

"It's the BENCH!" Sam shouted.

"THE BENCH OF FORGETTING!" John shouted.

"It's making us give up!" Sam said. Lepanto nodded slowly, and gave himself a great shake that started with his ears flapping wildly, descended to a madly waving trunk, and made the ground shudder as he stamped with his feet. He finally settled himself with a sigh, and looked from one to the other, himself again.

"This is the most dangerous place we have been," Lepanto muttered.

"The Book saved us," Sam said, and described how reaching for

it had freed him from the bench. "I think we should get going—I bet no bus ever comes here."

"Certainly no bus I'd want to get on," John said.

"Yes," agreed Lepanto. "Fetch the Book and we'll go under our own power!" Sam turned to get it, then looked puzzled. He looked behind himself, then behind Lepanto, and carefully searched under the bench.

"It's gone again," he said.

"It certainly has a mind of its own," John grumbled. He lifted his satchel onto his shoulder, and the three stepped away from the shelter and headed down the road towards Dread City.

As they walked first one, then the other, noticed the countryside race by on either side faster than they were moving. They stopped—and so did the fields and hills in the valley they were in. They exchanged glances, and started again: again the countryside flew by.

"Wow," breathed Sam. He picked up his pace, and the countryside on either side of the highway flew by even faster. This time when he stopped the landscape lurched ahead, then recoiled and stilled.

"We'll get to Dread City in no time if we make things go by that fast."

"Why can't we see ourselves going that fast?"

Lepanto shrugged at Sam's question. They started walking again, keeping their eyes on the flying landscape. They almost didn't notice how fast they came up on a bus ahead of them, and had to move to one side quickly to avoid hitting it.

They stopped.

The bus lurched and stilled.

Its occupants were silent and motionless, its exhaust hanging in the air thick as cotton candy. The bus driver had his eyes fixed firmly on the road, as if actively driving, but he was as still and gray as the rest.

Sam clambered in through the door that opened effortlessly at his touch. One man was frozen in the middle of a sneeze. A woman with an intense look of concentration was poised motionlessly in mid-stroke, her knitting needles frozen. No whistle came from the pursed, whistling lips of a little boy. Lepanto's voice stopped Sam as he reached out to touch him.

"Don't. We don't fit with them, or them with us. I wouldn't take any chances here." Sam drew his hand back, then clambered out.

"They're not alive," Sam said.

"They're not dead," added John.

"At least neither of those as we understand them," Lepanto added. They felt a prickling sensation on the back of their necks, and turned. A man with a great purple nose in a policeman's uniform hid behind one of the roadside shrubs.

"I thought we were being watched before," Sam said.

"I'm sure we are now," Lepanto replied.

They started walking again. Again the landscape flew past. Whenever they stopped a fraction of a second went by as the landscape flew past, recoiled, and stopped, resuming as they started up again.

The sun darkened gradually to a dense, Indian red that after a time darkened shade by shade to black. Stars appeared in the gray sky, red pinpricks that one by one also turned black, still visible as dots in the grayness overhead. Everything around them turned to shades of white and gray in a dull, even light without vividness or force.

Sam was about to point out how strange the sun looked, an arm raised, and stopped. His arm glowed. He looked down: his entire body glowed, his skin almost aflame in its vividness, not at all like the dense, opaque beet faced men who had haunted their dreams and adventures.

John took in Sam's piercing blue eyes, and blonde hair bright as sunlight. John too gleamed in this light, while when they turned to Lepanto his brightness almost hurt their eyes.

"Ooo," Sam breathed, stopping, taking in Lepanto, "how beautiful you look."

"How strange," John murmured.

Lepanto looked embarrassed. "I feel like I'm using myself up, here. Not all at once. Just—bit by bit." Sam and John nodded, for they felt the same. They were expending light, like suns, except they weren't suns, and their resources weren't unlimited.

"I'm hungry," Sam said. "What's in your pockets?" Lepanto rummaged for some time in his vest before he was able to pull out a small ham, a baguette that was no longer fresh, and a large, cellophane wrapped chocolate chip cookie.

"That's all," he sighed. John and Sam eyed them. They let Lepanto divide these, eagerly downing the ham, chewing on the bread, and happily feeling the chocolate chips in their third of the cookie melt in their mouths.

"Is there anything to drink?" asked Sam. Lepanto searched his pockets again in growing frustration, and finally brought out his kettle pipe. There was thick, aromatic caravan tea in the kettle which he let each sip. Sam almost gagged at the taste, but managed enough to wet his mouth and throat, as did John. Lepanto, with an unhappy sigh, emptied the last with his trunk.

"That will have to do." He didn't have to say for what: they understood only too well. Their hair prickled on their necks, and they spun around sure someone was watching, but saw no one.

"Come out come out wherever you are!" Sam shouted: "I'll show you a thing or two!"

"Sam," warned his father. "Let's not attract a crowd here." But he said it with a smile and was rewarded with one from his son.

"A little bravado is just the ticket, I think," said Lepanto. All had felt their sense of dread thicken as they moved forward, and had thrust it aside, each in their own way. "A good dance would do nicely," added Lepanto. He broke into a gay little rhythm.

> Da diddle-de dee!
> Da de de de de dee!
> Da diddle-de dee!
> Da de! da de! da dee!

The Elephant cut a caper, then began

> Gimme that old soft shoe I said
> the old soft shoe a razza-ma-tazz
> raaaaaza-ma-tazz! Ah-one, ah-two….

His shuffle gave way to firm steps. In a moment he danced gaily, joined by Sam after a moment, and then, a smile breaking through his stern expression, by John.

> A doodle dee doo! that old soft shoe
> nothing else will do oh raazza-ma-tazz!
> That's the dance my darling used to do!
> Razza-ma-tazz oh ma-taaazzz!

they sang, cutting a gay rhythm that made the landscape fly by. They danced faster, laughing when the landscape began to blur. Soon even the road flew by underfoot…. So they came laughing and dancing to the top of a slow rise, their laughter slicing through the dull air, and saw Dread City spread below them to the horizon.

They stopped, awed.

Wide highways carved through its different sections, full of trucks, buses, and cars of every description, as well as rail lines, some raised over the streets receding into a distant blur. They saw masses of people on the nearest streets. Here and there groves of brutal, solid towers of gray cement with monotonous rows of windows lifted upwards, surrounded by blocks of lower, squat buildings.

Nearer was a smattering of gas stations amid an unbroken line of motels starting just downhill and running into the first streets. To one side they saw an immense building with "Mall" spelled out in big black, block letters.

Overhead the air was full of planes and helicopters, some of the planes ascending, some preparing to land in an airport over that far horizon. Yet there was none of the electric excitement generated by a great city, and their sense of dread only deepened, for the planes hung motionless in the air.

The cars and other vehicles were strung out along the highways and through the streets in motionless strands, dull stones on stony necklaces.

No whistles blew from the trains.

No train moved.

No one moved in the press of people.

The black sun hung at permanent noon in the gray sky, dotted with black stars.

Absolute silence betrayed the nature of this city.

Utter stillness.

Grayness.

"I never expected this," John said finally. They nodded in agreement, mutely.

"Look over there," Lepanto said. They looked where he pointed to a section of the city they could just make out. After a moment they could tell there were seven hills clothed in ancient buildings, a great oval mass at its foot.

"If I'm not mistaken," Lepanto pointed, "that's the Roman Coliseum." John nodded. He could just make it out.

"That's ancient Rome," he breathed....

"There's the Eiffel Tower!" Sam pointed. They looked where he indicated. The shape was unmistakable. Surrounding it were a set of avenues and buildings that even at this distance suggested Paris in the 19th Century. As they stared they began to identify other landmarks. A suspicion grew in John's mind, but Sam voiced it first.

"I bet every city in the world is here!"

The other two nodded.

"Or imitations," Sam added. "It's all so gray. And what city is this one in front with all these square buildings?" The three stared again at the massive "Mall," and the nearer block of brutal towers.

"Moscow when it was communist, from the look of the mass housing."

"Then where," asked John, "is the Kremlin?"

"Probably out of sight behind those buildings."

"There's another Eiffel Tower!" Sam exclaimed, pointing.

He was right—in the far distance they could just make out its shape. They looked at each other, shocked as the same thought crept into all three minds at once.

"Every city," John said, "and every time," he added, giving that thought words.

"Yes," said Lepanto, full of sadness: "Every city in every era that ever was must be out there, every town, every village, and somewhere every hut and every cave and campfire…"

"All frozen in time."

"As if you don't die—don't disappear—" struggled Sam, "but come here, and, and—"

"Fade," said John somberly.

"Fade, and freeze," Lepanto finished, "forever." They shuddered.

After another long look John turned to Lepanto.

"Do they know?" he wondered: "Do they see—whatever way they look—and, like someone frozen, like in a dream, know everything?"

"That would be an awful doom," replied the Elephant with a shudder. He gave John a long look.

"No," he said finally, "I think instead they are still in mind, as well as body, holding their last moment of awareness in their minds, and frozen there."

"That would be awful, too," John said.

Sam shrugged anxiously. Neither vision seemed any better than the other to him. Adults, snuck into his mind: they always think the worst.

"No," he blurted out, surprising them from their gloomy thoughts, "you're both wrong. They are just blank."

"I'm not sure that's any better," John began, but Sam cut him off.

"Better than their heads full of thoughts, or," nodding at Lepanto, "with only one! Why should anything be going on? They're gray! They've faded from anything they need to do, whatever," he struggled to say. "Nothing's going on. The planes don't move, the people don't walk, the cars don't move: they've stopped. Just stopped!"

He wanted very much to be right. The thought of his mother suffering forever thinking things over without being able to do anything at all was too much to bear. He was relieved when Lepanto nodded slowly in agreement.

"Mmm, hmm. Stopped. Yes. That's it."

"My mother is down there, too," Sam said now, voicing the others' thought. There was nothing to say to that, but the other two now understood his vehement attack on their ideas. "Look," Sam added: "we're on fire!" In the gray all about them they flickered with a brighter color and energy than they had at first.

They eyed each other, and held out their arms. It was true, they had become living flames in fact, not just suggestion. Even their clothes flickered, as though sewn of flames, while their faces shone like the missing sun.

Sam smiled, suddenly very happy, his sense of dread for that moment lifting. "We made it. I said we'd get here. I said we'd find her, too. Let's go get her!" They nodded in agreement even as they smiled at his confidence. They had made it! Surely they'd been through the worst that could be thrown at them to stop them, and here they were anyway!

"But where do we start?" his father asked, stumped, for all that.

"Come on. We'll find a way. We always do!"

Lepanto shook his head.

Sam raced downhill trailing flashes of light.

XVI

Finding Madelyn In Dread City

F irst John and then Lepanto started after Sam. They felt watched and spun on their heels in one motion, but the purple-nosed man, the flaming red-haired man, and the man with different length arms all in police uniforms lay flat behind some low bushes, unseen. The travelers shrugged and resumed their quick pace, the motels and city outskirts flashing by. Soon it was the City's avenues and masses of motionless people that flew by....

Their earlier suspicions were confirmed as they read the signs marking the big intersections: "French Angle, 1800s" or "Sudanese Angle, Darfur Triangle, 2000s" or "Chinese Angle, Tang Dynasty." They turned now this way, now that, watching the streets change character and the crowds become French or Sudanese or Chinese or....

Modern vehicles gave way to areas with horses and horse-drawn coaches, to chariots, to litters borne aloft by straining, frozen bearers, to lithe hunters in a bare patch of landscape, then back to chariots, horses and horse-drawn carriages, and cars and buses. But only they moved in the entire panorama.

"They certainly look like they're doing things," Sam said.

They had reached "San Francisco Angle, 1905" and paused beside a stylishly dressed woman frozen in the act of flagging a horse-drawn taxi whose horse was stopped mid-motion, rearing. The women in the stores nearby were frozen in the act of screaming, the men in half-step as they struggled to keep their balance, their jackets flapping in an unseen wind. They saw the surrounding buildings in various states of collapse; tongues of black frozen flames lifted through their cracked ceilings.

"It's the great San Francisco Earthquake," John breathed. They looked at the women in the stores. Their hands held merchandise, but their eyes had a startled look, and some were about to be thrown off their feet.

"Wow," Sam breathed at the startling panorama in its moment of perpetual, frozen catastrophe.

They moved on and soon found themselves on Fifth Avenue, New York, December 7, 1941. Frozen masses hurried nowhere, the shops full, an era's last moment of innocence frozen in place.

"What's the point of all this frozen activity," John wondered, "all about to be changed forever?"

"If they had known," added Lepanto.

"It's like a bad joke," said Sam.

"But whose?" asked his father.

Neither of the others answered: instead, they wandered on from city to city, age to age, war and disaster, frivolity to frivolity, the weight steadily growing on their shoulders.

"Would anything matter even if it all speeded up?" asked Sam at last, giving voice to their unspoken thoughts, for so much of what they saw seemed so pointless, quick or frozen.

"I don't know," his father replied. But Lepanto gave Sam one of his long, appraising looks.

"Little," was all he said.

"We were becoming just like this," John sighed, "Just as frozen in time and place and action. There's only the appearance of life here."

"If that," added Lepanto. They looked at him. "What I feel," he added, "is the absence of love. There is only the repetition of what was always dead." John shuddered. But Sam filled with anger.

"How could you let mo—mom—my mother," he stuttered, "come here! What was wrong with you!" he demanded of his father, shrugging the weight of dread off his shoulders with his anger. He had heard his father's earlier explanations and apologies, but now that he saw Dread City his father's words were only a rain of pebbles.

"I didn't know, Sam. I was half here myself and I didn't know!" He gestured Sam to silence: "That's no excuse, I know! But," he went on after a moment, "you've brought us here, you've made us dream of miracles and made them real. You've changed us all from who we were when we started. Even so I'm sorry, sorry from the bottom of my heart."

Sam's throat tightened, and he flung his arms around his father who, after a startled moment, held him tight.

"Humph," came from Lepanto after a moment. "The time of miracles isn't done yet." But there was a smile on his face and a gleam in his brown and amber eyes. Sam nodded.

"Let's go get her," was all he said.

"Where?" John asked: "We can't go running from one time and place to another!" They sat on the curb next to a fruit vendor frozen in a shouting position behind a cart full of apples and oranges. Sam got up and looked at the gray apples and oranges, then picked up an orange.

It sat like a stone in his hands, and he almost tossed it back, then stopped: it began to change before his eyes. He stared. A faint flush of color strengthened as he watched: after a short time a ripe navel orange lay in his hands.

"Look!" he shouted.

None of them saw the beet-faced policeman with the huge purple nose poke his head out from around a corner, and pull back. They stared instead at the miracle of the orange glowing in Sam's hand.

Before John could say anything, Sam peeled the taut skin and broke it into sections, greedily swallowing its juice as he chewed its flesh. None noticed how the pieces of rind turned gray where they fell.

"Mmm…" He handed a section to his father. John took a bite, then another, wiping the sweet juice from his mouth, as Sam handed another section to Lepanto, who ate that tidbit with a sigh of pleasure.

"That's funny," Sam said, after a moment: "I feel hungrier." He took an apple, watched it in turn take on color until ripely red, and ate it. There was a puzzled look on his face. "I'm even hungrier!" He dropped the core on the street and reached for another gray orange.

"Don't," Lepanto warned suddenly, pointing at the core of the apple where Sam had dropped it. They watched it finish turning gray beside the gray orange peels. Lepanto got up, and now lifted an apple himself: it flared a brilliant red, and when he dropped it instead of turning to gray it collapsed into a puff of gray flakes.

"Wow," Sam said.

"I think you are putting your own life into that fruit but not getting all of it back," Lepanto murmured, bemused. "You'd have to eat core and seeds and stalk for that, and even then I think there'd be a little loss."

That struck Sam, and he put the orange back. It glowed a moment among the other gray oranges, but soon faded. They shook their heads. John sighed in frustration, and took in their surroundings with a growing interest.

"What is it?" asked Lepanto. John stood up.

"We're in the right city."

"But is it the right time?"

The three took in the buildings and sights around them, all typical of an area of north London right after the millennium. A hospital faced them across the street, its once bright glass façade now gray and featureless.

"There," John breathed, and shuddered. "There," he managed again, "is where she—where I last saw her—where I lost her."

They stood, silent.

"But just when in the 2000s is this?" he asked, looking around. "We need to find some kind of directory."

That was such an obvious idea Lepanto shook his head he hadn't thought of it himself as they set off to find one. Three misshapen policemen slipped behind the fruit stall as they left. The streets flew by from their quick pace until almost a blur in their urgency, and they had to force themselves to take slow, small steps so they could find what they were looking for.

A broad intersection came into view and, mincing steps carefully, they headed for the information kiosk in its center. They had overlooked such kiosks at other intersections. Here there were signs that pointed to "Colonial Mozambique Angle," "Mughal India Angle," "Sumerian Angle" and, behind them, "England Angle, London 2000."

A large map was mounted on one side of the kiosk, where another red arrow indicated their position. It swung out, showing another cross-section of the city: behind it was another map. To their dismay they discovered there wasn't just one "England Angle, London 2000" but more than they could count, as well as of every other 'angle.'

"But which one?" demanded Sam. "We'll never find her!"

"We could spend almost forever just searching one of these 'angles' room by room," John added in frustration, then moved around the kiosk to see if there was anything else that might be helpful.

"Here!" they heard him shout, and carefully moved to the other side. John stood beside a phone with rows of directories hanging above and beneath. "We'll look her up in the phone book!" They laughed at that despite themselves: a phone directory—here! Of course! John swung up the first directory and opened it, quickly thumbing through the pages as the others crowded in.

"No," he said, and let it drop. They took in the rows of thick, suspended directories…. Systematically John worked through them one after another, dropping each in turn back in place as he started the next, his index finger tracing down the right page for Madelyn without success. Their spirits sank with each failure. Finally John opened a directory nearly at the end of the bottom row. His finger moved down the page he turned to—and stopped.

"There…" he breathed. They crowded against him, alert again, peering at her name, phone number, and address: England, London 2000, 3: #16, 29 Hollow Rd." John stood, transfixed.

"What does that mean?" Sam asked, then: "what's wrong, Dad?" he added, seeing his father's expression.

"We lived there. For a time. Before you. Before she was ill. And then you came. And later she…" he broke off.

"So," Sam asked again, "what does it mean?"

"England Angle," John began.

"London 2000s," guessed Lepanto. "But what is '3' ?" Sam suddenly understood.

"I bet it's the third England Angle, London 2000s! Let's go find it on the maps," he added, inspired. They hurried back to the maps and searched through one after the other, frustrated because they could find no system to the City's arrangement.

"Why are they all jumbled together?" Sam complained in frustration.

"The city just grew," muttered John. Lepanto only nodded. "No central planning!" John added. "They just put one thing next to the other without any rhyme or reason." No one wanted to imagine who "they" could be.

"There!" pointed Sam triumphantly. Sure enough, his finger touched "England Angle, London 2000s, 3."

Carefully they traced their way back to the map with the red arrow showing them where they were.

"Phew," Sam said, "that's a long way, even with the way things move when we walk."

"Yes," said Lepanto, eyeing the maps and directories, "Here is everywhere, every year, every day, every moment that has been..." The enormity of the city pressed in on them. "Every life, every death, every moment, every city, endlessly..."

They were staggered.

"Wow," breathed Sam, not for the first time. "No wonder this place goes on and on! So," he added, squaring his shoulders, "it's a good thing everything hurries by when we walk." He laughed: "so let's take it at a run!" Lepanto gave a hearty laugh at his irrepressible courage.

"Run we will!" he said. "By heaven, we will make time fly!" They laughed with him, and as one dashed off.

No sooner did they start running than the streets disappeared behind them so fast they kept their eyes fixed firmly ahead to keep from becoming dizzy. Now and then they had to stop at a key intersection to check their route, then again flew forward so fast the cityscapes blurred behind and ahead from their mad pace. If they had been a moving line on a map, an onlooker would have been astonished at the distance they covered.

Nonetheless their breath began to labor before they reached their destination, and soon despite the way the streets flew by as they ran their progress began to feel painfully slow. They wondered if they had always moved through this blur, and finally slowed to a walk to regain their breath.

The cityscape lurched past them, shuddered, and stopped. All the while the sense of dread grew steadily heavier and moved from their shoulders to their hearts. Once they breathed calmly again they resumed their pace.

When they next paused Sam stumbled into one of the hapless pedestrians frozen in movement, knocking him over. The man fell in the same position in which he stood, like a toy.

"Sorry," muttered Sam, and grasped the man's hand firmly, not really expecting to be able to lift him, but although he was weightless and came up effortlessly Sam almost dropped him as wave of weakness rolled over him. He stepped back, swaying.

Lepanto and John stared at the man who had been gray when he fell but now was a faint pink.

"That's more dangerous than apples and oranges," Lepanto said. "Don't touch anyone again, at least not flesh to flesh." Sam nodded. There was a kiosk in the middle of the intersection, and they slumped down against it to rest, leaving the man frozen on the corner. There was a bus between themselves and the man now, so the policeman with a beet-colored face and enormous purple nose didn't see them as he approached the man with his tinge of pink.

"What's this?" he growled.

They heard his growl in the silence, and stiffened: first Sam, then the others peered under the bus just in time to see the red man reach out and touch the man. Even from there they saw what rough, careworn hands the policeman placed on the man, and how the man's hint of color drained while the policeman reddened.

"Don't do that!" shouted Sam, outraged. He dashed around the bus before John or Lepanto could stop him.

"What have we here?" the policeman said as Sam tried to push him back.

"Leave him alone!" he shouted again.

The man grabbed Sam: a dizziness swept over him, and he fell to his knees. But the policeman gave a cry, turned violently red, flashed, and crumbled into ashes. Lepanto steadied Sam while John poked at the ashes with his foot.

"He got a lot more than he expected," murmured Lepanto, looking at the ashes. A whistle blew, then another, answered by a third. They turned to see three of the misshapen men dressed as policemen running towards them, one with a large purple nose, another with a mane of flaming red hair that stuck out from under his cap, and a third with arms of different length.

"Stop!"

"Violators!"

"Trespassers!" Other whistles answered theirs.

"Follow me!" ordered Lepanto. He trumpeted, then charged directly at the three policemen with Sam and John behind. They burned so brightly in the gray that the three policemen stopped, then jumped out of their way. Sam, Lepanto and John raced on, determined to cover the remaining distance to Madelyn's address at a pace that would leave these far behind.

No sooner did they pass than the policemen followed, steadily falling behind as others joined their ranks. One glance back showed them receding into a distant pack as the cityscape flew past. Even as they became vanishingly small their voices lifted into a faint roar.

Sam wondered how they could shake them entirely before they found Madelyn, but as if he had read his mind, Lepanto now veered off to one side, then to another, trying to lose their pursuers. Yet even almost invisible in the distance they could not make them vanish entirely. It looked like there would be a fight against long odds once they reached Madelyn if they didn't find her quickly and depart even more quickly.

A grim look deepened on John's face echoed, he saw with a quick glance, by Lepanto and Sam. We'll see, John thought, we'll see indeed!

"Soon," Lepanto warned with a short breath, "we're nearly there." Sam stared at the tall buildings that had lifted before them, the river that lay dead under a bridge, and the steepening hills that flashed by as now John took the lead, guiding them. A turn. Three more blocks in a flash. Another turn.

They were near the top of a rise and turned down Hollow Road. The building they sought loomed before them and swayed side to side when they stopped, then settled in place.

"Violators!"

"Trespassers!"

"Stop!" came in faint waves behind them that grew steadily louder. Sam stared at the building.

"Let's go in," was all he said. John nodded and stepped in, but Lepanto was too big for the doorway, and turned to block their pursuers.

"Go on!" he ordered.

Sam and John nodded and ran up the stairway in the central hallway to the second floor. There a long corridor with monotonous doors faced them. On each door a name was stenciled in block letters. They might not have been able to make anything out in the dimness, but their glow filled the hallway with light.

"Like, and unlike," John muttered. "When we were here it wasn't this grim. There weren't this many doors, either," he added. Then Lepanto slithered beside them, as drawn out and supple as a Chinese dragon, filling the corridor.

"It's not where you were, only what someone else made out of it," Lepanto sighed. "Nothing here is what we think."

"Including you," said Sam, taking in the Elephant's bizarre, elongated body.

They heard a clamor outside the building now, and then the sound of many feet stomping up the stairs. For the moment they ignored them, eyeing the names on the doors as they walked or slid down the corridor.

"Hurry," urged Lepanto.

Sam stopped moving, staring at the door to his right.

The others crowded around him. He said nothing. Each read the sign, "Madelyn." Below was a small caption: "Sam's mother." Even as the first mishapen men appeared at the end of the corridor Sam tried to open the door: it was locked.

"Break it in, Lepanto." The clamor died in the corridor and one of the misshapen policemen stepped forward as the Elephant raised his arm.

"Are you so sure you want to do that?" he demanded. Lepanto twisted in a drawn-out, eel-like manner until he faced the policeman. Sam pressed against the wall, just able to glimpse past the transformed Elephant.

"We've come this far and not you or anyone else is going to stop me!" Sam said fiercely past Lepanto's long shoulder. The man kept his distance from Lepanto. He had to shield his eyes from the brightness the three travelers shed in this narrow space.

"Think what might be there," he said. That gave them pause. "Suppose she isn't in—or she is, gray as gray can be. What can you do for her?" A wrench of anxiety gripped John. Indeed, what could they do, he wondered? In their rush to get here no one had thought about what to do with a Madelyn as gray and still as everyone else in this awful place, if found.

The man saw the effect of his words and laughed meanly. Others laughed behind him.

"Whatever we find is what we came for," Sam said, angered by their laughter. "We are going to take her from here just like we got here, despite anything any of you can do! And we'll figure out how to bring her to life like we've figured out everything else!"

Their laughter died. Lepanto twisted around again and slammed a fist against Madelyn's door: it splintered and fell to the floor, revealing a cell-like cubicle with cot, a chair, and a desk. Sitting on the cot, her head in her hands, as if exhausted, or perhaps as though crying quietly, was Madelyn, gray as gray could be, still as all the other gray people had been.

"Mother," sighed Sam.

"Madelyn!" cried John.

"Stop!"

"Violators!"

"Trespassers!" The misshapen men rushed forward, their faces contorted with rage.

XVII

Escape

Lepanto faced the threatening, misshapen policemen, tusks lightning-bright in the dim corridor. The foremost hesitated at their sight, snarling at those behind who pushed them forward. Then Lepanto's trunk curled upward and he trumpeted a challenge that stunned them in that narrow pace, and charged forward.

He impaled the first policeman with a beet-colored face on one tusk as the other sliced through another with a flaming shock of hair. He pounded two more with his fists. Each flashed a brilliant red and crumbled to ashes.

Their attackers turned and pressed back down the corridor with frightened cries.

For a moment no one could move: then with the next red flashes from Lepanto's blows the whole mass gave way, Lepanto sweeping his tusks side to side, gratified by the piles of ashes he left in his wake.

He stopped at the landing as the last of their pursuers fled. Through the door he glimpsed a mob of them gathering, though now they showed no desire to move forward and recoiled in turn as the terrified remnants of the first attackers crashed into them.

Quickly Lepanto turned on himself to face John and Sam, who watched his contortions in this narrow space fascinated, brushed them aside, and reached into Madelyn's little room with an ever-extending trunk and lifted her out, careful to touch only her clothes as he did so.

He lowered her at their feet: she didn't change her seated position as she lay on the ground, even as the brilliant bands of color that

glowed where the Elephant had touched her clothes faded as they watched.

"There are too many out front," the Elephant warned, "we have to look for another way out. You carry her," he said to John, "but only touch her clothes until we think of what to do!"

John nodded and carefully lifted Madelyn, avoiding any contact with her flesh. He was shocked at how little she weighed, hardly heavier than a feather. Small roses glowed into life on her blouse, and a blue stain spread from his fingers across her skirt to eliminate its gray.

He was paralyzed with astonishment at actually having her in his arms. So many thoughts, images, and feelings rushed through him that he forgot to breathe. He had heard that people at the moment of death or facing great danger saw their entire life flash before their eyes, and it was like that now with Madelyn in his arms. The good and the bad, his love and his failures with everything in between ran through his mind.

"Dad," Sam breathed, his eyes aglow. John took a sudden

gasp of air.

"Be careful," Lepanto murmured. John nodded.

"Lead away," he said.

"That way," Sam pointed down the hall, hardly able himself to take in his mother in his father's arms, however gray, as well as the earlier spectacle of Lepanto driving their enemies from the corridor with brilliant flashes that left only piles of ash.

Lepanto nodded and followed Sam and John with his light burden to the end of the hallway. "Emergency Exit" read a neat sign in block letters, with an arrow pointing down. Sam stepped through the door onto the landing and stopped in surprise.

"What's wrong?" asked John.

"Look." First John, then Lepanto craned past Sam and saw stairs that circled downward as far as the eye could see. Opposite them was a neat sign on the wall, "You Are Forbidden To Leave The Place Of Abandonment."

John all but growled in response. They looked back down the hall towards the front where they heard a renewed clamor. They eyed the landing again: they could see it ended far above, but the idea of being trapped on the roof held no appeal for any of them.

"We have to go down," Sam said.

"Down to where?" muttered John.

"Into the heart of things, or under it," said Lepanto.

At least the landing was wider than the hall, and the stairwell as well: Lepanto looked more like himself as they started to make their way down, Sam leading. The clamor behind grew as the misshapen policemen found the corridor abandoned.

"Quickly," said Lepanto, and took the lead, his still elongated body filling the stairwell as he went by Sam with a hair's breadth to spare. His body stretched around several turns down at once even in this wider space. Sam and John followed happy to hear the clamor above reach a climax of frustration, then fade.

Down they raced.

Sam lost count of the landings as he listened for any renewed pursuit. He searched for signs of enemies behind each landing's door. At first he laughed, taking the stairs two and three and more at a time, swinging around the turnings. Once he slid down the banister until he bumped into Lepanto, who looked back with an amused gleam in his eyes. Then the Elephant picked up the pace of his slither as a challenge to the delighted Sam and breathless John with his light burden.

But as the landings passed one after another their descent lost its humor. Sam went from leaping and sliding to forcing himself to keep up with Lepanto. His breath came harder, and turned ragged, and his thighs began to tremble.

John simply matched their pace as he anxiously held Madelyn, her blouse now a blaze of color, her skirt a bright blue, but her flesh still deathly gray.

John was in a daze, unaware of the effort it took to keep up with the others. As her clothes took on color Madelyn seemed a little heavier in his arms, then heavier still as his breath came harder, too. Light as she was, distracted as he was to have her in his arms, his breathing at last turned labored, then ragged, and he grew aware of his legs' tremble from their never-ending descent.

"I will do this forever if I have to," he muttered to himself. "Now I have you again in my arms I will never let go," he added even as her grayness and lightness ate at his heart.

Only their own glow lit the way in their descent. Once they stopped to catch their breath and let their trembling muscles still. They considered the doorway on the landing where they rested, wondering what it could lead to after all this time. Sam opened it a crack.

A long corridor with neatly labeled doors marched into the distance, no different from the one on which they had found Madelyn. There seemed little sense going there. Worse, they could hear a faint clamor somewhere down that corridor. They shut the door, cutting off the sound.

Sam was appalled at how many rooms of gray people there must be in this one building. John and Lepanto looked at each other, as shocked. "It's like what we saw was only the tip of an iceberg," Sam added. "Do you think that's what all the buildings here are like?"

John shook his head, and Lepanto sighed at the thought the vast city they had seen was the merest tip of all there was. Everyone was here, from all times, in every condition. None of them could imagine how many that could be, but its endlessness filled them with horror.

Wordlessly they drew deep breaths and resumed their descent.

Sam felt they had gone down a mile, maybe many miles. He lost track of how many times they had to pause and wait for muscles to recover and breath to grow smooth before their next descent. He started to wonder how much more of this he could take as he turned around one railing after another.

He lost count.

He lost his sense of time.

He lost every sense but descent.

He was an automaton going down, turn, down, turn, down, turn, down, rarely rest, turn, down—and slammed into Lepanto.

The Elephant had stopped abruptly. A moment later John ran into them both and recoiled, barely keeping his balance and grip on Madelyn. Sam shook his head to clear it.

"Bottom," Lepanto panted.

They looked at each other, then at the door facing Lepanto.

"Exit If You Dare" was printed neatly across its top in

faded letters.

Carefully Lepanto tried to open it, expecting to see yet another corridor with labeled doors receding into the distance. But the knob refused to move, even when Lepanto grunted with effort.

He fumbled then in his vest pockets for what seemed endless minutes to Sam before finally pulling out a set of master keys. Each in turn failed to unlock the door. Further fumbling in his vest pockets produced a picklock set which, however, broke off in the lock.

"You wretched door!" he trumpeted loudly so that Sam had to cover his ears while John winced: then: "Stand back!"

They backed away from him as he backed up, then flung his full weight against the door. There was a momentary grinding, and Sam feared it would hold: then the door burst forward and fell with an echoing clang. He and John stared past Lepanto at the wide tunnel revealed.

Lepanto squeezed through the door, and sighed with relief as he stepped into the tunnel, assuming even more of his natural shape.

"Why did it have to be an elephant hanging in your room," he muttered, more to himself than to Sam. "Why not a lion, or tiger, or a bear, or some slender sylphlike thing of great beauty and greater strength, or a wizard with a staff to lean on and only a pointy hat to maneuver in tight places?"

Sam had caught his breath by now, and for a moment felt he should apologize, then laughed at the sheer absurdity of Lepanto's complaint. A pointy-hatted wizard indeed!

"Imagine," Sam said, "if it had been a whale!" Lepanto shook with laughter.

"Very well," he chuckled at last, as he half-heartedly tried to put the door back in place, "very well! We are what we are if just imagined that way! Let us go on."

They looked at John with his burden in her colorful clothes. John nodded at Lepanto's look, and, tired as he felt, still emotionally overwhelmed, resolutely followed the others through the tunnel. Gradually the concrete floor gave way to rougher hewn stone, as did the walls and ceiling.

"Do you think we're out of the city?" asked Sam.

"How fast do you think we're going?" added John.

But Lepanto shook his head: it was impossible to judge with only their light and the sameness of the walls. Soon all three felt they were being watched, though there was no sign of pursuit. They scanned their surroundings suspiciously as they moved, but the light they cast only went so far. Then Lepanto stopped.

"Look."

There, within a small niche in the wall, a small Watcher twisted in an attempt to avoid their light.

"You won't get far," sounded in their minds, clouded with pain.

"I've already come further than you know!" said Sam. "You see things and don't know anything!"

"Farther," muttered John, not "further."

They laughed and moved on, feeling a small spike of malice from the Watcher, occasionally passing others, each with the same result. More than once smaller tunnels joined theirs which they ignored, pushing straight ahead along what was clearly the major route.

They trusted to that as blindly as they had trusted to the wind when they came. They remembered what was written on the doorway to the stairwell: they had exited, and they certainly dared!

"Who can they be watching for?" Sam asked. "None of those gray people could come here—and who would come in here by choice?"

Lepanto gave him a look but said nothing. It was enough they were seen, he thought.

After another long passage of time the tunnels entering theirs diminished, then stopped. The Watchers grew fewer in number, and disappeared with their spikes of malice. The tunnel became cave-like, larger, but slippery as well, and tilted down even as it broadened.

In time Lepanto was able to resume his normal shape and flexed his arms with a sigh of relief, Sam one moment next to John to stare at Madelyn, then beside the Elephant looking where his brilliant glow lit way ahead. At times he ran there, a small beacon of light in the gloom.

At last Lepanto called a halt. Carefully John laid his burden aside, and slid to the ground with a groan. Madelyn was light, yet she was draining. He knew from Sam's experience with the fruit that even her clothes were draining his energy. What would happen if he touched her, if he took her hand firmly in his?

He pushed the thought aside, even as Lepanto watched him regain his own brightness as he rested. Then he looked at Madelyn, and Sam saw the wrinkles pile up on his great forehead, for Sam too saw how her clothes faded when no longer in contact with his father. No one said anything for a long time.

"Where is this leading?" John asked at last.

"I have no idea," answered the Elephant. "We still cast light which means we are still near Dread City. All we can do is go forward." He fumbled in his vest, pulling out one object after another, including the broken Flying Trapeze. But there was nothing to eat. Last he pulled out the globe, holding it thoughtfully in his hand before putting it back and picking up the other objects.

"We need to find water soon," Sam said, realizing how parched his throat felt the moment he spoke his need. John nodded with a gulp, while a wave of such thirst rolled over Lepanto he stood as though stunned by a blow. He was, after all, a large elephant, with an elephant's thirst!

Lepanto looked at the last objects in his hand: three small blue buttons.

"Here." He gave one each to John and Sam, and popped the last into his mouth. They imitated him, and after a moment their mouths dampened as their bodies tried to dissolve the buttons with a reluctant flow of saliva.

"It will help for now. And now, up. I'm sure they are behind us somewhere, thanks to the Watchers."

John stood and carefully lifted the faded Madelyn, then followed after the others, turning the button over in his mouth to tease out more moisture.

Lepanto set a demanding pace despite the way the cave floor roughened. Soon they could no longer walk around outcrops and boulders that had fallen from the ceiling but had to sidle carefully, or clamber over stones. The air was still, the footing slicker, yet no rivulets broke through the walls to relieve their thirst.

After several more hours passed not even the blue buttons kept their mouths moist. Finally John staggered to a halt with a low moan that stopped the others, and set his burden down. Madelyn's bright clothes began to fade and John's brightness to strengthen.

"How much farther can this cave go?" John muttered in frustration to no one in particular. Lepanto shook his head. He let the others rest while he explored ahead. Not far from where they stopped the cave changed, opening out on either side and arching upwards. Lepanto went on until he could no longer see the walls on either side or the cavern's roof overhead, then retraced his steps.

"The cave opens up into some great cavern just ahead. No water, though. Can you take her for now?" he asked Sam, nodding at Madelyn. John made no protest. After a moment's hesitation, Sam carefully lifted Madelyn, surprised in turn at how little she weighed, and confronted Lepanto, a determined look on his face.

"What are you waiting for?" he demanded.

Lepanto smiled, and John clambered to his feet shaking his head. They entered the cavern, surprised at the extent they sensed open around and above them.

But how could they keep their bearings to go straight? They searched the darkness for any sign until they made out a narrow trail ahead. Debris almost obscured it, but with their combined light they could just make it out. They looked at each other, recognizing how little used the path was, and set out.

The minutes stretched again into hours as they followed it until Sam began to think there was no end in turn to this cavern. He almost missed the endless stairwell down and the moments he still had had the energy to slide down a length of banister. His feet grew heavy and muscles already strained from those stairs went from a trembling ache into a heaviness that turned leaden.

His thirst turned fiery.

But he knew it wasn't just the strain of ever thirstier walking that wore on him. For in his arms Madelyn's clothes blazed with color and light, and he realized as John had that his own strength drained into these. He said nothing though as John and Lepanto glanced at how her clothes gleamed in Sam's arms.

John found the going hard even without the drain of Madelyn, and his sense of time grew amorphous. Had they been walking only a few hours? Or had it been for days? Had he been walking in darkness all his life and only now wakened to discover that dismal fact?

Lepanto fought his own silent battle, not tired, but ever thirstier.... He was relieved Sam hadn't imagined him as a whale! He laughed.

"What's so funny?" Sam forced out.

"Imagine," he explained as John and Sam looked at him, "if I had been a whale, like the time you teased me before: I'd be a fish out of water here!"

The others laughed then, too, and for a time the going was easier.

But then Lepanto imagined himself as a whale, immersed in water, water water. He thrust that thought away, and imagined himself instead as some rare desert creature, content to let months pass without a drink. Months, he thought, months without water?

"Oh no," he muttered.

"Did you say something?" rasped Sam.

"Nothing, months, nothing."

They trudged on.

The silence began to weigh on Lepanto's spirits too, and he worried for his companions. The button still worked in his mouth, but now as more of a tease than not, and he spat it out. He tried to whistle, and fought through his lips' dry stiffness until a sound came out. Then he searched for a tune, but his head was dull and nothing came.

"Whistle anything," Sam breathed behind him. "Whistle 'Row, Row Your Boat.' I don't care, but stop whistling nothing!"

Lepanto nodded. After a few false starts he managed "Row, Row Your Boat." That did liven the darkness and they stepped more lightly, but as the tune faded the thought of water turned into a river in all their thoughts. Sam remembered an old show tune about the Mississippi, how "Ol' Man River" just kept rolling on.

"Sing 'Ol' Man River!'" he blurted. Lepanto made a hoarse sound, then another, and then began to grate out the tune, abandoning the attempt to whistle. His voice strengthened and the words came more easily; soon he swept them all up in the river of his voice booming out the Great River Mississippi whose water water water rolled endlessly on.

But when Lepanto's voice faded on the last words he could sing no more. Now the silence settled on them heavily, broken only by the sound of their steps and their gasps.

They trudged on, aware in the silence how much greater was their sense of dread and how their legs were now heavy stones they struggled to lift with each step. Soon they leaned forward to move at all, yanking each leg forward in turn as if trying to pull free from knee-high mud.

Sam stopped first. He put his mother down and sank beside her with a groan. John sat by him, biting off his own groan. Lepanto paced on, realized he was alone, and turned back. Madelyn's clothes glowed between the three as though on fire, only slowly fading from Sam's touch. He didn't have the energy for even a whispered "wow."

"This is—" Sam finally breathed, "I don't know. The worst."

"As bad as the Watchers," asked John, "after we crashed?"

"Or the Sea of Faces?" asked Lepanto. They worried at Sam's heavy tone: they hadn't heard that from him before in all they had gone through, not even on the Bench of Forgetting.

Sam would have wiped away a tear if he had any to cry. He had carried Madelyn as his own fire drained into her clothes and seeped from those into her, keeping up with the others all this time until too tired to taunt them to carry on or to drive himself another step.

"We have your mother now, at least: think of that!" Lepanto said to encourage him.

Sam nodded: that at least was true, but to what point, he felt: they were all going to end up like her. He was too downhearted to say anything. They felt the weight of his silence. They stared at Madelyn. Even as her clothes faded she stared sightlessly, lost within a frozen thought.

Then she sighed, and her eyes shut.

They sprang to their feet, electrified. Lepanto knelt beside her.

"Sleep," Lepanto breathed, and brushed a hand over her. Her body relaxed and curled into itself naturally on the ground. They looked at Lepanto.

"How did you do that?" demanded Sam.

"I did very little," he answered; "it was mostly you." Sam's mind raced.

"But you made her move!" is what he came out with. None of the gray people had done that for himself or John. "Who are you, really?"

"I am what you drew," Lepanto reminded him.

"Where is the Book?" he demanded, as if the Elephant must know.

"Following your lives I'm sure," said Lepanto.

"Who are you?" Sam demanded again. "I drew you, that's true. So answer me!" Lepanto frowned in thought.

"I really don't know more than what I've already told you about myself. But..." He broke off.

"Go on!" demanded Sam.

"It's as much a sense as sure knowledge," Lepanto sighed, and held up a hand to stop Sam's protest. "But I feel I come from a land—a land that is undivided. The unlost unity. Someplace where the heart has wisdom, and the mind, heart.

"Yes, I know," he said in reply to their looks. "That sounds like poetry. Not something definite. Like somewhere that could only exist in a dream. Well then, that is the dream where you found me, Sam. You drew that dream! Just like being the wisest of Elephants with a fondness for dancing! Though," he added, "I don't feel like dancing just now."

With that they relapsed into silence.

He's right, Sam thought, I do have my mother. She moved!

Maybe from me! He stared at her. Even now her skirt and blouse still glowed with color, if not as strongly.

He stared around them, straining to see into the distance from the boulder they rested against, straining to hear any sound of pursuit. He would almost welcome that—it would mean they were going in the right direction and needed to be stopped. He heard nothing.

Then, very faintly, he heard a drip.

"Listen!" he did his best to shout. All three strained to hear anything in the darkness around them: silence.

Faintly, there was another drip.

"There," gestured Lepanto. He walked in the direction of the drip, waiting a moment for it to repeat itself.

"There..."

The drip was louder....

Lepanto stepped into a shallow pool near another pile of boulders. His glow lit the pool and gave its water a sheen. Even as he looked another drop fell, twinkling in his light, and splashed into the pool, making its glow quiver.

He lowered his trunk and drank deeply, ignoring the bitter, mineral and metallic taste. Water filled his trunk, his mouth, his throat, his whole being as he drank. At length he paused with a happy moan, the pool noticeably smaller. He fumbled in his pockets until he found a bucket, filled it, and made his way back to the others. Sam, then John drank his fill, each ignoring the bitter taste, at last sitting back with happy sighs.

Then Sam dipped his fingers into the water at the bottom of the bucket and wiped them over Madelyn's lips. Fascinated they watched her lips part and a few drops go within. Sam dripped more until it streamed from her mouth.

"Swallow," he begged, then did what he had been about to

259

do before they heard the drip in the distance, and laid his hands on either side of her head. He reeled dizzily—and Madelyn convulsively swallowed. Then he jerked his hands back, breathing hard. Madelyn lay motionless.

"Careful," was all Lepanto said. Sam stood again.

"Refill the bucket and let's go," he said. "She moved. There's water. We can't be in Dread City anymore."

The others looked at him, surprised as much by his renewed spirit as his words which were debatable, given how greatly they still glowed. But as Lepanto took in that glow he realized it had lessened, though whether from strain or distance from Dread City he could not tell.

He went back to the pool and refilled the bucket in silence and they set off again, hope growing in their hearts as they pondered the change in Madelyn.

But something was wrong. Each in turn felt that and after another step or two, stopped. They looked about them, but little had changed. Then they heard far behind them the ghost of a clamor of voices.

"They've found us," John said flatly. Sam shook his head. Lepanto's ears waved as he stared back.

"YOU CANNOT ESCAPE!" sounded in their minds so powerfully they staggered as though struck. The ghostly sound resolved into faint but distinct roars

"They're coming fast," warned Lepanto.

They turned and fled.

XVIII

The Battle Of Lepanto

B ut Lepanto didn't move. John and Sam stopped. The Elephant
eyed them instead, then fell to all fours.

"Get on."

They stared. Riding Lepanto had never crossed their minds. The
idea was—absurd thought first Sam, then John.

"YOU CANNOT ESCAPE!" sounded powerfully in their
minds again. Lepanto laughed.

"This is fastest," was all he said, then swung Sam with his trunk
onto his back, then Madelyn, whose clothes flared at his touch as
though set on fire, then John.

"Hold on," he warned.

Sam grabbed a fold of his jacket in one hand, and held feather-
light Madelyn in the other. John kept his eye on both as Lepanto set
off.

Riding an Elephant at his swiftest speed, even a magic Elephant,
wasn't much fun. The hard ground jolted them cruelly with every
step, while Lepanto's side-to-side sway threatened to throw them
off mid-bounce. Sam gripped Lepanto's jacket grimly as he held his
mother. It was only a little easier for John with both hands.

"STOP!" said a deep, distant voice. The roar of their pursuers
was louder, and echoed in the great vault. Lepanto moved faster. They
jolted and swayed as though back on their yacht in steep, choppy water.

"YOU CANNOT ESCAPE!" came the evil thought again.

"STOP!" bellowed the great voice.

"STOP! STOP! STOP!" echoed loudly in the cavern.

"How can they catch up so fast?" Sam shouted at Lepanto: in response the Elephant went faster. But when Sam looked to either side in the gloom for an escape route, he saw that Lepanto might be jolting ahead yet the landscape went by as though he crept.

He was mystified. Then Lepanto slowed for a moment before again surging forward, and Sam realized the ground went faster at the Elephant's slower pace…. If he went fast enough Lepanto would find himself running in place.

"Slow down!" warned Sam, then: "look at the ground!" Lepanto didn't understand at first. "It's the opposite of coming in," he shouted, "when everything raced by faster whenever we speeded up! Just walk!"

Lepanto slowed and then quickened, and saw what Sam meant. He slowed to a walk. Even at a normal pace the landscape refused to move by as it should although it went by faster than when he ran. They wondered how long that had been the case: probably from the start, Sam thought. No wonder their pursuers seemed to gain so quickly!

"Now what?" asked John, worried.

"Get the globe from my vest!" the Elephant ordered.

"In which pocket?" Sam asked.

"Always the one nearest!" he answered testily. "Hurry, they'll soon be here. Let your father hold Madelyn."

John took Madelyn from him. Carefully Sam leaned over, pulling up Lepanto's jacket and searching in the nearest vest pocket. As his hand slid in he wondered how he was going to hold the globe one-handed, but he lifted it out easily.

"First John," ordered Lepanto.

"YOU ARE FINISHED!" echoed and re-echoed in their minds.

"STOP!" There was no doubting the closing power of that shout.

John took the globe as Sam held Madelyn. He searched its depths for the light he knew was there. After a moment a bright curlicue twisted in its depths. He concentrated on that swirl of light until it broadened and drew closer, burning in the globe as brightly as Sam had ever been able to make it glow in the past. The dimness around them receded.

"Excellent," breathed Lepanto, "now Sam."

"STOP!" roared a loud, near voice. This time they heard what could only be the clash of great jaws as well.

"YOU CANNOT ESCAPE!" echoed deafeningly in their minds.

Sam held the bright globe in his hands. He remembered how Lepanto had made it shine.

"Glow," he cried, staring into it. For a moment it flickered, then flared brilliantly. "Glow like the sun!" he shouted with delight, and the globe's brilliance made him turn away.

"Splendid!" exclaimed Lepanto. He began to move again, and picked up his pace despite Sam's warning shout—for now the landscape moved by swiftly.

Cries of anger came from behind them, but now came no closer. So they fled across a cavern laid bare by the light Sam held over their heads, a bleak, rubble-strewn expanse so wide they couldn't see the far walls, while on its distant roof faint shadows leaped.

Now Lepanto ran effortlessly mile after mile while Sam's arms tired from holding the globe aloft even as he switched it from one hand to another. They twisted and turned as Lepanto avoided stones fallen from above into the faint path.

Pools of the bitter water like the one they drank from earlier were rare. Their urgent pace left no time to pause but at least kept their pursuers at bay, still unseen, although Lepanto couldn't go fast

enough to lose them.

Only once, chest heaving, did Lepanto pause by a bitter pool and suck at it in great gulps while they used their hands to take water from the bucket they had filled earlier. Its bitterness almost made them gag, but they got it down.

Then Sam poured a handful into Madelyn's mouth and watched fascinated, with John, as she drank it down when he briefly held her face in his hands, although he reeled from the drain of even that quick touch.

Lepanto refilled their bucket, sprayed them with his last gulp from the now dry pool, and resumed his grueling pace. But they could tell their pursuers had gained on them while they drank, if still invisible in the gloom beyond the light cast by the globe.

Time began to do odd things to their minds….

One moment they knew they swayed and jolted forward forever.

The next they saw from the sameness around them that they had only moved side to side and not forward at all.

Another moment was filled only with painful jolts.

All the while the globe grew heavier in Sam's hands until he could hardly lift it up.

At length two things happened. First, the globe began to fade with Sam, and although he soon had it blazing again, he sweated from the effort and with both arms numb he could only cradle the globe in his lap.

Second, even Lepanto began to weaken. No one can go on forever without rest, not even a magic Elephant who liked to dance and was very wise and had surprising resources in his countless vest pockets, however elegantly dressed. Even so Lepanto flogged himself on long after his pace became a labor, and then that labor an agony of gasped breaths and strained muscles.

He ran in a deep, sucking mud that clung to his legs that even the brilliance raining on them from the globe held by Sam no longer helped.

He ran on smooth granite that redoubled the agony of his jolts for his riders and sent sharp pains up his legs to his shoulders and hips.

He ran in breathless circles to avoid obstacles everywhere in the path....

His eyes misted with exhaustion, and that mist threatened to turn into a hard wall....

Yet even as the Elephant's pace slowed they sensed a change in the cavern: it started to narrow at last. That gave Lepanto the energy for a last burst that had the others hanging on for dear life as he jolted across the cavern floor. But that surge too faded and at last he could not force himself farther.

He stopped, head hanging, his chest a bellows of searing breaths.

"YOU CANNOT ESCAPE!"

"STOP!"

Jaws snapped with an echoing click. Still they saw nothing

beyond the glow of the globe, but knew that would not be so much longer.

"Oh Lepanto," sighed Sam who clambered down Lepanto's heaving side, holding onto his suit and pockets for handholds, then trying to embrace his great head.

"Here," John said, and carefully handed down Madelyn. "We've come so far," he said bitterly as he clambered down in turn as the Elephant's sides heaved, "to have to stop now."

Lepanto said nothing.

John sighed. "We could sure use the Book now." But that mysterious item was nowhere to be seen. Lepanto nodded, still silent as his chest bellowed, only pointing as he stood up.

They turned to see what he pointed at, and after a puzzled moment realized they could see the far wall of the cavern. It had come to an end. Lepanto shook his head, still breathless, and pointed again. They strained to see what he was pointing at, and finally Sam, with his sharp eyesight, saw a small, dark spot at the wall's base.

"Is that what I think it is?" he asked, and pointed it out for his father, who after a moment saw the dark spot too. "Is it the way out?" Sam demanded of Lepanto. Lepanto nodded.

"It is!" Sam shouted with glee: "it's the way out!" The globe, still in his hand, burned more brightly again.

Lepanto didn't share Sam's glee. He felt a moment of surprise, so certain was he a moment ago that they would all make it, only now realizing he was not meant to. Not if the others were to get away. First he, then the others turned to face their pursuers.

Three armies leapt over the boulder-strewn floor of the cavern towards them, the first made up of the policemen from Dread City with flaming red hair sticking out from under their caps, the second of policemen with beet-colored faces and enormous, purple noses, the third with policemen with arms of different lengths.

But they were nothing to their three leaders.

On one side was a great Watcher, even now trying to fill their minds with its sense of malice and triumph.

On the other half-strode, half-slithered the green sea-beast clashing its too-long jaws, revealed by the globe's light to be half dragon, half nightmare serpent with wings too small for flight.

In the middle strode a Mr. Nicholas as tall as the green beast, towering over his armies of misshapen men.

"That's far enough," warned Lepanto, speaking at last.

Mr. Nicholas laughed, but stopped while still a good distance away. He eyed Lepanto with a certain caution.

"I said we would meet again," sounded in their minds as the green monster ground his teeth. "I win our contest."

"We came, when we couldn't," Sam said fiercely, "and we are leaving the same way!"

"Not yet." The beast smiled in anticipation. Sam did not flinch.

"I don't know how," he said honestly, "but you won't win." The beast made an odd, choking sound they realized after a moment was laughter.

"YOU CANNOT ESCAPE!" The Watcher focused entirely on John. He groaned. "YOU ALWAYS KNEW YOU WOULD FAIL!" John ground his teeth. "BRING HER TO ME!" John took a stiff step forward.

"Dad!" shouted Sam, and lunged towards him, but Lepanto held him back.

"Let him do this," he said. Sam hesitated, looked into Lepanto's curious brown and amber eyes, and slowly relaxed, the thought flashing across his mind that those eyes must see something in his father that hadn't been there before.

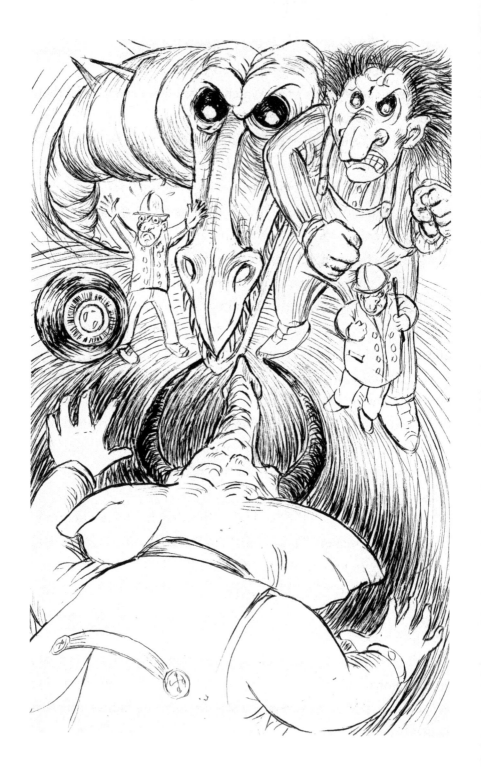

John looked sorrowfully at his burden. How lovely she was, even gray. How badly life has treated me, he added to himself.

"YESSS…" echoed in his mind. "How you betrayed her! How you betrayed yourself! How you betrayed Sam!" With each lacerating thought John took another step away from Sam and Lepanto.

"YESSS… You deserve nothing. Nothing! Only to join her, to become gray and lifeless as her, forever close yet more distant than the stars are from each other. NOW, GIVE HER TO ME!"

John took another reluctant step forward, groaned, and stopped.

"What can you give her?" he breathed. Again Lepanto had to restrain Sam with a nod of his head.

"PEACE: WHAT CAN YOU OFFER BETTER? YOU DROVE HER AWAY BEFORE! YOU—LET—HER—GO!"

John gazed into Madelyn's face, and stepped back. That Watcher's reproaches were true. Then. He was no longer the same man.

"I know," he sighed. "But I won't now." He stared defiantly at the Watcher, and the beast, and Mr. Nicholas. "Not now," he repeated, taking another step back. "I can give something even greater than peace."

"WHAT IS THAT?" filled his mind

"I can give her love." He stood again beside Sam and Lepanto who each gave him an affirmative nod.

"LOVE!" the armies echoed.

The Watcher spun in merriment. "YOU! THE BETRAYER! HAHAHAHA—!" But he broke off as Sam shouted,

"We win again!"

"I know you now," added John. "You give nothing. You just take. But we," and his glance included his companions, "can give."

"No one leaves here!" Mr. Nicholas said, furious. All this time Lepanto had stayed still, but now he laughed.

"Are you so sure? We came, when we couldn't. We found Madelyn, though told we wouldn't. And we are leaving, although we were told that was impossible, too. Sam has been right all along. You have been wrong."

And he laughed again, merrily.

"Who are you to question me?" Mr. Nicholas thundered. "You are smaller than my foot!" The armies of Dread City laughed. The beast ground its teeth. The Watcher spun again. A few stones fell from the distant roof with a crash.

"You are mistaken," replied Lepanto, who stepped in front of John and Sam and Madelyn. They stepped back from Lepanto, startled.

"You hardly rise to my knee!" roared Mr. Nicholas. But he was quite wrong, Sam saw, astonished: Lepanto clearly rose to his waist.

Doubt shone in Mr. Nicholas' eyes. The beast was taken aback. The Watcher rolled backwards. The armies of misshapen men grew silent.

Lepanto bent down, took the globe from Sam, and faced Mr. Nicholas as he looked into the globe, then flung it soaring towards the roof; there it hung large as a harvest moon, shining with a brilliance that was not so much hard to look at as hard to escape.

The misshapen armies groaned—in that light they looked gray. The green beast lost his brilliance and became a deep, dun green barely a step from the black of shadow. The pain from the Watcher filled their minds as it spun in that light, unable to escape, and burst abruptly into a rain of translucent fragments.

"We are evenly matched," Lepanto rumbled, standing even with Mr. Nicholas.

Sam and John would have been amazed at Lepanto's transformation if their attention was not riveted on Mr. Nicholas, for

Lepanto's globe revealed his true nature.

His clothes were worn shreds baring much of his body, now a dark red, now a near-burnt-black body that had gone through some unimaginable torture. His flesh had melted and frozen as though he had been through the "FLESH TO STONE" oven many times without turning to stone, enduring only torment instead, and in no uniform way, for sharp shapes jostled with flowing sags.

It was hard for John and Sam to say what they were looking at unless they kept the whole in focus. The damage was greatest in Mr. Nicholas' face where his features had melted and frozen, melted and refrozen unevenly, at once ludicrous, hideous, and tragic.

"I could use a bit of a dance," Lepanto rumbled, shifting his weight but not lifting his feet for fear of bringing down the cavern's roof. "A song would do," he said to Sam. "Sing 'Blue Suede Shoes'."

John laughed at the absurd request, but Sam shook his head. He didn't know that song.

"Ah well, hmm, then 'Lucy In The Sky With Diamonds'?" Again Sam shook his head. "Well now," Lepanto rumbled, ignoring the renewed roar from the armies behind Mr. Nicholas, and the beast's clashing jaws, "a Christmas carol. Something simple."

"I'll have her," grated Mr. Nicholas, "or else—"

"Silent Night," Lepanto rumbled, ignoring him. Sam looked doubtful: a song now? Really? But Lepanto's certainty stilled his doubt, and he nodded: he knew that song at least, and took a breath.

His voice quavered at first but gathered strength as he sang in a boy's pure soprano. Mr. Nicholas forgot what it was he was going to say as that pure sound filled the cavern: the beast's head sank slowly, and silence spread from the nearest ranks of the armies of dull, gray men to the farthest. Sam's purity of tone made John's heart ache, too.

No one knew how long it was since Mr. Nicholas or his minions had heard such a sound or seen such innocence, but while that sound endured they could not move. Sam thought he must stop after the first verse, but the words for the next formed in his mind as he needed them. He glanced at Lepanto, certain he was feeding them to him, and went on.

When he finished the last verse all was still in the great cavern. Not far from them Sam saw there was one of the bitter pools of water. A single drop splashed into it from the cavern's roof, its sound alone in the stillness of that somber place.

"Now," sounded clearly in Sam's mind, "take Madelyn, and go into the tunnel!"

It was Lepanto. Rebellion flared in him: he was not about to leave the Elephant alone. "Go," rang clearly in his mind, and then, softer, "I must stay. Don't worry. I can take care of myself. As for Madelyn—what you desire you must give," Sam heard, obscurely.

Now, in John's mind as well and with a force that compelled obedience, Lepanto ordered: "RUN!"

XIX

The Long Journey To—

"**N**OOO!**"** Mr. Nicholas shouted and the beast's jaws snapped together as Sam and John with Madelyn in his arms broke the spell as they turned and fled without a backward glance towards the tunnel, driven by Lepanto's "RUN!"

Only as the tunnel closed around him did Sam risk a quick backward glance.

He saw Mr. Nicholas raising his arms to strike Lepanto as the Elephant hurled himself forward with a resounding, trumpeted cry, his appearance more a scintillation of light than the familiar figure of their adventures.

The brilliance of his collision with the ruined figure of Mr. Nicholas was blinding. The beast bit itself in agony, and the gray, misshapen armies flashed like a string of firecrackers set off that left nothing but ashes behind.

"RUN!" now rang out again commandingly.

Sam flew after his father deeper into the tunnel. He was blinded by Lepanto's collision with Mr. Nicholas and bounced from the walls and stumbled over the floor's roughness, that "RUN!" compelling he and John onward with Madelyn in his arms.

Darkness and distance swallowed the sounds of battle as they ran deeper into the tunnel whose floor bore upwards gradually and whose walls slowly narrowed, that "RUN!" a whip across their shoulders, a wind at their backs, a terror in their hearts.

They ran on after their legs rediscovered their weight and

turned leaden, a leadenness they ignored, their hunger and thirst and exhaustion forgotten too as that "RUN!" drove them on. They ran even when their speed was no more than a jog, then no more than a walk which in turn became a desperate weaving forward as they pivoted on one foot to drag the other ahead.

At last John stopped, gasping, and let Madelyn slide to the ground. Sam pivoted one more step and froze into place. Then he and John collapsed in slow motion. Their harsh breathing alone broke the silence.

They were alone somewhere in the heart of the world.

"Lepanto," Sam gasped, now able to feel the grief that command to run had overwhelmed. What had happened to him? Who knew how many other armies Mr. Nicholas could still summon to the field? What would happen if the beast turned from itself to Lepanto, too? "Lepanto!" he repeated.

"Knew—what—he—was—doing!" John gasped. That stopped Sam.

"But—alone—."

"Whoever—whatever—it was you drew—back then, Sam—has more tricks in his pockets—…" John gasped to a stop. Sam understood. He nodded. Somehow the Elephant would manage. There was none of the weight in his heart he was sure he would feel if Lepanto had fallen. He said so in a more normal voice. John nodded in the dimness.

His last view of Lepanto filled Sam's mind again, the glittering form barely guessed through the light, a form itself of light unfolding and spreading within light, the fearless charge.

"Who is he?"

John shook his head. They sat in silence, straining to hear sounds of battle or pursuit. But there was neither. His father looked long and hard at Sam, remembering how his voice had reached out with its purity and frozen their enemies in the cavern.

"Lepanto is something—someone—in you," he said at last. "Maybe in me, once, too, and maybe a little bit again." Unexpectedly, he gave what sounded like a laugh. But Sam saw nothing funny in their situation.

"Sam, Sam," sighed John at Sam's look. "Lepanto, if we know anything at all, really is someone who dances in the face of danger." They both remembered his dance in the Sea of Faces.

"Not always at the best times," muttered Sam.

"No."

"No."

Slowly their breathing became normal. Still there was no sound of pursuit.

"I do think we're getting away," Sam offered at last.

"Things do seem a little more normal," John replied. Then he looked at the dark tunnel, at Madelyn, at Sam, at the way the two of them still glowed. "Normal!" he snorted. "Normal!" and laughed.

"What's so funny, Dad?" asked Sam. That provoked more laughter from John: Sam shook his head, then laughed himself. Then it was all too funny and he laughed hard. When he was done he felt better. John shook his head, and was about to get up when a sound stopped him.

"What was that?" He looked back down the tunnel, straining to hear signs of pursuit.

"Not there," Sam said. He pointed at Madelyn. The silence hummed in their ears. Then Madelyn moaned. They knelt beside her but as the minutes stretched out she made no further sound or movement. But they both felt a new charge of energy and hope that made them forget their weariness.

John lifted Madelyn and with one will they hurried along the cave determined to put even more distance between themselves and any pursuers. They didn't speak, but hope flooded their hearts with a growing certainty that the farther they got from Dread City the more normal Madelyn would become. But John remembered, troubled, how at home she had faded.

In the dim light they still cast time seemed a moment forever drawn out, then moments that flew past one another like water over rapids. As one sense of time alternated with another their difference blurred, and when Sam tried to see if they were going faster than their steps, or slower, he couldn't tell.

On they walked, Madelyn's one moan now driving them as before Lepanto's "Run" had.

There was little change in the tunnel: the same rough but manageable floor, the same warm, dank air, the rough walls, the darkness that enfolded their glow.

Time stretched out as they walked.

Time contracted as they walked.

They lost any sense of how long they had been walking—perhaps a minute, perhaps days. At times they felt all they had ever done was to walk in the darkness casting a little light, a gray woman in bright clothes now in one set of arms, now another.

Their one sure measure of experience was their thirst which crept softly into mind then became steadily more insistent. They had left their water behind with Lepanto and had not found even the slightest drip along the tunnel's walls or from its ceiling.

Yet even as their thirst grew and their limbs wearied they settled into a robotic pace that carried them forward.

Thoughts of Lepanto distracted them, and of Madelyn, whose one moan continued to tantalize them. Sam kept replaying his last glimpse of Lepanto, impossibly tall and brilliant, twisting forward as

he charged, until Sam realized his charge really was a dance into battle. That made him smile, his dry lips cracking. Maybe his pounding feet brought down the cavern roof, burying his enemies and, Sam thought sadly, himself. But if the battle had brought down the cavern's roof, then their tunnel's entrance was blocked.

That made sense of there being no pursuit. There was only one way to go, he realized, whatever had happened: forward.

He trudged on.

John tried to lick his dry lips, forgetting thirst too as he remembered the last glimpse of Lepanto he stole over his shoulder as he dashed into the tunnel. He was all brilliance sweeping forward, twisting forward, why, John thought too, dancing up to Mr. Nicholas!

He glanced at Madelyn, whose rescue the Elephant had made possible, despite everything: she lay in his arms, her face in such calm repose against one shoulder, as though in a deep and pleasant dream. Her presence concentrated his thought.

How were they to bring her back, further? And if they did: if, somehow, she awoke: if she knew him, how would she see me, he wondered? As the man who had failed her? Or would there be a new hope, a new chance? He was so caught up in the tension between those thoughts he forgot all else until driven past endurance he stumbled and nearly dropped her.

He caught himself, then felt a wave of thirst fall on him as he sank to his knees. Sam staggered on a step, stopped, and turned to watch him, the dull expression on his face giving way to alarm.

Gently John laid Madelyn down. In slow motion Sam sank to his knees opposite John and Madelyn. His head sagged, and his arms hung motionless by his side as now the same wave of thirst broke over him.

Long moments passed as their breathing calmed and the

numbness wore off their legs, replaced by an ache and a tremble they couldn't stop. Madelyn lay silently in the gloom, her clothes still gleaming. Sam reached out and silently held the material of her skirt, amazed at how brightly its blue shone in the tunnel. The roses on her blouse glittered. He expected both to fade and was not disappointed as their brilliance dimmed as neither touched them longer.

Sam was frustrated: maybe there was no pursuit because there was no escape, no chance for his mother. At some point they would set her down again in this cave and fade beside her. Then something Lepanto said swam into his mind. As for Madelyn—what you desire you must give.

"As for Madelyn—what you desire you must give," he muttered, wondering what the words meant.

"What did you say?" asked John.

"What Lepanto said to me when we ran. In my head. They were his last words." John repeated them.

"What you desire you must give." He had heard those words, too.

"Bringing her home this way was never my idea," Sam added. "I never did get a chance to draw a way home in the Book." John nodded.

"Unfortunately Lepanto said a lot of things we don't understand," John added. Sam watched him touch a rose on Madelyn's skirt: it flared, then started to dim when he withdrew his hand. But Sam straightened after a moment.

"Look at that rose, Dad!" John looked, puzzled, then it struck him too: it had only faded a little when he withdrew his hand, while the other roses which should have grayed by now held a good deal of their color, and her blue skirt was still solidly blue, if no longer a brilliant blue light.

"Remember the apple and the orange," Sam breathed, "in Dread City? At that fruit stand?" John nodded. "Remember how they faded all the way after I dropped the core, and rind?"

"And how the policeman you touched," John added, slowly, piecing it together, "didn't fade, but almost burst into flame and turned into ashes."

"Like those others did at Lepanto's touch in the hall. Remember him telling us not to touch moth—mother's skin?"

"Yes."

"Maybe he meant in Dread City! But we're not there now! Nowhere near its center, anyway! No, we must be a long way away! And look—"

"It's like what we give she keeps, now," John murmured, puzzled, lightly fingering her blouse.

"As for Madelyn—what you desire you must give." Sam lifted her into his lap.

"Careful—" John started.

"We need to do this now while we still have this glow, while we're still somewhere we can do this, before the Book suddenly shows up," he said, inspired, "and we see it's all filled!"

And he pressed his cheek to his mother's.

A wave of weakness swept over him like when the red man grabbed him, but he held Madelyn firmly, warm cheek pressed to cool.

"Mother," he whispered, "you said to come, and I did: now you have to come back to us. You have to come back. Come back, mother," he repeated, "come back," over and again as his own glow faded. "I'd do anything for you," he whispered, the words catching in his throat, "anything. Come back... I WANT—MY—MOTHER—!"

Sam held on as long as he could, murmuring those words, until his mother slid from his helpless arms and the contact was gone and he sank to the ground with a groan. But now John lifted Madelyn in turn.

"She's heavier," his father breathed. Sam was so drained he could barely move his eyes to watch his father. His glow was gone. But Madelyn's cheeks were now a pale pink although she did not speak or waken. John took a deep breath and pressed his face against hers in turn.

Weakness swept over him.

"Forgive me," he said, "I'm so very sorry for letting you go: never, never again, I swear!" All his faults swept through his mind, missed opportunities, anger, loss, selfishness, all the reproaches he had step by step leveled against himself in their adventures as doubt had been faced and hope embraced, and a hard-won honesty cleared the guilt from his mind.

He felt a clarity of emotion that canceled all his ambivalence and redeemed all his failings.

"Live with my life. Live in my love."

"Live with our love," Sam breathed.

John fought his blurring vision, his muscles, the growing numbness that spread through him, and tightened his embrace. He fought his giddiness and then the heaviness that seeped outward from his heart so that it felt impossible to hold himself upright, even sitting, let alone hold Madelyn to him—and only set his jaw more firmly and pressed her cheek harder to his until, with his last strength, he laid her down and fell back against the tunnel wall.

The darkness was absolute. John's glow was gone, too. But the soft sigh that came from Madelyn electrified them. They crouched over her and felt her snuggle against John with a deep, regular breathing where there had been none before.

They feared her breathing would slow and fade, but it did neither. Instead she slept soundly. Sam reached out to lift her and was astonished by her weight.

"We did it!" Sam gasped.

"To Dread City and back," John answered him, hopeful too as Madelyn breathed steadily against him. To have achieved this, and not make it back now seemed unbelievable to him.

"Not all the way, but soon!" Sam breathed fiercely, feeling the same certainty.

"Soon," John agreed in the darkness.

But now their glow was gone they noticed the darkness was not absolute, for here and there were patches of phosphorescence on the cave's walls that gave a faint light. They could just make out the smile on Madelyn's lips.

Hope was a sun in their hearts and tears swelled in their eyes and ran down their cheeks as though thirst had never been heard of and water was as common as the air they breathed. In the face of her smile nothing would make them give up now. Sam staggered to his feet.

"Let's go."

John carefully lifted Madelyn. She felt like a person now and would have been harder to carry except for the exultation in his heart. They set off side by side with vigorous steps aided by the occasional phosphorescence, sensing their way forward blindly in its gaps, their senses sharpened by the darkness.

Their exultation was a long time fading, for every time they felt thirst or tiredness force their way into consciousness now they had only to look at Madelyn to get a fresh burst of strength that carried them on.

But that couldn't go on forever.

First thirst again slid into mind, gentle as a wave running up a shore and fading into the sand, then ever more insistent. Even as they fought off thirst the tiredness in their long-suffering muscles grew insistent. They were tormented by the memory of all the uncounted miles they had run or walked since leaving Dread City.

Then hunger added its own insistence to the others. They had given so much of themselves to Madelyn. They scrabbled at the patches of phosphorescence on the walls, hoping to peel away some form of glowing plant life to suck for its moisture or eat for its flesh, but the phosphorescence was mineral in nature, and if damp, gave them nothing to lick from their hands.

They hadn't eaten since that last, odd meal Lepanto found in his vest. Was it earlier in the day? A week ago? A month? Despite themselves they ran every incident of when they had eaten through their minds as if the thoughts themselves were food.

At last they fell into an exhausted sleep. When they woke, their muscles if stiff were at least usable. They said little, just took in each other's grim determination, and started off again, Madelyn in John's arms.

They rested now and then when their muscles congealed. Once recovered they set off again, repeating this pattern until after another stop they fell asleep, unsure whether it was morning or night. When they awoke they had no idea how many times this had happened.

Had they been at this forever?

John's back became one large, strained muscle, then a fire from his neck to his thighs which he ignored with a fixed determination, for Madelyn neither woke nor faded.

She grew steadily heavier in John's arms although he thought it must be his weakness that made her feel that way, but when Sam asked for a chance to help, he couldn't lift her on his own. With a sigh John swept her into his arms again, memory tormenting him with how he had done that in happier times in the past, memories that also gave him renewed bursts of strength as he dreamed of doing it again in the future.

One such burst of energy carried him a great distance up the tunnel's sloping floor that left him breathing harder when he had to pause. For a moment he looked at Sam without comprehension: then a smile cracked Sam's lips.

"We're going up more!"

That thought renewed their hope and from some hidden reserve they found a new burst of energy so that they climbed steadily forward, delighting, at first, in the ground's upward tilt until the torment of their swollen tongues and their hunger and burning muscles overcame energy and hope. Again they staggered to a stop, rested, slept, woke, struggled on, rested, slept, woke, struggled on.

Time now became one thing only: a blur.

At least they were certain from the silence behind them that there was no pursuit, although a thought grew steadily in their minds there was none because none was needed.

Maybe the cavern wall had had many tunnels: maybe if they had looked closer, they would have seen the others, and tried to pick out one more promising. Maybe there was no way out in the one they had taken.

Maybe, in a last flash of consciousness before they turned completely gray, they would feel themselves being carried into Dread City, each to his own deathly cubicle. Madelyn didn't waken, because she would never waken: they had done what they could, and it was not enough.

But they were also glad she hadn't woken here.

The darkness at last became a heaviness itself however momentarily relieved by the glowing patches, while each breath grew harder to draw down raw throats into burning lungs. They were nauseated by the air of the cave. They grew lightheaded with hunger and wondered if they were going in the right direction: only the upward tilt of the cave kept them oriented.

Even if we escape this cave, Sam wondered, will we be among

the Watchers? Or among the centaurs and their stony charges? By the wreck of our sailboat with a long sea voyage ahead of us and no way to sail, Mr. Nicholas racing up behind us?

Does this cave just go in a great circle, John wondered, one too gradual to notice, so we'll just end where we started? Or, given the way it's going up are we going to come to a door we'll stagger through to find ourselves on the top floor of one of those brutal skyscrapers in Dread City?

At length the moment came when they were uncertain they moved at all or only did so in the dreamlike desire of their minds.

The inevitable happened. John stumbled, and sank to his knees.

"No more," he somehow gasped out. Sam stood still as a stone.

"We can't stop!" he tried to shout, but couldn't form the words. Tears of frustration tried to form in his eyes, but they were tears of dust.

John let Madelyn slide from his arms and sank beside her, too drained even to despair.

Sam envied Lepanto his brilliant battle. That was a better way to end than this, unable even to bend his knees to sit in this endless cave.

Lepanto....

The image of that dancing elephant strengthened in his mind. He remembered once more Lepanto's wild dance in the Sea of Faces, remembered how he smashed through the deck with a last fling, how a wave of faces rolled over the boat to swamp it.

How angry Lepanto had been! Sam groaned in place of laughing. They hadn't sunk: they'd overcome that storm. What would the Elephant say now? He'd have some funny way of putting things to encourage them. What you can carry you can walk, or.... Sam shook his head.

He just wouldn't give up.

286

"I hear something," he gasped, gesturing back. John looked at him slowly. When did it become possible to see, he wondered, for the darkness was not as heavy as it had been. Then he took in the meaning of Sam's words. He forced himself up.

"No, never! They will never get her again!" he ground out.

He lifted Madelyn and set off with jerky, determined steps. Sam stumbled after him, suddenly as full of fear as if he really had heard something.

They swayed forward side to side like drunkards, using the cave's close walls to keep themselves upright. After a time it became clear in the silence that there was no pursuit, only more cave, endless cave, always going up.

Still John pushed on, fueled by the fear he would never start up again if he stopped now. The same fear kept Sam in motion behind him. Their feet slapped on the ground, while their breaths grew hotter in their already inflamed throats.

John shook his head, his pace a series of lurches until each grew slower and he only moved forward by again twisting side to side to swing one leg forward, then the next. Finally he only swayed in place no matter how hard he swung side to side.

Flames raced up his back again. Madelyn was a lead weight in his arms.

"Ohh," he groaned, and sank down, falling across Madelyn. Sam staggered on a few feet more until he swayed in place like John had, then he too sank down.

Ragged breathing....

Silence....

No pursuit....

None needed....

Just time, just grayness to come.

This was it.

This was the end.

Sam flung out an arm in hopeless anger. It hit the wall of the cave. He flung out the other. It slammed against the other side. The cave had closed in on them.

Something is wrong here, he thought: when did the walls get so close together? There won't be enough room to walk soon, he told himself, then remembered they were past walking, past help, past anything more, past.

He raised his arms over his head preparing to bring them down on himself in his frustration, and kicked out spasmodically: and touched a third wall. Furious, he lashed out: this was the end, indeed! Bitterly he flung his arms about in a final, angry spasm.

They struck the cave's three sides, with rungs of steel jutting from the third.

Three sides?

Rungs of steel?

That focused his mind! He twisted with sudden energy and felt several more rungs rising from the ground. Astonished, he pulled himself up: the rungs went straight up the wall. He ignored his burning muscles and climbed up without the energy to lift his head and so banged it against the top.

He dropped down, furious at the blow. That fury finally brought him fully to his senses.

"Dad!" he croaked, "it's the end of the cave! There's a ladder up!" When there was no reaction from John he staggered over to him, gasping. John was barely conscious. Sam shook and shook him until he struggled to sit up with a groan and a complaint.

"Stop," he muttered, "stop."

"Wake up! I found the way out! Wake up!" Sam insisted, not

letting go of him. "There's a ladder. WAKE UP!"

The words finally broke through John's daze, and he let Sam pull him to his feet.

"A ladder?" His voice quavered.

Sam led him, staggering, to the cave's end and guided one of John's hands onto a rung. His father stiffened, then tried to stare up through the gloom but could not see where the rungs ended.

"How far?" he croaked.

"Not far!"

John took a shaky breath and clambered up until he hit his head against the top too, and slid down. The blow cleared his mind in turn. They looked at each other.

"There can't be a ladder up without a way out," Sam said.

XX

The Heart's Desire

John climbed the rungs again more cautiously until he felt the cave's ceiling. There he felt a rectangular opening with a stone covering that blocked the exit from the stairs. If they could move it aside they would be out. It didn't matter where, he thought: anything must be better than this.

He pushed against it with his hands without effect, then lowered his head and strained upward with the weight on his neck and shoulders as his legs tried to straighten on a lower rung.

He groaned when the stone refused to move even after he

redoubled his efforts. Then Sam squeezed beside him and added his strength and they both pushed, straining as hard as they could against that stone, ignoring the pain in their necks and shoulders. Nothing— then the stone ground a little to one side....

They relaxed, exchanged looks, and flung themselves against the heavy weight overhead with renewed energy and, gasping, inch by inch pushed it aside. When the opening was wide enough first Sam, then John poked his head into the darkness above.

They saw a room that seemed bright after the tunnel, although they could barely make out more than dim shapes on the floor or against a wall, and a stairway up to a door where light blazed through the crack at its foot to their dark-sensitive eyes. They fought to silence their breathing. Were they in the house where the old woman turned children into stone?

They heard a mechanical, whining sound in the distance, and a low gonging, and froze. But no one came to investigate the sound of the stone being pushed aside. The other sounds went on unchanged.

Something tugged at the edge of their memory. They looked at each other, puzzled. After another long moment Sam climbed into the room. John went back for Madelyn. Awkwardly he lifted her up rung by rung. Sam caught her under her arms as John lifted her head above the floor and dragged her into the room as his father pushed from below.

Then John clambered up. Carefully they stretched her out. They turned to the stairs.

Neither gave word to their fears, just looked at each other, saw the same dirt-stained, crack-lipped strained expression on each other's face, nodded, and put their feet on the stairs.

"Creak," went one. They froze.

"Crack!" went the next, loud as shots to their ears. They

froze again.

There were still no footsteps above, only the same puzzling sounds.

Just let there be a man with a beet-colored face waiting for them, John thought: he'll be sorry! I'll smash his big purple nose!

Just let that witch be there, Sam thought, I'll have her in her oven in no time!

"Creak!" went the next step, and the next again "crack" in turn until Sam pressed an ear to the door as he reached it. He heard the puzzling sounds, took a breath, glanced at his father, turned the doorknob and stepped through.

He stopped.

John pushed past him at a half crouch expecting the worst, but stopped, too.

Facing them was a machine designed to take three eggs, a dab of butter and a quart of milk from the refrigerator, crack the eggs over a bowl on the counter, discard the shells, add milk, stir, light a burner of the stove, and then empty the contents into a frying pan with the butter to make scrambled eggs.

It was jammed, eggs at risk as the motor whined and the arms tried to crack them.

The grandfather clock beside the refrigerator gonged relentlessly. Two place settings were laid neatly on the table by the window. Outside the sun shown brightly in the canyon. They were in their kitchen in the Last House.

They were home.

They took another step. Madrigal lowed loudly from the barn.

Something dripped.

Two sets of eyes fixed on the sink faucet and stared fascinated as a drop swelled on its tip, dangled, extended downward, hung

tantalizingly—and dropped with a splash.

They flung themselves forward and turned the spigot on full. John shoved Sam's head under the stream of water as he lapped away happily, then pulled him back to thrust his own under that delicious stream, lapping the water in turn. The cold water stunned them with a pure flow of liquid fit for a god to drink.

John pulled back and held Sam.

"Only sips now," he whispered huskily. Sam nodded, thrusting his head back under that heavenly flow, savoring its rush over his head, and, as he stood back, down his neck and back.

At last John walked over to the clock, opened its cabinet, and stopped the pendulum to end the gonging. He reset the time and let the pendulum start its tick-tock again.

Sam turned off the mechanism to make eggs as John returned the butter and eggs to the refrigerator. All the other clocks had run their course and were silent.

They turned and soaked in the blue and green world through the window, then as one walked stiffly to the front door and out onto the porch. They heard the stream working its way down the canyon towards the ocean that glittered distantly in a brilliance of light that made them shield their eyes.

Awkwardly they clambered off the porch, turning to stare at the house. The faded colors on the Victorian fretwork struck them both.

"Needs paint," John whispered.

"Color!" was all Sam could whisper, with a choked laugh.

Then they hurried back to Madelyn, leaving Madrigal to low a little longer. Carefully they carried her up to the kitchen, then up the next flight to John's room where they laid her in John's bed after Sam drew back the quilt.

She settled with a happy sigh. Sam drew the quilt up to her shoulders. They both stood by the bed, staring at her resting, at a loss what to do, exhaustion settling on their shoulders again and dulling their minds. They nearly fell asleep standing.

Vaguely Sam thought he wanted to sing and dance as he started to drift off. He tilted to one side, but startled awake as John collided with him. They looked at each other, and clambered awkwardly back to the kitchen.

Sam again ran water over his head, dared a few more mouthfuls, then stood back for his father.

Finally John too stood back, the water dripping down his front and back, a ridiculous smile on his parched face. Refreshed, their eyes met, and they embraced, their arms tight around one another's bodies, joy a brilliant sun in their hearts, uplifting and painful and both at the same moment and beyond any words.

Sam pulled away with the rumble in his stomach filling the room.

They made an enormous feast to satisfy their eyes, though they could eat little. They emptied a jar of pickles in a bowl, heated the beans, fried the eggs, sliced cheese, set out left-overs from their last chicken meal, toasted bread they spread handsomely with butter and jam, and poured milk to the brim of their glasses. Sam took a drink, though less than he thought he could—but John suddenly froze.

"The milk—it's not sour." Sam stared. "We've been away months…"

They heard Madrigal lowing from their barn. As one they rushed out to milk her. She moaned with relief as they milked her, swollen and in pain but as clearly not neglected for the months they had been away.

"Someone must have milked her while we were gone," John whispered.

"Who?"

They could think of no one who would have come by to check on them. They went back to their feast. Everything smelled fine. Nothing had gone bad in all this time.

"Something's not right," John muttered. He walked into the living room. There was his pipe where he had last left it. He picked it up.

"No dust," John muttered. He hesitated when he went to replace it, then tossed it into the fireplace. He looked at Sam, then looked out.

Silently they went back out and climbed up the long driveway to the road. There was a single ad in the mailbox. Three papers lay on the ground. After a moment Sam handed the papers to his father. John opened them, reciting their dates.

"Three days," he whispered. "We've been gone three days."

Wild surmises filled their minds. Three days for many months of travel. Sam didn't understand. John shook his head.

"Three days," he repeated.

"Here," Sam said finally.

"Here," his father nodded: "here."

Stiff-legged they went back to the house. They settled back down to their feast but could still only nibble.

"We have to go slow, Sam," John sighed as he sat back. Then he went upstairs to his room where Madelyn slept. He sagged down on a chair: in a moment his head sank onto his chest and he slept.

Sam clambered up to his room. There hanging from the ceiling and turning slowly in the room's drafts were a green dragon with a too-long head, a model of the schooner on which they had sailed to the Far Land of Fear, and Lepanto dancing in an elegant Edwardian suit on a Flying Trapeze.

Sleep hurled him onto his bed.

They slept all day, all night, and another day and night for good measure. Madrigal thought they'd left her again and lowed in renewed misery. At last Sam stirred, rolled over, and slowly took in the three figures hanging above him, focusing on the Elephant.

It must have been a good foot-and-a-half in height hanging there, spats on his feet, the well pressed Edwardian suit and many-pocketed vest, a hat doffed in one hand, a cane in the other, trunk curled, tusks gleaming, one foot raised above the other as if caught in mid-step, all precariously balanced on the Flying Trapeze.

How very odd, he thought in that awakening moment, warm in his bed, stretching his rested limbs. Then he flung off the covers and stood with a start.

He was grimy and itched and every muscle was stiff, and he flung himself into the shower and fresh clothes then raced down to his father's room.

John was just stirring in his chair with a groan. As his eyes opened he took in nothing, then Sam, then Madelyn. Memory flooded into his mind in turn too, and he stood with a jerk.

They looked at each other, then at Madelyn: she looked entirely

normal, but still slept.

The same question shaped in each other's eyes: would she ever waken? Or would she lie there breathing normally, a faint flush of good health on her cheeks, forever?

"We should try to wake her up," said Sam. John nodded, hesitated, and reached towards her.

"Maddy," he breathed, and jumped back startled as she sighed, turned, and opened her eyes. They were blank at first, then filled with Sam and John.

"Mother!" shouted Sam joyously, and flung himself into bed beside her: after a startled moment her arms closed tightly around him. She was soft, so soft, warm, so warm, and smelled faintly of flowers. She hugged him close for a moment, staring at him in surprise and wonder.

"Sam? Sam…" she breathed, and kissed him, surprise giving way swiftly to tears of joy mingling with his. Then John swept them all up with a roar that made them mix their tears with laughter.

"We did it!" Sam gasped, "we really did it!"

"Yes," said John, full of wonder, "by never giving up, and believing!" Sam looked at John proud at how he had changed.

They laughed and cried, their joy making up for all their trials and pains and fears and doubts, even for the loss of Lepanto. Finally Madelyn pushed them away, and struggled to sit.

"What did you do?" she asked, her puzzled look deepening. John and Sam exchanged looks, unsure where to begin.

"I have had such a dream," she added, interrupting their look, "such a strange dream." She stopped, taking in John and Sam again. "So sad. So happy."

She held Sam at arm's length. "How you've grown! Why, you're the biggest five year old I've ever seen—" and stopped.

"I'm ten," Sam said. "Almost eleven. Not a boy any more."

"No..." She tried to take him in, and John, puzzled. "Such a dream... What have you two been up to? How did I come here? I was in a dark, gray place, I was...and now...I'm here..."

Her face darkened.

"Yes, you are here," smiled John.

"You're home!" exulted Sam, and he and John laughed as though laughter would never go out of style.

"It's a long story," John got out to Madelyn's bewildered expression. "I'll never let you go again," he added, abruptly in dead earnest as he tightened his arms around her, "never. I'm so sorry—" he began, but Madelyn put her fingers to his lips.

"For what?" she asked, and frowned as her memories began to return. "I was in a different room—white—there were machines—"

But before John could try to answer there was a loud rumbling from his stomach, followed by an impressive echo from Sam's.

"Time," he sighed. "One thing at a time. I'm too hungry to think!"

"Me too!" said Sam. They all laughed, and John kissed her. Sam looked down, half revolted, half happy.

"Time," Madelyn agreed, "time for everything. In fact, now you mention it, I'm famished too! I feel like it's been years since I had a good meal!"

"Come on," John said, lifting her up. They smiled at each other, and kissed again.

Sam groaned. They laughed at him.

"It's so—I don't have any words for this," sighed John.

"What about me?" said Madelyn. "Was it all a dream? Is this—where I—"

"This is home," Sam said firmly.

"Home," she whispered.

"No matter what all the beet-colored, big-nosed, hairy-headed, long and short armed men in Dread City want," Sam bragged. Madelyn's expression clouded.

"Time," John said hurriedly. "Breakfast. All in good time," he reassured her with a look to Sam.

But he and Sam stood thunderstruck: those men....

Mr. Nicholas....

The cave....

The ladder....

The stone they'd left to one side!

John let Madelyn stand, then he and Sam turned as one and rushed down the stairs.

"What's wrong?" Madelyn said to their swiftly disappearing backs, and hurried after them.

John and Sam took the stairs two and three at a time in their rush, dashed across the dining room into the kitchen, ignored the whining, jammed machine and gonging clock, flung open the door to the cellar and leaped down the stairs blinking to help their eyes adapt to the cellar's gloom.

Madelyn was at the cellar door as they hurried across its floor to where the stone lay to one side of a square of darkness.

Sam stared down that dark well and strained to hear any sign of pursuit, but he saw and heard nothing. John also strained to hear any sign of pursuit, but aside from his and Sam's breathing and the blood pounding in their ears, there was the same absolute silence there had been since the crash and fury of battle had died in the tunnel.

"What are you two doing?" Madelyn asked from the top of the stairs. Sam and John said nothing as together they strained to push the stone over the entrance.

"They're somewhere there," John said.

"He's somewhere there," Sam added, without having to say whom. They looked at the stone.

"That didn't hold us," said Sam, "and we were so tired and weak."

They looked around the room, ignoring Madelyn with her hands on her hips.

"Will you two tell me what you are up to!" she demanded.

"We have to cover this," was all Sam said. There were a few boxes of books to one side that they dragged over the stone, and an old dresser they tilted over on top of these.

"We'll have to seal it," Sam said.

"This will hold it for now," John replied.. "Let's add that stone too." He pointed at a small gray lump off to one side. "Everything counts."

"Will you tell me what you are doing?" Madelyn demanded

again, starting to come down the stairs as Sam went to pick up the small stone and add its weight to the pile. But he found it was just some gray rags, and kicked at them in disgust. His foot hit something solid. He pulled the rags away and found the Book in his hands.

"Look! The Book!" he cried.

"What Book?" asked Madelyn, edging down the stairs.

"It's a magic Book," explained Sam. "It's filled with everything—everything since you called for me to come and get you in Lepanto's tent." Madelyn stopped on the stairs, a hand to her brow.

"Yes… I was so alone. I so wanted—I didn't know what—" She smiled at Sam. "I so wanted you. Your bright face and hair…were all that was left in my mind."

"It was enough," he said.

"Let's take this upstairs and have a look at it, then." She held out her hands for the Book. "You say it explains everything?"

They nodded as she turned it over in her hands. First one, then another stomach rumbled.

"After we eat, I think," she smiled, and as one they went back to the kitchen.

With a will they again fixed the jammed egg-cooking mechanism, made toast, fried eggs, poured milk and orange juice, fried bacon, ham, and scrambled more eggs and cooked pancakes and in an inspired moment made waffles they coated in syrup, topping the pancakes with apple sauce and brown sugar. They added portions of cereal for each, with more milk, made tea, and….

Everything looked good to them.

The table should have collapsed from the weight of it all. Yet again Sam ate far less than he thought he wanted, as did John, while Madelyn could only nibble, pushing eggs and pancakes and waffles and fresh fruit about on her plate as though with so much to choose from she couldn't make up her mind to eat anything.

The truth was privation had not only made them hungry but shrunken their stomachs, so their eyes feasted but their bodies managed only tidbits. They still drank sparingly too, John and Sam's tongues awkward and throats raw too so their voices had yet to lose their husky edges.

With a sigh Madelyn pushed her plate aside.

Her eyes were drawn to the window where she had leaned the Book. The three of them stared at its singed but rich leather covers. John and Sam moved their chairs beside hers.

"If anything can explain what happened, this is it!"

She looked at Sam and smiled, then traced the title that was now printed cleanly across what had been a blank cover, "Orpheus Rising" with "By Sam And His Father, John" printed below it, and below that, "With Some Help From A Very Wise Elephant Who Likes To Dance."

Madelyn turned the cover. It was different now, for even the first adventures were embedded in a clear, type-set text that replaced the original, neat writing.

"The light shatters off the glass facade of the hospital under the noon sun as John stands at a loss, eyes slits against the glare.

"How did I get here, he wonders?

"He can't take it in, the plaza, the people, the buses on three sides, why he stands like an idiot squinting at that blinding facade.

"And remembers.

"She was gone," Madelyn began to read, the three somber until, after a pause, she reached,

"A Dream Called Life."

"Somewhere an alarm goes off; then another followed nearby, and a third more distantly. Soon each room in the house rang.

"A groan came from a small shape that could just be guessed

under the twisted covers in a third story room under a pitched gable from which a green dragon hung with a too long head, and a two-masted yacht, a schooner, while an unlikely elephant who perilously tap danced on a flying trapeze hung by them. The elephant was elegantly dressed, and wore spats."

The sun streamed through the windows and moved across the kitchen wall as Madelyn read on, their three heads close together while the canyon's green gleamed, and the stream gurgled audibly beyond the open window. They paused only to milk Madrigal.

Adventure followed adventure until they took a silent break for lunch after "Through the Upside-down Ocean," then read on until tea time, before resuming with "John Finds His Courage—." They nibbled through dinner, then continued in the living room.

Madelyn was fascinated by John and Lepanto and Sam's adventures when they were separated after the schooner crashed, and perhaps even more by the way their thoughts were so clearly recorded.

John was at first embarrassed by that, then ashamed, then felt a slow, reluctant pride grow as his will firmed and resolve hardened until at last he was able to face the great Watcher and Mr. Nicholas and the beast and defy them. Madelyn gave him a look that left him glowing inside.

It was late that night when she read the last words that showed them sitting in the living room reading the last words. But it ended oddly: there was still room on the page, and there was no "The End" written.

There was a long silence.

"Now at least I know what you two have been up to, although it will take a deal of thinking about." John began to say something but her hand brushed lightly across his lips to stop him.

"I think everything has been said, except..." Sam and John looked at her.

"Except I am very happy." They held one another wordlessly then as the joy that had swept over them in the morning swept over them again.

And they cried.

"Now," she said at length to Sam, pulling back, "bring me a pencil." He ran to get one. The Book was still open on her lap when he handed it to her. She began drawing a picture.

"What are you doing?" asked John.

"Sssh," she smiled, and went on drawing.

Soon they saw it was their cellar and the stone sealing the entrance to the cave but without the bric-a-brac they had piled on it. She added instead an iron loop to the stone, and other loops surrounding it in the floor, then drew chains from each to the central loop, all locked with large padlocks.

"How's that?" she asked. They nodded, pleased with her effort.

Beside the locks she wrote, "No one may come through here."

Sam looked doubtful. He took the pencil and added, "Except Lepanto." And laughed.

෨෧

Time would pass, the past be accommodated, understanding deepen, and love.

Time in its fullness would bring someone like George to the family, and later a sassy girl who exasperated Sam but whom he secretly admired.

Life would resume its ordinary ways, except they would be happy.

Happiness is wonderful but does not make for a good story which needs conflict, suffering, and striving.

Even the loss of Lepanto would lessen night by night for Sam as he stared at the Elephant hanging from his ceiling, remembering his last brilliance as they fled into the tunnel.

He would search that brilliance in his memory, recall how Lepanto's tusks had become swirls of light within light, achingly bright: and he would sense in Lepanto's brilliance great shapes unfolding, like wings, he thought one night, except wings upon wings, until he realized he had no word or image for what he had seen.

Still, he fell asleep with a smile on his lips, the darkness opening and closing over him as if breathing, or as if great wings beat behind its veil.

The next morning he was sure the Elephant had shifted his feet on the trapeze.

They never saw Mr. Nicholas delivering newspapers or as a half-melted, half frozen figure of terror again.

Just now Madelyn marveled at Sam's bright eyes and glowing good health despite all he had been through, and her fingers interlaced with John's. Sam nodded, and lifted the pencil a last time. At the bottom of the page under his mother's drawing he wrote in big letters,

and closed the Book.

ABOUT THE AUTHOR

Lance Lee is a poet, playwright (*Time's Up and Other Plays*), novelist (*Second Chances*) and writer on drama and screenwriting (*A Poetics for Screenwriters*, and *The Death and Life of Drama*). His six previous volumes of poetry are listed under "Also by Lance Lee." His seventh, *Elemental Natures*, draws together a selection of thirty years of lyrics, sequences, and prose, with new work. His poems appear widely in America and England, between which his family is split. A past Creative Writing Fellow of the National Endowment for the Arts, his home is in Los Angeles, where he has also taught at a number of leading universities. As an environmentalist he was instrumental in forming the California State Park system in the Santa Monica Mountains.

portrait by John Robertson

ABOUT THE ILLUSTRATOR

Ellen Raquel LeBow has illustrated among others Robert Finch's *Special Places....* LeBow finds certain archetypal icons deeply compelling be they personal, ancient, or contemporary and draws what awes her. Much of the art in Orpheus Rising was made by carving through black India ink brushed over a board coated in white kaolin clay to expose the white clay. The lines are meant to give the illusion of drawing with light. She coordinates ART/MATENWA, a project that brings sustainability through art to women in Matènwa, Haiti. On the founding board of Wellfleet Preservation Hall, she splits her time between Wellfleet and Cambridge, MA with her long-time partner Seth Rolbein and their two goddaughters Hernitte Riviere and Woodmyha Rafa Lima.

Due to printing exigencies the images on pages 70, 190, 244, 268 and 293 have had to be modified. The originals may be viewed at lanceleeauthor.com/images/orpheusrising.html

ABOUT THE DESIGNER

Kate Cooper is a website developer, graphic designer and photographer based in London, UK. As a multi-disciplinary designer, Kate works with an extensive variety of digital media and print art forms, and has produced many wonderful collaborations for clients and industries including charities and non-profit organizations, artists, travel, education and construction. When she is not working, Kate is an avid traveler and is happiest on the road, exploring with her camera.

This book was formatted using Adobe InDesign, set in 12pt Adobe Caslon Pro, and printed by Ingram Lightning Source.

CPSIA information can be obtained
at www.ICGtesting.com
Printed in the USA
LVHW010721141021
700377LV00003B/153/J